NEW EROTICA 6

The Nexus imprint is the largest collection of erotic
fiction published in Britain. The list is as diverse as it is
cutting edge, boasting a wide variety of themes, fetishes,
locations and sexual interests, while ensuring that only the
most arousing stories are published.

With the *New Erotica* series, we hope to give the reader a
taste of the variety of the imprint – from Aishling
Morgan's fantastical world of priapic beasts and warrior
women to Yolanda Celbridge's Sadean stylings. Virtually
every erotic activity is celebrated – from bondage to
watersports via depilation and orgies – in explicit detail.

We publish two new titles every month, to add to our
extensive backlist, so if you're unsure which to choose,
then this collection is a good place to start. We hope you
enjoy it as much as we enjoyed putting it – and all the
other Nexus titles – together.

It's always worth checking out what's new on our erotica
website: *www.nexus-books.co.uk* You can order books from
there, too, so there's no need to miss out on our great
offers.

Have fun!

T0315539

Other Nexus Collections:

EROTICON 1
EROTICON 2
EROTICON 3
EROTICON 4

NEW EROTICA 1
NEW EROTICA 2
NEW EROTICA 3
NEW EROTICA 4
NEW EROTICA 5

SATURNALIA

NEW EROTICA
6

Extracts from the best of Nexus
plus two original stories

First published in 2002 by
Nexus
Thames Wharf Studios
Rainville Road
London W6 9HA

Copyright exists in the following works:

The Point	© Penny Birch
Intimate Instruction	© Arabella Knight
Pet Training in the Private House	© Esme Ombreux
Drawn to Discipline	© Tara Black
Beast	© Wendy Swanscombe
Caged!	© Yolanda Celbridge
Whip Hand	© G. C. Scott
Angel	© Lindsay Gordon
The Last Straw	© Christina Shelly
Slave Acts	© Jennifer Jane Pope
Slave-Mines of Tormunil	© Aran Ashe
Dolls	© Aishling Morgan

The right of the Authors to be identified as the Author of the
Works has been asserted by them in accordance with the
Copyright, Designs and Patents Act 1988.

www.nexus-books.co.uk

Typeset by TW Typesetting, Plymouth, Devon

ISBN 0 352 33751 6

Printed and bound in Great Britain by Clays Ltd, St Ives PLC

CONTENTS

THE POINT

Penny Birch

Penny Birch is currently the most prolific author on the Nexus list, and probably the most filthy-dirty too. Her stories are largely autobiographical, based on her own activities, and those of her game friends, in over ten years on the fetish scene. She's a founder member of the Birch, Bottoms and Lovitt Pony Club, a worthy institution which serves the needs of lovers of human equestrianism. Regular readers of fetish fiction will know that her books are realistic and extremely horny missives from the furthest reaches of human sexual behaviour.

The Point is a brand new story from Penny, one that you won't find in any of her previously published books. Why not check out her website at *www.pennybirch.com*

THE INDIGNITIES OF ISABELLE
  (writing as Cruella)
PENNY IN HARNESS
A TASTE OF AMBER
BAD PENNY
BRAT
IN FOR A PENNY
PLAYTHING
TIGHT WHITE COTTON
TIE AND TEASE
PENNY PIECES
TEMPER TANTRUMS
REGIME
DIRTY LAUNDRY
UNIFORM DOLL

I expected the dinner party to be a disaster from the start, or at best dull. Marjorie Burgess was one of those women whose principal interest lay in arranging other peoples lives for them. She worked in the administration block at the university, something in management, a big, raw-boned woman, matronly, kind in a slightly sharp fashion, bottle blonde, perhaps fifty although unlikely to admit it. I'd met her on my first day, while trying to sort out the endless bureaucratic niceties my position as senior lecturer seemed to bring with it. At the time I'd have been grateful for any help at all, and accepted hers. She had bustled through the process with remarkable efficiency, complaining in a constant undertone, but refusing to stop until I was finished.

Since then we had met occasionally, at first casually, then socially at the Christmas party. I also met her husband, a whiskery, cheerful man, considerably older than her, who'd been something quite senior in the military, but was now retired. As I am never good in new social situations, and was still finding my feet in the department, I readily accepted the invitation to join their table. Before the evening was through I'd been invited to dinner in the New Year, which I could hardly refuse.

For some reason best known to herself, she considered it her duty to try to pair off her unmarried acquaintances, which I was sure was what she had in mind for me. I was also sure her choice for me would be some dull but well-meaning man, somebody she considered a 'safe choice' as she put it. I was wrong. It was worse.

Possibly she had detected something of my submissive nature, but if so, she had entirely got the wrong end of the stick. Aside from the two of them and myself, three people had been invited to dinner. There was one other female, Ivy, a mousy-haired woman smaller even than me, and so shy she barely seemed able to bring herself to speak. She was quite clearly intended to partner Angus, a big, loose-limbed Scot, with red hair and a speech impediment.

That left me with the other man, Graeme, tall, dark, square jawed, absolutely confident, and utterly condescending. Physically, he had considerable appeal, and I could see that he would be able to handle me very easily indeed. Characterwise, it was a very different story. Within ten minutes of meeting he had clearly decided that he was going to bed with me later, and that I would be grateful for it.

With Ivy and Angus already staring at each other in a sort of dumb adoration, and both host and hostess constantly moving between kitchen and dining room, I was left with little choice but to talk to him. The only sensible thing to do seemed to be to hit the drink and pray for oblivion. With luck he'd attempt to take advantage of me and I'd be sick down his front.

Whatever else was wrong, Edward Burgess' choice of drink could not be faulted. He'd opened Champagne as we'd arrived, two bottles of vintage Pol Roger. Neither Ivy nor Graeme drank, and Angus only moderately. I was already feeling slightly tipsy by the time we sat down, me between Graeme and Edward Burgess, opposite Angus. The meal started with a soup that contained more than a little sherry, along with

4

hock, then went on to pigeons individually roasted in little pots, washed down with Burgundy. Haggis followed, served with a tot of malt whisky and a Rioja, which left my head spinning and my stomach a little round ball beneath my dress. The conversation had not improved, but I had discovered one interesting thing. Edward Burgess had been a Colonel in the army.

There was a scandal, about the time I was born, involving a Colonel who made a habit of inviting girls to crew on his yacht, and then spanking them for their errors. A newspaper had exposed him, labelling him a pervert, and he had sued. His argument had been, that while he had indeed spanked the girls, he was not a pervert, as 'any red-blooded Englishman was bound to want to spank a young girl's bare bottom'. It was a wonderful phrase, enough to make me wet just reading it, and it had stuck in my head. Ever since then, the rank of Colonel had held a peculiar fascination for me.

It was easy to see Edward Burgess as a spanker too. He had the right sort of hands, big, rather heavy, with long fingers, good for spanking, and good for getting into little crevices once I was properly contrite and pliable. There was also his moustache, which was big, bristly and, frankly, offensive. Being spanked by a man with a really offensive moustache always adds a certain, special something to the sense of humiliation that comes with being punished and then molested by my persecutor. Sadly it was unlikely to happen, and I had to content myself with fantasy.

Ivy and Angus failed to put much into the conversation. Graeme more than made up for it. He never stopped, and he had an opinion on every possibly subject, even those he evidently knew nothing whatever about, including women. Marjorie had been doing her best to steer the conversation onto relationships and marriage all evening, and as she had become increasingly drunk her efforts had become increasingly open.

She had finally succeeded, although perhaps not quite in the way she had anticipated. Graeme was holding forth on changing views on female sexuality.

'. . . nothing ever really changes, of course,' he was saying, 'whatever the feminists might want us to believe. What every woman wants is a stable, monogamous relationship with a man who can provide for her and her children. It's simple biology – the survival of the fittest, the selfish gene. Sex is irrelevant, simply a tool to ensnare a suitable husband, then for reproduction. Of course they say they need it, to egg us boys along.'

'You're right, of course, dear,' Marjorie put in. 'I think far too much attention is paid to sex nowadays, especially by the media. And naturally a stable relationship is what every sensible woman wants. Don't you think so, girls?'

Ivy made an odd little noise in her throat. She was blushing. Angus was looking concerned and protective.

I should have followed Ivy's example. I didn't.

'Leaving the relationship issue aside for a moment,' I said, 'I can easily demonstrate that Graeme's argument is specious . . . well, ludicrous frankly. Ethology is not a particularly exact science, so I won't attempt to explain the current position on the relationship between human behaviour and evolution. It wouldn't be necessary anyway. Just consider the physiological evidence. The clitoris has no function save the provision of sexual pleasure. QED.'

'A vestigial penis,' Graeme answered.

'Oh for goodness sake, at least get the appropriate GCSE before you start pontificating on human biology. A vestigial organ is one in which the primary function has become redundant, generally leading to evolutionary degeneration. If the clitoris is a vestigial penis it would imply that our female ancestors had penes, which is plainly absurd.'

6

He didn't answer. Angus was the colour of a beetroot, and Ivy little better. Marjorie was looking worried. The Colonel was smiling.

'Shall we have dessert?' Marjorie said hastily.

She made for the kitchen, leaving absolute silence, until Graeme spoke again.

'It's all very well using long words and clever arguments, but the fact remains that women have no real need for sex, not in the way men do. They only use it as a tool, to get what they want. No woman ever has sex simply because she enjoys it.'

'Rubbish!' I answered.

'It is true,' he insisted. 'Can you prove otherwise?'

'What, by having sex with you, I suppose?'

He laughed.

'Right into my trap!' he went on, and laughed again, unnecessarily loud. 'You have just proved my point, Penny. You see, you know that I cannot possibly do anything other than decline that invitation . . .'

'It was not an invitation!' I exclaimed. Again he laughed, and continued.

'A challenge then, if you prefer, a challenge to me to escalate, and one you knew I couldn't not possibly accept, not within the bounds of social acceptability anyway. Therefore you say it, calling my bluff in the sure knowledge of success. Now, if you had thought there was the slightest chance of my raising the stakes, you would never have dared to say what you did.'

'Why not? I could still have turned you down.'

'Not without losing the argument, you couldn't.'

'No. Has it ever occurred to you that my not wanting sex with you might simply be something to do with you, and nothing to do with my enjoyment of sex?'

'No, no. You don't understand. I'm not saying you wouldn't enjoy it. In fact I know you would. I'm saying you have no real need for it and so would not do it without some gain other than the simple pleasure of the act.'

7

'Then fair enough, you have trapped me, because whatever I was to do now, you could argue that I did it to prove a point, thus providing my ulterior motive.'

He just laughed. I bit down my anger, determined not to allow myself to be goaded any further. Our argument had already soured the atmosphere. He seemed oblivious, and wouldn't let it lie.

'She knows I'm right,' he said to the Colonel.

I held my peace, with difficulty. At that Marjorie Burgess returned from the kitchen, bearing a tray with six elaborate looking cream puddings on it, along with a bottle of deep-orange wine. I asked what it was, in an effort to change the topic of conversation.

'It's called cranachan,' she explained. 'It's a Scottish dish. Cream, honey, raspberries, and liqueur whisky, on a bed of oatmeal.'

'Delicious, and Tokaji, a favourite of mine.'

'It's an 'eighty-four,' the Colonel commented, 'five puttonyos . . .'

'You missed the end of our little discussion, Marjorie,' Graeme interrupted him. 'I absolutely trounced Penny. Didn't I, Penny?'

'No,' I answered. 'You did not. You simply manoeuvred me into a situation from which I could not prove my point. That does not mean you are right.'

He laughed again, that same irritating bray.

'Quite the little spitfire, isn't she?' he said. 'Still, whatever she may say, she knows I'm right.'

'Are you trying to goad me into some sort of sex act?' I demanded.

'There you go again with your little dares,' he answered me. 'It doesn't work, Penny.'

I took a spoonful of cranachan. I was boiling inside, absolutely furious, and humiliated too, although not in a sexual way. Sober, I would have stayed quiet, but with more than a bottle of wine inside me, not to mention the whisky and sherry, my feelings got the better of me.

8

'I can prove it,' I said. 'I can prove it by giving pleasure to another woman, by bringing her to orgasm. She would have nothing to gain but pleasure.'

I shouldn't have said it. I knew I shouldn't have the moment the words were out of my mouth. Every one of them froze, looking at me as if I'd just suggested bestiality or cannibalism, Ivy in particular. I realised she thought I was propositioning her.

'Look, I . . .' I began, but she just ran.

Angus followed, knocking his bowl of cranachan over as he went, to spill out onto the table opposite me. I had to say something, and followed. Marjorie was ahead of me, after a dishcloth, and Ivy simply grabbed her coat and left, so all I got was a dirty look from Angus and the door more or less slammed in my face.

I stood in the hallway, swaying slightly. I was cross with myself, but furious with Graeme. Not that I wanted to face him, as I could just imagine the sort of self-righteous and condescending stance he would take. What I did want was water, and, rather than return to the dining room, I went into the kitchen. Marjorie Burgess was there, at the sink, soaking a cranachan smeared dishcloth in water. She turned to me, a glare of absolute fury.

'You have absolutely ruined my dinner party!' she snapped. 'How could you say such things?'

'Me?' I demanded. 'What about that bastard Graeme?'

'How dare you!' she yelled. 'Graeme is my nephew!'

She just snatched at me, grabbed me by the hair and wrenched me forwards. It took me completely by surprise, and she was a lot bigger than me. So I went, screaming in shock as I sprawled across the sink, banging my head on the tap. It hurt, and it was still running a trickle, right down my neck. The knock left me dazed for a second, by which time she had taken my arm and twisted it violently up into the small of my

9

back. I realised I was going to be spanked even as I felt her hand touch the back of one thigh, groping for the hem of my dress. I squealed in outrage, twisting my body in an effort to get free, but succeeded only in snagging my dress on the tap, turning it full on, and spilling one breast out.

Water exploded over my head even as my dress was jerked high, right up to my waist, putting the lacy black panties I'd chosen on show to her, and for all I knew, the men too. I screamed in protest, getting a mouthful from the water running down around my head. She'd dropped the dishcloth, and my bare breast had gone in it, slimy with cranachan, a disgusting feeling, which was pushed right out of my head as her hand locked in the waistband of my panties.

'You're coming bare, young lady,' she snapped, and pulled.

They were down. My bum was bare, showing to the world, pink and naked and quivering, complete with smack marks from my last punishment. I went wild, kicking and screaming and cursing, but only succeeded in showing off my pussy and bumhole as my panties were tugged firmly down. She left them there, indifferent to my tantrums, around my thighs, inverted, to frame my bare bottom in rucked up dress, suspender straps and lowered panties. She set to work, slapping me hard, just as I heard her husband's voice raised in surprise.

'Marjorie!?'

'Hey!' Graeme put in, and went quiet.

She didn't answer. I did, with a fresh scream and a desperate lunge to the side as her hand came down hard on my bottom for the second swat.

'Stay still, you little bitch!' she swore, and twisted my arm harder still, even as she applied the third swat, the hardest yet.

A fourth followed, laid full across my bum cheeks, and a fifth, lower, catching my thighs as well as my bum. With that I lost control completely.

I've been spanked a lot of times, by a lot of people. Marjorie Burgess was one of the worst, really hard, merciless. Her big arm was going up and down like a piston – smack, smack, smack – until my screams had turned from outrage to pain and my overriding emotion from humiliation to a burning self-pity. It hurt so much, every blow slamming into my poor bare bottom, to jam my body into the sink. My buttocks were wobbling crazily, my tits shaking to the same rhythm, with a mixture of cream and water dribbling from the bare one. My feet weren't even on the ground, but high and wide, kicking in a frantic, futile response to my pain. With the men watching from behind me, I tried to stay knock-kneed, to keep my pussy and anus hidden from them. It didn't work, the pain was too much, and I gave what must have been a thoroughly dirty and undignified show of my whole bottom, every detail.

I don't know when I burst into tears, but it was long before the end. I usually cry when I'm spanked, and I don't see why I shouldn't. I do love being punished, but that doesn't stop it hurting, and this time it wasn't even supposed to be erotic, but a genuine punishment. I had every right to cry. My tears didn't stop her, she just carried on – smack, smack, smack. She might not even have noticed, with her anger and the way the water was cascading down over my head, but she must have heard my cries change in tone; the broken catch, and the snivelling, miserable gulps that came between my screams.

By the time she finally stopped I was completely broken. She let go and I sank down, to my knees, no longer caring for the blatant display I was making of my bottom. After all, they'd seen everything, and there was no possible doubt that they had wanted to.

I'd realised it was a set-up from the moment she'd told me my panties were coming down. If my spanking had really been given in anger she'd have left them up.

After all, they weren't very big, and left most of my bum cheeks sticking out at the sides anyway. Even if she had been determined to get me bare, she'd only needed to have tugged them down, or just pulled them up into my bum crease. People who tell a girl her panties are coming down for a spanking are getting a kick out of doing it, a sexual kick.

There were other things too. The Colonel's lack of resistance when he found his wife beating me, Graeme's knowledge of how to make me angry. They knew what I was like. I had no idea how, but they knew. They'd done it well too, because I was in that glorious state of utter, wanton submission that comes only after a really good spanking. Even if it had been genuine I'd have masturbated, although obviously not in front of them. As it was, it was only fair I give them the rudest possible show.

All three were there, Marjorie standing over me, slightly out of breath, the men further back, at the edge of my vision. I could barely see through my tears, and I was still snivelling a little, with mucus running down my lip. So I gave them a little wiggle to show that I was OK, and to express my thanks for the spanking. None responded, just watched, which was fine by me. Pushing out my bottom, I found the wet crevice of my sex, and began to masturbate.

I must have looked a fine sight, kneeling there, one cream smeared tit hanging out of my wet dress, my hair sodden, my bare bum stuck out, both cheeks smacked red, my anus on show in her little nest of hair, my sex lips showing and my fingers busy between them. It certainly felt good, and my need to make a real display of myself rose with my pleasure.

There were parsnips on the worktop, left over from the neeps, big ones, fat at the top, and tapering to narrow ends. It was too much to resist. I snatched up at them, pulling three down. The fattest went up my

12

pussy, stuffed in, big end first. I was so wet it slid up on the second push, to leave me stretched and gaping, with half of it sticking obscenely out of my hole. The second I put to my bumhole, thin end first, easing it into my little sweaty ring, and up, until it began to hurt. Well plugged, I went back to masturbating, now in a squat, thighs wide, sat on the parsnips so that I could push them slowly deeper as I frigged.

As soon as I touched my clitty I knew it wasn't going to take long. I began to rub, my other hand going to my chest. I pulled out my covered breast, smearing cream across the sensitive skin and pinching the already hard nipple. With the orgasm rising in my head I began to buck and wriggle, squirming my bottom on the intruding parsnips, alternately snatching at my slimy breasts and the hot, rough skin of my smacked buttocks. I began to mumble, thanking them over and over again, until at last it hit me and I screamed out in pure, uncontrolled ecstasy, my whole body going rigid as I came.

I held it as long as I could, and collapsed, purring happily to myself, thoroughly content, my eyes closed, my mouth set in a happy smile. Remembering Graeme's argument, now obviously designed to wind me up, I laughed, and spoke as I turned to look at him.

'I think that proves my point, don't . . .'

I trailed off. He wasn't smiling, he was staring, open mouthed. So was the Colonel, his face set in an expression of absolute outrage, one muscle twitching in his cheek. Above me, Marjorie Burgess was also staring, her face frozen in astonishment.

I realised that the punishment had, after all, been genuine.

INTIMATE INSTRUCTION

Arabella Knight

Arabella Knight is one of our most evergreen authors, whose tales of dominance and discipline have delighted Nexus readers for a few years now. Her wayward young characters are taught how to behave and soon develop an appetite for the pleasures of punishment. In this extract from *Intimate Instruction*, her latest Nexus book, young Emma Wyndlesham arrives at Lament's Hall, an institution to which the upper classes consign their wayward daughters for discipline, and ends up as the victim of a painful case of mistaken identity . . .

Also by Arabella Knight from Nexus are:

THE ACADEMY
CONDUCT UNBECOMING
CANDY IN CAPTIVITY
SUSIE IN SERVITUDE
THE MISTRESS OF STERNWOOD GRANGE
TAKING PAINS TO PLEASE
BROUGHT TO HEEL

They were in a spartanly furnished study. A desk, good Adam period chairs, a patterned carpet. A large blue vase of early daffodils and, incongruously, framed photographs of fifties and sixties female tennis stars, softened the hardness of the room. Orange flames flickered in an open hearth, their dancing light reflected in the polished walnut of a chest of drawers.

Emma stood before a desk. It was littered with open files and scattered sheets of paper – the only note of discord in the neat room around her. Seated at the desk, gazing at Emma steadily, was a handsome woman in her early forties. Her steel grey hair was swept back into a severe chignon. She wore a crisp blouse, pearl buttoned, with a small cameo fixed at the throat. The woman's pale blue eyes scanned Emma unblinkingly as she asked for some identification. Emma, giving her name and the purpose of her business at Laments, produced her driving licence.

The grey hair gleamed as the woman bent her head down to study the licence. Emma caught the whiff of jasmine perfume across the polished leather of the desktop.

'And what did you say your purpose at Laments was?' The pale blue eyes gazed up unblinkingly. The lipstick-free mouth was resolute, suggestive of a firm, dominant personality. The sensual lips were pursed.

Emma explained once again, producing the paper-work she had been assigned to serve and handing them across the desk.

'Ah, the Wigmore girl.'

Emma frowned. Clearly this stern woman could be no relation of the Right Honourable Rebecca. Emily's thoughts stole back out on to the terrace to the scene she had glimpsed through the leaded window. Had it been Rebecca receiving the severe spanking? Emma felt a little confused.

'You're wet, girl.'

Emma, her panties soaked after witnessing the spanking, blushed.

'Slip off your Barbour and shoes and take a chair by the fire.'

Wet. Raindrops glistened on her Barbour as she peeled it off. Suppressing a fleeting grin, Emma accepted the invitation, obediently kicking off her shoes and making herself comfortable by the blazing fire. She turned her face and hands towards the heat. Sniffing delicately, she savoured the slightly pungent aroma from the pearwood logs crackling in the hearth.

'You shall see the Wigmore girl in a few minutes. This matter must be dealt with at once. There must be no delay, and no scandal. The girl's parents are out in Tokyo,' the silver-haired woman added, tidying up the files on her desk. 'Sir Joseph and Lady Wigmore are launching an important business deal in Japanese television.'

Those Wigmores, Emma thought, recognising the name. The family owned several theatres as well as a growing media empire.

Emma grew impatient. 'Are you Rebecca's aunt?' she asked politely, knowing that the woman at the desk certainly wasn't.

'*In loco parentis*. And you may rest assured that I will see to it that the account is settled and that the Wigmore family name is fully protected.'

Emma replied that was exactly what NVK always strived to achieve.

'I am so very glad to hear you say so, my girl.'

Brushing aside the mild annoyance of 'my girl', Emma struggled to decode an elusive clue the woman had let slip. *In loco parentis*. The phrase stirred in her brain.

'Laments,' the stern woman continued, rising from her desk, 'is an institution which takes in young ladies who, like the Wigmore girl, require guidance and training.'

A private school. A girls boarder, Emma thought. 'I see. Private, I mean public school?' Emma smiled.

'An institution,' the suave reply cut in, 'where the emphasis is placed on appropriate training. Training,' she continued, patting her chignon, 'and correction. The girls come to us the despair of their parents. Conventional methods have frequently proved profitless. They are wayward, spoiled and badly in need of discipline.'

Discipline. The nude blonde, bare bottomed, being given a hot, red bottom in the drawing room. Emma gulped.

'Laments, of which I am the Head,' the woman continued, approaching one of the framed photographs of tennis amazons on the wall and straightening it affectionately, 'provides such girls with a very strict regime, a bracing lifestyle along with what I deem to be the undoubted benefits of intimate instruction.'

Intimate instruction. Emma's thoughts returned swiftly once more to the bare-bottomed spanking in the drawing room. Its fascination haunted her. Just one remembered glimpse of the firm palm sweeping down across the suffering, upturned cheeks was enough to juice her prickling slit. Intimate instruction. So. Little miss hot-cheeks was a pupil here at Laments, benefiting from a little spot of one-to-one tuition.

'Felicity Flint,' the Head said, approaching Emma, extending her hand.

Emma rose, smiled and shook hands – wincing slightly at the firmness of the other's grasp.

'We'll have the Wigmore girl in now, I think.' As she strode back towards her desk to use the intercom, Emma noted the athletic, tanned legs. Powerfully thighed, tautly muscled. The Head, she observed, wore white ankle socks and white laced-up pumps. As Emma watched the Head bend down to speak, she fleetingly wondered if any of the naughty girls ever felt the fury of a supple white pump across their bare, quivering buttocks. Probably.

'Miss Watson.'

'Yes, Dr Flint?' a metallic voice replied.

'Come to my study.'

'Yes, Dr Flint.'

Moments later, there was a polite tap at the door.

'Enter.'

A slender, soberly dressed woman came into the room. Emma spotted the cruel mouth at once – and the narrowed, green eyes behind the flashing lens of horn-rimmed spectacles.

'Miss Watson, my secretary. Absolutely invaluable.'

The green eyes widened and the cruel mouth slackened to a simper.

'As good as a second pair of eyes and ears to me.'

The glasses flashed as Miss Watson inclined her head, bestowing a curt nod towards Emma.

'Winkle out the Wigmore girl from whatever she shouldn't be doing, will you, Watson? Bring her straight here.'

'The Wigmore girl? Early Bed, I believe. Late for French from showers. Is anything the matter, Head?' Miss Watson asked, shooting a suspicious glance at Emma.

'Nothing that cannot be settled here and now. The Wigmore girl, if you please, Watson.'

'At once, Dr Flint.' She scuttled away.

The Head fingered the cameo at her throat, then slowly undid the single pearl button at the cuff of her right sleeve.

'How many girls do you have here at Laments?' Emma asked, feeling somewhat obliged to make conversation. How do you administer their punishments, she really wanted to know. A cane? A real yellow length of bamboo whippy cane? A whippy cane that would bite into their peach-cheeks, leaving pink stripes across the proffered buttocks and stinging salt tears in their sorrowful eyes?

'Eighteen,' she heard the Head's voice say. Emma concentrated on what was being said. When Dr Felicity Flint spoke, it was wise to listen, Emma felt. 'With a staff of five. Under strength at the moment. With such a generous SSR –'

'SSR?' Emma interrupted, instantly wishing she hadn't.

'Student-to-staff ratio, my dear. It allows for the intensive tuition I mentioned earlier, and of course the girls' parents are both willing and capable of paying for this unique provision.'

Emma felt a response was appropriate. 'Your girls are very priviliged.'

'Possibly, but I fear that they do not always appreciate that fact.'

Remembering the shiny-sore red bottom in the drawing room, Emma suspected that Felicity Flint was perfectly correct in that observation.

'How old are you, girl?'

Emma, startled, answered at once. 'Twenty two.'

'Hmm. Five years older than our youngest, three years above our oldest girls, of which the Right Honourable Rebecca Wigmore is one.'

The door to the study opened.

'And here she is.'

Miss Watson entered, shepherding a dark-eyed nine-teen year old.

'Thank you, Miss Watson.'

The secretary, eager to learn more, hesitated at the door.

'Good night,' Dr Flint added, the note of finality unmistakeable.

Scowling resentfully at Emma's fleeting smile, Miss Watson withdrew, closing the door behind her. She'll listen at the door, Emma thought, recognising the prying type. Hadn't the Head mentioned something about eyes. And ears.

By the desk, the Right Honourable Rebecca Wigmore stood, head bowed, her long dark hair curtaining her pale face. But Emma saw the gleam of the dark, wary eyes. The girl shivered, scantily clad in a tight, white vest and tiny shorts. The vest, short sleeved and deeply scalloped at her bosom, rode the swell of the firm breasts with a taut stretch of cotton. The peaks of her prinking nipples were clearly defined beneath the soft fabric. Emma's tongue slowly thickened as she noted how the tiny shorts sculpted the young girl's delicious pubic mound.

'In bed, already?' the Head barked.

'Early Bed, Dr Flint. A half forfeit.'

'A half forfeit, eh?' rejoined the Head, feigning a note of surprise. 'What for?'

Rebecca stubbed the toes of her right foot into the patterned carpet. Emma, privy to the answer to the Head's question, wondered if the girl would risk a lie.

'I'm very much afraid that an Early Bed is far too lenient a punishment for such slacking. Late for –' Dr Flint paused briefly '– let me see. Friday evening. Why, French conversation.'

'Yes, Dr Flint.'

'An Early Bed from Mme Puton?'

'Yes, Dr Flint,' Rebecca whispered, delicately tracing a fraction of the floral pattern in the carpet with her toes.

'I shall speak to her tomorrow on the subject.'

The Head turned towards the flickering fire and briskly introduced Emma and the purpose of her presence. Emma rose, eager to see the transactions completed.

'NVK work this way to spare you any –' she began.

Dr Flint broke in sharply, taking charge.

'I understand that you have been using this credit card, the existence of which I was wholly unaware, and in addition to this you actually had the temerity to exceed an agreed credit limit by some two and a half thousand pounds and,' the Head concluded, her stern voice rising in anger, 'no arrangements have been made for any repayment of the accumulated debt. Is this correct?'

Crushed by the tirade, Rebecca merely nodded and bowed her head in shame.

'You actually broke your credit agreement and failed to make any attempt at repayment?'

Rebecca's silence confirmed her guilt.

'But you know the rules perfectly well, girl. You seem to have been flouting them pretty freely. We will go carefully into the exact details of when and where you used, or rather abused, this credit card in a few moments.'

What kind of hornet's nest have I stirred up here, Emma wondered. Were the girls here at Laments gated, forbidden to visit the nearby villages and towns? If so, poor little Rebecca was really in the shit.

'May I say, Dr Flint –' Emma began.

Again, the Head curtly ignored her. Emma, hovering uncertainly by the fire, was now anxious to complete the business and get back into The Beast and on the road to London.

The Head took her seat behind the desk and spread out the NVK paperwork, smoothing it down against the polished leather desktop with her broad palms.

Summoning Rebecca towards the desk with an impatient snap of her fingers, she instructed the shivering girl to read and then sign them.

'I will see to it that Miss Watson makes an immediate payment of one thousand pounds on Monday morning. These papers,' the Head continued, retrieving her fountain pen from Rebecca's nervous fingers, 'will be forwarded to the family solicitors. In the absence of Sir Charles and Lady Wigmore, I believe that to be the most prudent course of action. Epsom, Epsom, Darkling and Epsom, isn't it girl?'

'Yes, Dr Flint.' Rebecca's penitent whisper was scarcely audible.

'Well, that all seems fine,' Emma conceded. 'There's just the credit card. My instructions –'

'Ah, yes. The credit card,' the Head broke in, once again marginalising Emma. 'Where exactly is it, girl? No. Let me think. In your swimsuit?'

Rebecca glanced up, amazement battling with fear in her dark eyes. 'Yes. I hide it in my costume, Dr Flint.'

'Carefully tucked away in your locker, I presume.'

Rebecca merely nodded.

'Then we shall have to go down to the pool together after I have punished you and destroy the wretched thing.'

Punished you. Emma's tongue worked busily, trying to lubricate her dry mouth. What precisely did the stern Head mean by those delicious words. More strange forfeits? Early Beds? What if Rebecca was about to be spanked? Emma supposed that she wouldn't be around to witness it this time.

'Place that chair over there, in the centre of the carpet, Rebecca.'

The girl picked up the chair and obediently positioned it on the spot indicated by the Head's jabbing forefinger.

'Across the chair, girl. I am going to cane your bottom.'

Emma clenched her hands into tight little fists of excitement. Her nipples stirred, thickened and kissed the lace of her taut brassiere cups. A caning. It was going to be a caning.

'Hadn't I better –' Emma murmured.

'Stay where you are by that nice warm fire, girl. Much more comfortable, I'm sure, than out in the nasty rain.'

Stunned – but secretly thrilled – Emma slumped back down in her chair. She watched, somewhat shyly, as Rebecca bent down over the chair, planting her hands, palms down, on the polished seat. Head bowed, thighs squeezed together, she presented her rounded buttocks up for their impending pain.

'Laments,' the Head purred, approaching the gleaming walnut chest of drawers, 'dispenses all discipline immediately. Instant punishment could almost be our motto. It's the best way, I find. Sometimes, of course,' she added conversationally, 'the miscreant benefits from waiting anxiously for an hour before being beaten. Endless moments of delicious dread. Sixty minutes of sweet torment. Such waiting heightens the girl's anxiety and foreboding. Before I bare the naughty bottom, the wrongdoer has already imagined and suffered every stinging swipe, every searing slice, of the cruel cane.'

As the Head paused to open the second drawer down, Emma clenched her buttocks furtively, inching them up from the seat of her chair to ease her soaking panties clinging to her flesh.

'But in this particular case,' the Head grunted, rummaging in the deep drawer, 'prompt punishment is called for. Ah, there it is.'

She had been pawing the interior of the drawer. Emma heard the dry, eerie rattle as the Head's fingertips encountered the length of bamboo. So did Rebecca – who whimpered softly. The cane was extracted from the darkness of the drawer and brought out into the light. It sparkled beneath the electric lightbulbs above: twenty-two inches of venomously supple wood. The Head closed the drawer with her elbow. The smooth, worn wood slid home silently. Emma watched, more openly and with lively interest, as the Head shouldered her cane, stepped up to the framed photographs of the last generation of female tennis champions, smartly saluted them with the quivering stick, then turned to address the proffered buttocks of the bending girl.

'Shall we say six for actually using the credit card, such usage being, as you know full well, Rebecca, forbidden during your stay here at Laments and six,' the Head added, inspecting her cane closely for a few seconds then swishing it down to test its whippiness, 'for risking the good name of your family by flouting the credit limit and failing to make provision for repayments?'

After the flurry of words, a loud silence filled the study. Suddenly, a pearwood log settled in the embers, sending a shower of orange sparks whirling up the dark chimney. Emma, spellbound as she followed the pre-punishment preparations, almost toppled from her chair.

'But first,' Dr Flint murmured, reverently placing her cane lengthways down across the polished leather surface of the desk, 'I require you to give me full details of how, where, when and with whom you used the credit card.'

Stepping forward two paces, she reached down and placed her capable hands at the waist of the bending girl. Rebecca eased her tummy down, bent her knees a fraction and jerked her bottom up obediently to allow her tiny shorts to be dragged down slowly. The Head's slender fingers left the shorts at the lower thighs. They remained there, binding the soft flesh in a restricting band, clamping the bare-bottomed girl's legs together and rendering her exposed cheeks above perfectly poised and positioned for punishment.

Gazing at the dark cleft between the perfect peach-cheeks, Emma was struck by a sudden thought, prompted by a glint from a pearl button on the Head's bloused bosom. She had known all along, Emma realised, watching the Head roll up the unbuttoned sleeve of her blouse. She unbuttoned that cuff five minutes after I came into this room. Rebecca's fate had been sealed – and her punishment decided – even before the dark-haired girl had been dragged from her Early Bed by the eager Miss Watson.

The double echo of a blisteringly spanking hand rang around the spartan study. Emma blinked, almost angry with herself for not concentrating properly and, in consequence, missing the first two spanks. The echo had died. All that remained to attest to the fact that they had occurred were two pink blotches which deepened to a darker crimson before Emma's wide eyes. Smack. Smack. The Head stood up after delivering two more crisp spanks across the soft cheeks. Rebecca mewled in response, her buttocks reddening angrily as she squeezed them.

'Well, girl. Speak. I'm waiting.'

Under the threat of the hovering hand above her bottom, Rebecca quickly confessed to using the credit card in Brighton. Two more severe spanks elicited two shrill squeals and a full confession. Times, dates and places all spilled forth. Names were named. Less than half of it made any sense to Emma, although she was able to work out that Rebecca had taken three of her friends from Laments in a hired car to Brighton and back – before dawn – on at least a dozen memorable jaunts. Lavish meals washed down by champagne had been enjoyed. The hire car, plus waiting time and tip, must have cost at least a hundred. That, Emma realised, calculating rapidly, accounted for the earlier cash withdrawals before the hole-in-the-wall had dried up.

The Head ran her fingertips lightly over the punished rump, then briefly thumbed Rebecca's hot cleft. 'Vintage champagne? Lobsters?'

Under a staccato of five more merciless spanks, Rebecca yelped out her guilt, confessing unreservedly more details, more damning facts.

Stepping back from the spanked girl, Dr Flint rubbed her hot palm against her thigh before snatching up the bamboo cane.

'Twelve, we agreed, did we not?' she whispered, depressing the spanked cheeks under the thin whippy stick's yellow length. 'Legs straight. Up on your toes, girl.'

The Head raised the cane. Emma saw the white line its pressure into the hot flesh had left slowly fill with crimson.

'Bottom up a little more, girl. Come along. Get it up,' she rasped, tap-tapping the curved flesh mounds imperiously with the quivering tip of her cane.

Rebecca, sniffling, obeyed instantly, straining to present her smacked bottom up to her punisher's satisfaction. Dr Flint took a half pace back, levelled the bamboo in against the swell of the beautiful buttocks, swept the whippy wood up then lashed it down. Emma's soft gasp was drowned by the sound of the slicing swipe across the soft cheeks, and the loud sorrow-sob from the lips of the punished girl. A second, a third and then a blistering fourth stroke followed. Rebecca's squealing became one long howl of anguish. Emma held her breath, painfully, until the fifth cruel stroke had whipped down, bite-slicing into the striped buttocks. Criss-crossed with vivid weals, the flayed buttocks jerked and writhed. Emma glimpsed the wet fig of the thrashed, bare-bottomed girl as she twisted across the chair in an agony of torment. Emma breathed out softly, surrendering to the ache in her pent-up lungs. Her loud sigh was silenced by the brutal swish and searing swipe of the sixth stroke.

Rebecca screamed softly, wriggling and writhing as if in orgasm, bucking her hips and squeezing her cheeks as if sucking up a ribbed anal dildo into the wet warmth of her sphincter. Emma sat still. To move an inch – dragging her wet slit against her cotton panties – would, she knew, trigger a climax almost at once. Ashamed, deliciously disturbed and sexually aroused by the strict discipline being dispensed to the bare-bottomed girl across the chair, Emma was filled with the pleasurable discomfort of her new found self-knowledge: she enjoyed watching another female being punished. She found strict discipline delightful, and took pleasure in another's pain.

Rebecca wriggled frantically, her striped bottom describing erotic arabesques as her slender hips writhed.

'Stop that at once, girl,' Dr Flint snapped, trapping and taming the whipped cheeks beneath the yellow cane she had just lashed them with. 'Now get down right across the chair for the next six strokes. Hurry up, girl,' she thundered impatiently, 'you know what I want.'

Rebecca squirmed as she lowered her breasts over the far edge of the polished wooden seat and sank her belly into the shining wood. Her bottom, now horizontal, was deliciously poised, forming a tempting target for the cane. The bamboo twitched eagerly in the Head's firm grasp.

Struggling to avoid coming right then and there on her chair, Emma gazed directly on Rebecca's re-positioned buttocks: longing to kiss each perfect peach-cheek then bury her hot face down between the hotter twin mounds of red-wealed flesh and tongue the deep cleft between them.

29

Almost swooning, Emma gripped the sides of her chair to steady herself. She felt her pulse plucking at her soft throat, sensed the hammer of her heart. Her swollen tongue seemed too thick for her mouth. She sat, her brain spinning, as the Head commenced to administer the second stage of the punishment.

Dr Flint gripped her cane firmly and angled it above the bunched buttocks directly below. The first six strokes had been swift and searing, planting scarlet stripes across the helpless cheeks in rapid succession. The concluding strokes were, Emma felt intuitively, to be slow; more deliberate and more measured.

One. Emma counted silently, surreptitiously smoothing her fingertips down over her pubis as the thin cane sliced into the rubbery spasms of punished flesh.

Two. Emma whispered it softly, her dry lips peeling slowly apart as she murmured the count. Two. Two nipples, now burning peaks of pain, aching for the fierce cupping of her crushing palms.

Three. The third stroke instantly conjured up three sounds: a shriek from the punished; a snarl from the punisher; a moan from the voyeur.

Four. The cane whistled down, kiss-lashing the upturned buttocks savagely. Rebecca slammed her hips four times into the chair in a frenzy of violent ecstasy before the Head planted her white pump firmly down on to the whipped bottom. Writhing beneath the pinioning pump of her dominant tormentress, Rebecca squirmed in agony, sobbing aloud. Emma, her slit now weeping freely, yearned to bring her fingers to her wet heat.

'Come here,' the Head instructed, shouldering her cane and summoning Emma to her side.

As if in a trance, Emma rose from her chair and approached. Dr Flint took her pump away from Rebecca's bottom and replaced it on the carpet. Emma glimpsed the chevrons of the ribbed sole working a herringbone pattern against the crimson flesh. Shrinking back slightly from the sight, at such close quarters, of the cane-striped cheeks, Emma looked up into the Head's clear gaze.

'Here. Take it.'

Emma was offered the cane.

'The girl is due a further two strokes. She has caused you a good deal of inconvenience. Her bottom is yours. Stripe her. Stripe her well.'

Gripping the cane and thrilling to the potent malice of the whippy wood, Emma succumbed to hesitation, guilt and indecision. She wanted to administer the two remaining strokes, wanted to swish the bamboo down across the already striped buttocks of the bare-bottomed, bending girl. She yearned to hear the thin whistle of the slicing strokes, and ached for the grunts from Rebecca's lips as her soft cheeks suffered. But, inexplicably, Emma found, to her frustration and confusion, that her arm could not raise the length of cane up above the shivering buttocks below.

Felicity Flint, scrutinising Emma carefully, nodded judiciously and stepped in, smartly retrieving the situation. A true dominant, she was anxious to maintain control at every stage of the discipline. Any lapse – or unscheduled pause in the proceedings – could shift the carefully orchestrated balance of power between the punisher and the punished.

'You are tired,' she murmured.

Emma, with a fleeting pang of reluctance, surrendered the cane to the Head. She nodded, avoiding the piercing gaze of Dr Flint's pale blue eyes.

Swish, crack. The remaining two strokes were delivered instantly with consummate skill, leaving Rebecca squealing and writhing in renewed anguish.

'Remain exactly as you are across the chair for two minutes, girl,' the Head instructed. 'Gin and T or sherry?'

Emma, lost in her own thoughts as she gazed down intently at the red-wealed buttocks still wriggling in pain, did not think the partly heard words were being addressed to her.

'I could get some tea or coffee rustled up, of course,' Felicity Flint continued.

'Oh,' Emma blinked. 'A G and T would be fine.'

The Head, after carefully returning the cane to its dark lair in the polished walnut drawer, fixed two gins, splashing the tonic in expertly. Emma heard the ice cubes clinking against the sides of the tumblers.

'Bottoms up.' Dr Flint arched her right eyebrow up.

Emma blushed, then drank deeply. She watched over the rim of her tumbler as the Head raised her own glass up once more in a salute to the photos on the opposite wall. Emma, shaken by recent events, found herself toying with an empty glass.

'Another?'

Coming to her senses with a determined effort, Emma shook her head. 'Driving.' She shrugged.

'Let's not even discuss your dashing back to London at this late hour,' Dr Flint countered suavely, commandeering Emma's glass and refilling it generously. 'There. You'll stay. It's settled. We'll have some supper when I have completed our business here.'

Settling down on to her chair by the fire, Emma realised that she was to remain at Laments overnight. Supremely confident in all her decisions, the Head had spoken with an air of finality without any discussion. Emma had not even agreed.

'Come along, girl,' Emma heard the Head admonish the snivelling credit card cheat, who was struggling unsuccessfully to yank up her tiny shorts over her whipped cheeks. 'Take me to your locker at once.'

Emma watched as Rebecca wiped a silver tear from her eye with the back of her hand. Snuffling as she answered, her whispered words were indistinct.

'Oh, come here, girl.'

Emma turned, alert to the new timbre in the Head's voice. It could have been one of the tennis aces framed upon the wall speaking, encouraging a colt who had just missed an ace. Felicity Flint had spoken with an unsuspected tenderness.

'Shorts down. Let me see your bottom.'

Rebecca obeyed, thumbing down her shorts obediently until the tight waistband cupped her punished cheeks – causing their swollen curves to bulge deliciously. The Head kneeled, her stern face a mere three inches from the buttocks she had just blistered with the cruel whippy wood.

Emma watched, fascinated, as the kneeling Head brought her tumbler of iced gin and tonic up against the naked bottom, pressing the cold glass into and then rolling it across the hot double domes. Rebecca gasped aloud, jerking her whipped rump back into the healing balm.

'You have been a very naughty girl,' Dr Flint murmured softly, removing the glass and, after raising it to her sensual lips, sipping slowly from it. Rebecca waggled her reddened bottom impatiently, signalling her desire for the return of the tumbler.

'Haven't you?'

'Yes, Head.'

'But you have been punished, and I note that you did not lie or attempt to deny the offence.' The Head skimmed the frosted glass teasingly across the quivering cheeks.

Rebecca whispered her penitence softly. She inched her buttocks back, seeking the touch of the cold glass against her punished flesh. The Head crushed the tumbler along the dark cleft. Rebecca whimpered happily, shuddering at and basking in the delicious aftercare.

'And you did deserve to be beaten, didn't you?'

Rebecca remained silent. It was a sulky silence.

'So,' the Head whispered, her voice returning to its tone of velvety venom, 'you resent your stripes? There will, I must warn you, girl, be more stripes for you, and your wicked accomplices.'

Emma saw Rebecca's cheeks clench in fearful anticipation of further punishment.

'But more of that tomorrow.' Dr Flint rose, finished her drink with one hand and jerked up Rebecca's tight shorts deftly with the other. 'Now take me to that wretched card and let me destroy it.'

More stripes. Sitting alone by the glowing embers in the hearth, Emma nursed her second strong gin and T. She sipped from it meditatively, relaxing as the drink warmed her. She felt drained. Exhausted. Grudgingly glad not to have to take The Beast back through the rain to London. And her slit seethed. She must, she thought, get some privacy soon and attend to the heat that was becoming increasingly more urgent between the juncture of her slippery thighs.

Emma's desire for the relief and the release of a climax clamoured loudly in her brain and at the base of her tightened belly. The roller-coaster events of the last couple of hours had left her with so much to feed her fantasies with, so much to fuel her scrabbling fingers frantic at her pussy.

One more peep at that cane. Dare she? Emma skipped across to the polished walnut chest of drawers and opened up the bamboo's resting place. Her fingers found the thin length of cane and dragged it into the light. Glancing down, Emma shivered, vividly remembering Rebecca's red stripes. Emma knew that she must hold the cane once more. It quivered in her tightly gripping fist. She swished it, thrilling to the vicious slice as the bamboo sang its cruel note of suffering. Emma's mouth dried. She sipped her iced gin and T.

The study door opened. A stern-faced woman, in the lemon vest, black short, pleated skirt and laced pumps of a gym mistress, entered the room. Her sharp, hazel eyes darted from the deserted desk to Emma.

'What are you doing in here, girl? Where is Dr Flint?' she rasped.

Emma, startled by the sudden entrance and abrupt tone, gulped – and had to wipe the gin trickling from her chin. The cane dropped silently at her feet on the carpet.

'Felicity has just gone to –'

'Felicity?' the gym mistress thundered. 'How dare you be so impertinent. All girls, without exception, address members of staff here by their correct title, understand? What were you doing with that cane?'

The svelte, athletic woman approached, her pumps treading the patterned carpet with silent menace. 'Is that gin?' She sniffed suspiciously.

'Gin and T,' Emma, struggling to explain, managed.

'Bend over this instant, girl. You may be new but there's simply no excuse for this outrageous behaviour.'

Emma, so shocked she almost giggled, stepped back. 'You don't understand –'

'I said bend over. At once,' the gym mistress hissed. 'Unless you learn to obey instantly your time here at Laments is going to be painfully unpleasant,' she grunted, wrestling Emma expertly down across a chair and pinning the struggling girl down with her right pump.

'No, don't, get off,' Emma screeched, no match for the lithe and strong gym mistress.

'Silence,' snapped the stern woman, pulling out a white hankie and forcing it into Emma's mouth – silencing her shrill protest.

Pinning Emma down by the nape of her neck with one hand, the gym mistress unfurled a coiled leather belt from her skirt pocket. As she dragged it out, a silver whistle spilled down on to the carpet. Emma spluttered into her gag and wriggled violently beneath the pinioning hand at her neck and pump on her upturned rump. But the gym mistress, snapping the length of leather ominously, was clearly adept at dealing with girls who struggled to evade the lash.

'Rule number one for new girls at Laments,' she hissed, planting her feet apart and deftly baring Emma's bottom. 'Obey all rules. Understand?'

Emma squirmed but found all struggling futile. She was bared and prepared for the bite of the leather. Helpless, she tensed, dreading the moment the hide would caress her buttocks.

'Stop struggling or I'll double your six to a dozen, girl.'

Emma's outrage collapsed into raw fear. The gym mistress was implacable – Emma knew that she was about to receive six searing strokes across her poor, defenceless little bottom. But with the knowledge came a guilty thrill.

Crack. The length of hide sliced down, bequeathing a deep pink band of pain across Emma's clenched cheeks. It stung and burned. Emma squealed.

'What on earth –' Dr Flint's voice demanded imperiously as she strode through the door into her study.

Crack. The gym mistress lashed the leather down once more, adding a second pink swathe of pain to the deepening crimson of the first stripe. 'Nothing to worry about, Head. Found this new girl in here drinking your gin –'

'No, stop –' Dr Flint commanded as the leather strap was raised aloft. 'Let her go at once.'

'Head?' came the challenging response. The leather quivered above Emma's bottom, its tip dangling teasingly across the surface of her whipped cheeks. 'Let her go?' echoed the gym mistress, lowering the strap down across the crowns of the punished buttocks.

'Not a new girl,' the Head gasped, coming to Emma's rescue at once.

'But then –' Emma's tormentress countered, baffled.

'Oh dear,' Dr Flint purred, palming Emma's bottom gently. 'Not a very good welcome to Laments, hmm?'

The gym mistress furled up her strap and pocketed it. Stooping, her lemon vest bulging as her unbrassiered breasts burgeoned, she snatched up her silver whistle.

The Head assisted Emma from the chair. 'Never mind. Time for a bite of supper.'

Deciding the incident to be closed, the Head picked up the cane from the carpet. 'How did this get there?'

Emma blushed.

'She was playing with it when I came into the study,' the gym mistress remarked.

'Was she?' the Head murmured. Giving Emma a playful tap on her bottom with the tip of the yellow bamboo, she returned the cane to its resting place in the chest of drawers. 'I am sure we shall all three of us look back one day upon this little misunderstanding and smile.'

Dr Flint and the gym mistress laughed brightly. Emma, still in shock, sore bottomed after the stinging leather and – to her discomfort and puzzlement – disturbingly aroused, did not laugh. She did not even return the Head's attempt at a winning smile.

'No sulking, now. Mistakes will happen,' Felicity Flint reasoned, her tone brisk and reasonable.

Emma attempted a political, if uneasy, smile.

'Marion, my deputy,' the Head continued, making the introductions and explaining Emma's presence at Laments.

'The Wigmore girl did that? Do we know her accomplices, Head? They too must be punished.' Marion remained unapologetic. Her manner was, Emma felt, annoyingly bracing.

A flash of anger darted across Emma's face, clouding her grey eyes. This gung-ho gym mistress had just bared her bottom and swiped it twice with a strap. No apology. Just dismissing the incident as trivial. Like Dr Flint had said, a mistake. Bloody assault and battery, Emma thought. And now all they could talk about was the institution, and the prospect of further punishments.

Felicity Flint glanced at Emma. Noting the frown beneath her visitor's blonde mane, she motioned to Marion, dismissing her.

'Ready for supper, I'm sure.'

Emma wanted a fuller apology. An apology for the outrage visited upon her poor little bottom. But the Head's pale-blue eyes held a let's-have-no-more-nonsense challenge in their gleam. Emma decided to play safe. She smiled weakly, surreptitiously fingered her panties back into place at her cleft and followed the stern Head obediently out of the study to supper.

PET TRAINING
IN THE
PRIVATE HOUSE

Esme Ombreux

Esme Ombreux is one of the original practitioners of fetish fiction. Her first novel for Nexus, *One Week in the Private House*, took erotic fiction to new horizons of flagellant behaviour – and sold out within weeks of its first publication in 1991. Since then, Esme has added another four novels to the series, set in the timeless but familiar – and fiendishly kinky – world of the Private House. She also edited the first two New Erotica collections for Nexus. All in all then, an erotica CV worth writing home about! You can write to Esme at *esmeo@postmaster.co.uk*

We're looking forward to publishing Esme's next full-length novel soon. In the meantime, here's an extract from *Pet Training in the Private House*. Here Jessica, newly arrived in the suburb of Hillingbury, is put through her paces by Matt, an instructor at the local health club with a rather unusual exercise regime.

Also by Esme Ombreux in Nexus:

ONE WEEK IN THE PRIVATE HOUSE
AMANDA IN THE PRIVATE HOUSE
DISCIPLINE OF THE PRIVATE HOUSE
AN EDUCATION IN THE PRIVATE HOUSE
CAPTIVES OF THE PRIVATE HOUSE

B y the time Jessica arrived at the Hillingbury Health and Exercise Club it was already late afternoon. Once again there would be no time for her exercise programme: she would have to report to her mentor, tell him everything that she had done during the day, and hope that he had time to punish her and use her.

She had been in a state of arousal for so many hours that she felt disconnected from the world. It seemed as though she had floated, rather than walked, from her house to the club. As the rain had stopped at last, and the sun was out, the raincoat had seemed inappropriate, and she had put on a skirt and a blouse. She was still wearing the stockings and ankle-boots from the morning's outing.

Her breasts, bottom and sex were naked under her summery garments and, of all the sensory stimuli surrounding her as she walked to the club, only the sensations in these erogenous zones managed to hold her attention. In fact she couldn't stop thinking about those sensitive parts of her body, and things that she hoped Matt would do to them. Her bottom, in particular, wouldn't let her forget that it hadn't been spanked since the morning, and then not much. Her skin was tingling with anticipation. And she had become so used to the weight and size of the plug that she had worn in her anus for most of the day that, now it was no longer there, she missed the uncomfortably full feeling.

'You're late again,' Matt said, as soon as they were alone in his office. 'Don't bother to explain, I know you have other commitments now. Undress, please.'

He seemed more austere and remote than ever. It seemed impossible to believe that he cared for her in the slightest. And yet he insisted, each time she left, that she must return. And, as she stood before him, naked but for her stockings, with her hands clasped behind her head, she could see that he desired her.

He walked behind her to lock the door and, instead of returning to the desk, without warning he grasped her wrists in his left hand, bent her over, and delivered six hefty smacks to her buttocks. Jessica hardly had time to breathe, still less to enjoy the painful sensations, and the spanking was over almost as soon as it had begun.

There was no explanation for the punishment. Matt pulled off his T-shirt and his shorts, sat at the desk, and gestured to Jessica to stand at his left side.

'Report,' he said, and positioned a pen in readiness over a blank notepad.

Jessica drew a deep breath. He had hardly looked at her since she had arrived. Did he know, she wondered, how much his disdainful attitude excited her? Was his severe, almost contemptuous manner an act, designed to inflame her perverse desires? Or was it that he truly didn't care?

As she gave a detailed account of her activities during the day, Jessica consoled herself with the thought that Matt must like her, at least a little: he couldn't keep his hand off her. While he wrote copious notes with his right hand, his left was roaming across and between Jessica's blushing buttocks. She talked, falteringly whenever his fingers dipped into the wet channel of her sex, and he wrote without pause, even when she

42

described the events that had taken place in Mrs Smythe's bathroom. He seemed imperturbable.

She couldn't keep her eyes from his manhood, rising like a domed tower between his hard, flat stomach and the front of the desk. She wanted to touch it, and her wish was granted when she began to tell him about the toys in Mrs Smythe's playroom. He stopped writing and pushed his chair back a little.

'You like to have something to play with, do you?' he said. 'Play with that. Continue your report.'

Leaning forwards, with her hand curled round his hot, hard shaft and her right buttock cupped in his left hand, she managed to resume her account. Now that she was holding his erection she felt more disoriented than ever by the strength of her desire. It wasn't enough to have his manhood in her hand: she wanted it in her mouth.

He stopped writing, abruptly, when she told him about the plug that had been inserted into her anus. His hand fell from her bottom.

'Bend over the desk,' he said. 'Legs wide, bottom up.'

He pushed his chair back and stood beside her. He wasn't satisfied with her position. Wordlessly he pulled her arms behind her back and pressed her breasts against the surface of the desk. He slapped her thighs further apart. With the fingers of his right hand he held apart her buttocks. Then, as she had expected, he used his other hand to inspect her little hole. As his fingers pressed and probed a wave of shame swept over her. There was nothing, she realised, that she would not let this man do to her. It didn't matter how much or how little he cared for her, or if he cared at all. Her devotion to him was absolute, unconditional.

She gasped as his finger slid into her. He murmured, as if the ease of entry corroborated her story. A second finger worked its way alongside the first, and Jessica

43

sighed. She realised that she had made another dis-covery about herself: she loved the feeling of having her anus penetrated. It was so perverse, so intrusive, so satisfyingly filling.

Matt's fingers pushed further in, and Jessica wriggled her bottom.

'You're leaking,' he said. It was true: she could feel the wetness seeping from her sex.

Without extracting his fingers from her, he spanked her again. Another six hard smacks, right in the middle of her bottom, his hand landing on the inside under-slopes, his fingers spanking her wet vulva.

Still his fingers remained inside her. His elbow, resting on her back, kept her pressed against the top of the desk. He sat on the desk beside her, with the notepad on his knees and his feet resting on the seat of his chair. 'Continue your report,' he said.

How was she supposed to remember what had happened earlier that day, when all she could think about was what might happen next? Each little move-ment of his fingers made her think she was about to come. And she didn't want to come yet, even though she had been denied orgasms all day. First she wanted to submit to the harshest punishment he could administer, and then she wanted to lick his penis until the fountain of his semen flooded her mouth. Then, at last, she would masturbate for him, in any position he desired.

With many hesitations and pauses to catch her breath, Jessica completed her daily account.

'Very interesting,' Matt said. He pulled his fingers from her anus. 'You seem to have enjoyed having a toy stuffed up your arse.'

She lifted her head and reached for his erection. 'Yes, I did. And your fingers, too. I expect that's very, very naughty.'

He watched her hand moving up and down his shaft, and then turned his blank gaze on to her. 'You can't

44

get what you want by being nice to me,' he said. 'I'm not susceptible to bribery. After all, you have to obey me. I can have anything I desire from you. If you want something specific, you'll have to ask for it.'

It was true. He knew exactly how and when to remind her of the lowliness of her position. 'Please, Mentor,' she said. 'I just want you to punish me. Very hard, please. I've been thinking about it all day.'

'But of course,' he replied, smiling at last. 'I rather enjoy disciplining you. And I think I can provide something appropriate, even with the limited resources here. Stand up. Go to the middle of the room. Adopt the "beg" position, as you've described it to me, but with your hands crossed behind your back.'

Jessica liked all the pet positions she had been taught. Every one of them was so indecent. 'Beg' she found particularly humiliating and exciting: once she was squatting, with her knees spread wide apart, it was difficult to move, so she felt very helpless. Putting her hands behind her back, instead of together in front of her, made the position even more difficult to maintain.

Matt advanced towards her. In one hand he was holding a metal cylinder welded to a square base; in the other a disappointingly small cane.

Jessica hoped that Matt would order her to suck his penis: she was at just the right height. But he placed the metal square, with the cylinder rising vertically from it, on the floor behind her.

'This is part of one of the old machines from the gym,' he said. 'I retrieved it, as I suspected it would be useful again. I want you to lift your bottom up a little, move back, and then lower yourself on to the tip of the cylinder. I want it up your arse, of course. Don't worry, the top is round and smooth. And I'll put some of this lubricant on it. You'll have to lean back a little. I'll support you.'

Jessica wasn't worried. From the moment she saw the cylinder she had hoped that she would be required to take it inside her. And Matt was going to hold her! She would have to be careful not to swoon in his arms.

The cylinder was wider than Matt's two fingers; wider than the phallus that had been lodged in her anus for most of the day. But with Matt holding her steady she rested the funnel of her bottom on the tip of the thing, and she felt herself open, and a little of the cylinder was inside her. She couldn't help crying out. It was stretching her, and hurting her. As with the phallus, however, the pain receded, leaving her with the familiar and welcome sensations of being stretched and filled. She was very conscious that her shoulder was resting against the hard muscles of his chest, and that his erect manhood was pressing against her thigh.

'Keep your hands behind your back,' Matt said. He was kneeling beside her, and although he moved away from her a little his strong left arm remained around her shoulders, holding her upright and preventing her from sliding any further on to the cylinder. 'Shoulders back. Chest out,' he said, and he began to whip her breasts with the cane.

For a moment Jessica hardly knew what was happening. The pain was so sharp that she couldn't catch her breath, and so immediate that she wanted to curl into a ball to protect her vulnerable breasts. This wasn't like any punishment she had taken on her bottom: it was crueller, more intimate, and the wristy flicks of the cane were like wasp stings.

But with Matt's arm around her shoulders, and by clenching her hands around her arms behind her back, she succeeded in keeping still. She tossed her head from side to side, and heard herself uttering a succession of gasps and cries. She glimpsed Matt's face beside her: he was frowning with concentration as he flicked the cane as rapidly as he could, giving her no time to recover her breath between the strokes. The tip of the cane caught one breast and then the other. He was aiming for the most sensitive areas, around and just below her nipples. Through the stinging pain she could feel her breasts jiggling and dancing as they were whipped.

There was a pause. Matt tightened his grip around her shoulders, and then allowed her to lean a little further back. Jessica groaned as the cylinder penetrated further into her. Matt's right hand, still holding the cane, cupped her sex, and the tip of the cane nudged into her wide-open vagina. She could feel that she was dripping wet. Her breasts felt hot and swollen, and her nipples hardened suddenly. Her body shook with tremors of desire. She knew that if Matt were to move his hand, only a little, she would start to come.

'You seem to be enjoying this,' he said, and he brought up his hand and resumed caning her breasts.

Now each sharp lash was sheer pleasure. Jessica arched her back, to present her breasts and to push her bottom down on to the cylinder. Jolts of electric energy ran through her body. In a lucid moment she wondered whether it was possible for her to reach a climax this way.

'That's enough,' Matt said. Jessica sighed and moaned as he helped her to stand, and the cylinder slipped from her anus.

She stood with her head bowed and her long hair falling about her face as she recovered her breath. She kept her hands behind her back. She gasped when Matt's fingers touched her breasts, and the surge of pleasure was so intense that her legs almost gave way.

'They'll be sore for a while,' Matt said. 'But I don't think there will be marks. It's getting late, but I suppose I should allow you to have a climax. From your report it sounds as though you've had a frustrating day. So you can masturbate now. Use the cylinder up your arse, if you like. You seem to enjoy it.'

Jessica was so desperate for satisfaction that her hands went straight to her sex before he had finished speaking. It was wonderful to touch the hot, wet, secret places between her legs, with her breasts and her anus still throbbing insistently.

But she wanted more. She wanted Matt. With a sob she took her hands away from her sex. They were wet with her juices. She lifted her head to look at her mentor. 'Please,' she said. She reached out and grasped the shaft of his manhood. 'Please?'

He shrugged. 'Very well,' he said. 'I can't deny that it's pleasant to fuck you.' With effortless strength he took a rolled-up exercise mat from behind the door and threw it on to the floor, where it unrolled. 'Kneel,' he said. 'Then bend over. Head down on the mat, bottom up.'

Jessica was so excited that she thought she might pass out. This, even more than the punishment, was what she had been waiting for all day. She arranged herself in the position he wanted. She placed her knees as far apart as she could, and drew them up to her shoulders, so that her bottom was as rounded and open as she could make it. She pressed her face and her sore breasts against the mat, and shivered with pleasure.

He was going to fuck her again. Even the sound of the coarse word excited her. Not her mouth, this time. Her sex. A proper fucking.

Her hair was spread in a pool all round her head. She could see nothing. She was a vessel, containing nothing but yearning desire, waiting to be filled. She could imagine how she looked, abasing herself on the floor, her bottom and her vulva so prominent that the rest of her might as well not exist. She was nothing but sex; she wanted nothing but sex.

She heard him kneel behind her, between her calves. Then, suddenly, the hot, blunt tip of his erection was pushing between her labia, and then he was inside her, pressing further in, filling her vagina before she had time to recognise the succession of sensations that flooded through her.

48

He moved back and forth inside her, unhurriedly, and even though he didn't touch her in any other way Jessica was in a state of bliss. If she had been a cat she would have purred. Matt's long, thick member seemed to be growing even bigger and harder.

He withdrew it, until only the tip was nuzzling against her sex-lips. Her vagina felt empty, and she murmured with disappointment.

'I'm sure that was very enjoyable,' Matt said. 'But it isn't what you need. I think we should keep to today's theme.'

Before Jessica could decipher his meaning, she felt the tip of his penis slide from between her labia and up, into the funnel of corrugated skin around her anus.

He was going to use her there.

'I should have whipped you here, as well,' Matt said thoughtfully. 'Never mind. There's no time now.'

For a brief moment Jessica wondered whether she should object, struggle, cry out. Everything was happening too quickly. Before today she had never allowed anyone to put anything into her anus – well, nothing more than the tip of a finger, anyway. Now she was expected to accommodate Matt's rigid, engorged penis.

She relaxed. There was, after all, nothing she wanted more at that moment than Matt's manhood. She felt it test the resilience of the little ring of muscle, and she sighed as the hole opened, and the head of his penis slid into her. I'm losing my virginity all over again, she thought.

She cried out as the pain began, and then her cries became groans of pleasure as the pangs lessened. He was well inside her now, inching into her with little thrusts of his powerful hips. He felt larger than the plug she had worn at Mrs Smythe's; larger even than the metal cylinder she had squatted on while he had caned her breasts. He was like a heated metal bar inside her. Each time he thrust forwards she felt a spasm of pain that melted into the spreading, deepening pool of her blissful delirium.

It's as if I'm being spanked inside my bottom, she thought; it's punishment and pleasure combined. It's humiliating enough to be used this way, but it's utterly degrading to enjoy it. I'm such a naughty girl. Because I certainly am enjoying it. Oh, yes. I hope it feels as wonderful to Matt as it does to me. I want him to use me like this again.

She could no longer think coherently. Her whole body was alive with electric tremors, and she was moaning helplessly in time with the deep pulses of pleasurable ache that spread from her breached bottom. Matt was fully inside her now: the thick base of his erection was stretching open the ring of her anus, and his hairs were scratching her buttocks. His body was bent over hers: she felt the hard pips of his nipples press into her back. He was panting, and uttering little guttural noises. Even as she rode the rising waves of pain and pleasure, Jessica smiled: at last she had succeeded in breaking down the wall of his indifference.

He curled an arm under her stomach. 'Up,' he grunted, pushing her ribcage upwards. 'I want your breasts.'

She did her best to comply. Before the tips of her breasts were clear of the mat, his hand was grasping them. Had he forgotten that they had just been caned, or did he intend to cause her more pain? He wasn't gentle: he grabbed and kneaded the sore flesh, and then, as if regaining his self-control, he began deliberately to pinch and twist the nipples.

More pain; more pleasure. It felt as though a taut wire stretched from her nipples to her rectum: a wire alive with electric shocks. The sensations were too strong, too much, too wonderful to bear. Matt was holding her, he was surrounding her, he was inside her.

She was a limp, helpless doll. She was nothing but waves of sensation crashing faster and faster on the shore.

'If you want to come,' Matt said through gritted teeth, 'touch yourself now.'

I'll come anyway, she thought, if you keep on doing the things you're doing. But he was her mentor, and she had to obey. It was difficult: she had to prop herself on one elbow and insert the other arm under her body, reaching back and up until her fingers found the strands of viscous liquid hanging from her sex.

The effort had brought her to the surface of her lake of pleasure. One touch of her fingers on the petals of her sex was enough to send her diving back down into the dark, warm, liquid, pulsing depths.

One touch, and she was starting to come. Her fingers pressed and rubbed frantically, matching the pulses of pleasure-pain, the regular thrusts of Matt's invasive penis, the insistent pinching of his fingers around her sore nipples. The hard, hot bar inside her was suddenly still, and she could feel the cataract of semen forcing its way through the tight ring of her anus as it sped towards its explosive expulsion into her bowels.

An avalanche of emotions swept over her and carried her away. It was as if every pathway in her brain had been thrown open simultaneously. She forgot where she was; she forgot who she was. She just experienced wave after wave of emotion: love, shame, loss, delight, even fear. She realised that her body was shaking and she was uttering loud cries. She felt wetness on her face, and knew she was crying.

She slumped slowly on to her side and lay, curled up, on the mat. She was aware of Matt looking down at her. She felt his hand on her cheek.

'Are you all right?' he whispered. 'I think you lost consciousness for a moment.'

51

If Jessica had not felt so drained of energy she would have sat up and kissed him. He was concerned about her; he cared for her.

'Mmm,' she murmured, and nodded. 'Yes, thank you, Mentor.'

'Good,' Matt said, standing straight. 'It's bad for business if the members pass out. It's very late. I have work to do, and you have to return home. Whatever that anal plug was supposed to prepare you for, I'd say you're ready for it now.'

He left the office. Jessica dragged herself to her feet. He was right: she had to go home. She was so happy that even the tiredness was wearing off. Her life kept on getting better and better. Suddenly she laughed. What would Brian say, she wondered, if she were to tell him that today she had watched one of her neighbours being given an enema; and then she had spent most of the day naked, playing with the most unusual toys and with the neighbour; and that finally she had had her breasts caned and, for the first time in her life, she had had anal sex. She knew what he would say. He wouldn't believe her.

She laughed again, and with shaking fingers she began to dress.

Field agent's report to the Private House
From: Matt
For the attention of: Mistress Julia

I am aware that the enclosed report is merely a factual, if detailed, account of the activities that Jessica told me about and of the meeting I had with her late in the afternoon. I decided to write this separate note of my observations and opinions.

Thank you, first of all, for responding quickly and positively to my request that I be allowed to remain in Hillingbury and in charge of this operation. I am very sorry that today's events have already demonstrated that your faith in me is not merited.

I have allowed my feelings for Jessica to cloud my judgement. It's true that I have said nothing to her, but after my treatment of her this afternoon I cannot believe that she will want to see me again. I still don't know what possessed me. Jealousy, I suppose. I couldn't bear to hear the happiness in her voice as she told me about the fun and games she's enjoyed as a 'pet'. I was determined to show her that submission entails more than being naked and playing with toys. And she is, Mistress, irresistibly submissive.

Even if she returns to report again, I don't think I can maintain this charade. Every time I write to you I am betraying her confidence. She thinks that I will keep her secrets; instead I send them all to you. What will she think of me when she finds out?

I understand that you must send another agent to complete this assignment. I will remain here until I am relieved of the post, and I will continue to report.

I can't bear to think that I won't see Jessica again.

DRAWN TO DISCIPLINE

Tara Black

Tara Black is a newcomer to the Nexus list. Her second novel, *Ritual Stripes*, was published in June 2002, and builds on her reputation as a writer of CP novels with an up-to-the-minute flavour. That reputation has been established by the novel extracted here – *Drawn to Discipline*, which takes a realistic look at corporal punishment as practised by flagellants from Leipzig to LA. Tara Black touches on the politics and contradictions of CP and SM, but don't let that put you off! She's a hot, arousing read who helps explain why generations who have never been brought up with institutionalised CP still find it a perennial turn-on!

In this extract, student Judith Wilson finds out first-hand about the Nemesis Archive – an institution at which she's landed a job – and its intriguing brief: the documentation of perverse female desires!

'S o you're saying this isn't going to make our fortunes as a porn vid?'

'Honey, she gets a cool swishing and she's got a peachy big butt, so that's say six out of ten, maybe seven at a pinch. But when he sticks her you don't even see which hole he's in, only his ass blocking the camera, and he keeps his fucking pants on! So that makes a total score of three, tops. I make better tapes than this every weekend. Talking of which, it's time you came along to star on one – and we'll have *your* sweet ass good and bare. Now *that* would have to be worth a few bucks!' Marsha hooted as Judith went red, wrong-footed by the lady's deadpan humour.

'I'm sorry. Don't get mad, Jude. I can't resist getting a rise out of you. Just remember I'm not letting on *what* I do between Saturday night and Sunday morning, but I'll tell you it's usually with just one lover. That's l-o-v-e-r. I want you for a *friend*, girl.' The voluble American pecked quickly at Judith's cheek, conciliatory, and Judith smiled. It was impossible to be cross with Marsha for long. Together they picked up the drinks they had just bought and were carrying them over to the corner table when Judith spotted a familiar black face on the steps down into the basement bar. For a second she was blank, then it came back. It was the girl who tried to pick her up in the Ladies before, oh, God, before . . . It was a full month ago yet to think

57

about it still made her sick. Gwen, that was her name. Judith called it out and the young woman looked across and waved.

She bought a beer and came over, and Judith did the introductions. 'I've seen you around,' said Marsha, looking from her to Judith and back with a twinkle. 'The Phoenix folk are following me about on my night off.'

When they were sat down, Gwen took a sip of her drink and said to Judith, 'So that guy you were dating got up to his old tricks again.' For a moment Judith gawped – how on Earth did Gwen know what had happened to her that night? – then the penny dropped. 'Didn't you hear? He's been done for assault – some lady up north – and it ain't no first offence neither. So the bastard'll be going down for sure. Good fucking riddance.'

'For a while,' said Marsha.

'Then you didn't hear he got me,' Judith said.

Gwen looked horrified. 'Jesus fuck. Me and my big mouth. Oh, honey, I had no idea.'

'Don't worry about it. Just a bruise. But it was a shock I could have done without. And it led to me losing the job I had.'

'Oh, fuck. You were at the archive, yeah? The place the feminists wanna close down?'

'Some *so-called* feminists,' Marsha put in with a snort.

'I don't get it. How could him hitting you put you out of work?' Gwen continued.

'Well, only indirectly. Oh it's a long story, let's just say I was late the next day and there were consequences.' Judith saw Gwen had a curious look that was asking for more. 'OK, OK. Much as I'm caught up in all this discipline malarkey, I just couldn't – wouldn't – take a leathering from the boss. So I had to leave.'

'Wow! So she practises what the stuff on her shelves preaches, eh? Hey, that's cool. Kinky stuff. It kinda gives me a funny feeling to think about it. And that's funny-nice, I mean. I ain't never done it, but offering your bare bum up to be slapped is a fucking sexy idea.' She stopped and put a hand to her mouth. 'Honey, you lost your job over this and I'm rabbiting. Fuck, I'd be chicken, too, when it came to the point of pulling my pants down.'

Judith looked away. How was it everyone else could be so at ease with this subject when it tied her up in knots inside? Then with relief she saw a second figure she knew at the far end of the bar and seized the opportunity to switch the conversation into different channels.

'Hey, Melissa! Over here.' Heads turned at her raised voice, then she said, half to herself, 'Wait a minute, she's supposed to be in Germany. That's why I took over.'

Marsha stood up, looking for once distinctly sheepish. 'Er, Liss is with me for a couple of nights, then she's back to Bonn. Stay where you are, I'll go and get a round in.'

Judith smiled at the hasty disappearance; it was rare to see her friend embarrassed. So here was this weekend's lover for them all to see: they'd had their Saturday night and Sunday morning and by the look of it there was another night to come.

When the two of them came through with the drinks, Judith could sense Gwen's keen interest. The sexual rapport between the wiry American with the iron-grey crew cut and the Glaswegian blonde with the startling red fingernails was an almost material presence at the table and while Liss muttered to Marsha in a low voice, gesticulating, Judith felt breath in her ear and a hand on her thigh.

'Cor, see them. Makes my knickers wet to watch. You wanna follow their example out the back, hon?' Startled, Judith swung round, only for the black girl to dissolve into giggles. 'You should see your face, Jude. But it ain't really a joke, you know that.' She gave the bare flesh below the short skirt another squeeze, then Melissa leaned forward and spoke to Judith.

'How you getting on at the Meni? I hear you care for the janny even less than I do.'

Judith laughed. 'He'd hate being called that, the way he fancies himself as *superintendent*.'

'Aye. That'll be superintendent of young lassies' bums. But he never got his paws on me. When he tried it on I stuck a nail file in his ribs. Let the shit believe it was the point of a knife. Kept his fucking distance after that.'

Gwen's eyes were popping out. 'Jeez, Jude, are you safe working there? I mean, what is it this outfit actually does?'

'Good question,' said Judith, looking at Melissa. 'It's some weird deal altogether. All I know is I deliver stuff from this depot two streets away. There's books – some of their own publications – and then there's, well, straps and, er, things. All securely wrapped and I haven't dared have a proper look yet.'

Melissa exchanged looks with Marsha and again Judith had the feeling they knew something she wasn't being told. All Liss said with a shrug was, 'No use asking me. I was never given the big picture at all, just what I was doing.'

Who do you think you're kidding, thought Judith, with you swanning about their European branches?

Gwen was clearly fascinated. 'So you're taking supplies of your actual *implements* –' she stressed the word with relish '– to all the discipline freaks around the area? I like it, sister. I would say that's a step on from just reading manuscripts.'

Judith smiled at her enthusiasm, but, before she could press Melissa to spill more of the beans about the mysterious Eumenides company, a group of the univer-

60

sity's more orthodox feminists sat down at the next table. Marsha may have affected loathing of their company but it was clear the attraction of a bit of verbal fisticuffs outweighed it, especially when the beer was flowing.

'Your recruits get younger every time, Marsha. You sure these are old enough to drink?'

The lanky redhead meant *them*, and Judith felt Gwen stiffen beside her. She stood up and took the black girl's arm.

'Time to do your eyes, girl, and I'm bursting with all these beers. Come on.' Inside the Ladies she said: 'Marsha loves a barney, but I don't want to get into it. I'm too confused in my own head to join a scrap. And you looked ready to deck Carrot-top.'

'Too fucking right.' Gwen leaned forward and examined herself in the mirror, her camouflage combat trousers tight across the prominent rump. 'Actually, the make-up will do. But thanks for getting me out of there, honey. We don't really wanna get barred from this hole.' She straightened up and they looked at each other without speaking. Judith could feel that her own sexual attraction had returned.

'Got to pee.' She dived into a cubicle just as another woman came in to use the mirror. When she emerged they were alone again and Gwen said, 'I think we know how we feel, right? Thing is, there's a guy staying at my place next couple of weeks and I kinda said, well, I sorta promised . . .' She broke off with a grimace. 'To be honest, it's a fucking mess and I'll be glad when it's all over. *No* chance will it work out. But I don't wanna make you an offer when I ain't properly free.'

Judith was touched by this plain speaking and turned on more than ever. Following her out of the lavatory, she tried to keep her eyes off the firm protuberances of the girl's behind and her thoughts away from what they would feel like under her hands. Shit. First Jeanie, now

61

Gwen. Women were obviously becoming the business in her life.

At the table the argument was raging, though Judith judged they were a few drinks away yet from the stage of gratuitous insults. The tape was lying by her bottle and she picked it up, raising her voice to explain that Gwen and she were going to leave them to it. Marsha winked lewdly and was straight back into the fray, but Liss leaned over and spoke.

'I shouldn't really stick my oar in, but I'd be careful if I were you, hen. You may think you know her nibs quite well, know just how she's gonna take it when she gets this from you, but . . .' She shrugged and emptied her glass of vodka. 'Whatever. It's not *my* funeral. Who's for another?'

The two young women walked side by side through the park before their ways diverged. By the pool they stood and kissed for a while then stopped as if by mutual decision.

'I'm off work, Tuesday,' said Gwen. 'Any chance I could see your place?'

'The boss is away all week. Hey, why don't you come out delivering with me? There's room on the back of the bike.'

'Fuck, that'd be great. Will I get to see some of these imp-lem-ents?' Gwen drew the word out.

God, she is hooked on this topic, thought Judith. 'It's 16 Markham Street, top flat. Be there at 8.30 and we'll walk over to St Mary's. OK?'

On the Tuesday at 9.15 Judith came back outside with three packages, two of which were metre-long tubes taped shut at the ends while the other was a smallish cardboard box. 'Well, even I can guess what those two are,' said Gwen, 'but what's the third one? Hey, it's quite heavy. Go on, Jude, let's have a look.'

'No way.' Judith shook her head firmly. 'They're very keen on things being properly sealed till they reach the customer. However, if you're patient you may get to see what's in the box.' As they walked round to the garage she explained that it was to go to a model school out in the country and they were to wait while it was inspected in case it didn't suit.

In the garage, Gwen was impressed by the shiny red Vespa. 'Wow! These things are cool.' Judith stashed the items in the paniers, the ones that could only be canes sticking up obtrusively. 'We'll get rid of those first,' she said, before we head out of town. 'Put this on.' She handed over a helmet and thought it suited Gwen a treat, dressed as she was in a leather jacket, black stretch leggings and boots. Then they both climbed on and, with the feel of the black girl's body pressing into her quickening the pulse, Judith started up and drove them out into the back lane.

As they reached the main road Gwen yelled into Judith's ear, 'When you get your test, then?'

'Don't ask silly questions,' Judith said over her shoulder and as she did a nifty right turn almost under the wheels of a double-decker bus she heard from the back a shout of 'Fucking hell!' and what sounded like: '*Now* she tells me.'

The long packages were dropped off in suburban streets, the first to a shifty-looking man who looked even shiftier when he saw it was two young women who had brought his order. The second was taken by an older woman who was anything but embarrassed by their presence or by what they had brought. She opened the tube on the doorstep and swished the cane several times appreciatively, seemingly careless of what the neighbours might think. Gwen was goggling at the sight, but since the item seemed acceptable Judith grabbed her elbow and steered her out of the gate, claiming they had a busy schedule. Who knows what kind of trial the woman might want if they hung around.

It took the best part of an hour to reach the final address after a wrong turn that petered out at a farm entrance, but eventually they swooped into a driveway past a sign reading MANNERLY MODELS. At the baronial entrance Judith rang the bell and the door opened almost at once.

'Ah! The delivery from Eumenides. *Entrez, entrez, mes chéries.*' He was a slim, well-muscled man in his forties with a shock of black hair and discreet, minimal make-up. In a silk shirt open to the waist and satin trousers that sheathed his thighs, he bubbled over with conversation as they followed him into the entrance hall.

'I'm afraid I'm not Mannerly. Courteous at all times, I hope, but not mannerly.' His laugh had a manic edge. 'Place is named after a distant ancestor of mine, an aristocrat, no less. Queer as a coot. Lovely man. Used to pick out a stable lad at the end of the day, leather his sit-upon then bugger him silly. They all adored Lord Mannerly, used to vie with each other for the privilege.' Eyeing his somewhat startled audience, he let out a heavy sigh, as if in mourning for those paradisal days long past. 'However, our girls are very lovely and I do get a little bottom-warming in now and then, if nothing else. Which is where you come in, darlings, so please follow me.'

He led the way through a small gymnasium where three young women were exercising at the wall bars, past a dressing room where several others were sitting in front of mirrors, into a classroom that contained perhaps a dozen desks. Then he stuck his head back out of the door and called: 'Ladies! When you're ready, *s'il vous plaît.*'

He took the package from Judith and began opening it on the table at the front of the room, talking all the

64

while. 'I should have said that my name is Boswell, but they all call me Bozzy, so please follow suit. That is Bozzy, not Bossy, though I'm sure I am at times. *Mes jeunes filles* can be so scatterbrained.' Tittering, he took out the contents, which uncoiled into a strip of what looked like leather and weighed it in his hand.

'I needed this because my pupil – ex-pupil, I should say – Marlene cut my old one up into little pieces and threw it in my face. Took a kitchen knife to it as if it were some kind of vegetable to be chopped. Then she walked out.' By this time the students had all appeared and Bozzy turned to them. 'These young ladies have kindly brought me my new strap and I was just telling them about Marlene's outrageous behaviour. *Très, très folle*, given all the opportunities of work your Bozzy is going to find for you. I mean it's not as if I ever really *hurt* your sweet bottoms, do I, darlings?'

His question was obviously rhetorical and the aspirant models pouted coyly to each other in a way that went straight to Judith's loins. Meanwhile, the director had examined the strap minutely and spoke again. 'They told me that this instrument has a rubber core under its leather surface and it certainly feels a little heavier. So I think we require a trial. After all, I can't buy something that might be *too* painful for my dear pupils, can I?' He appealed to the class who chorused, 'No, you can't, Bozzy,' in what was clearly a well-practised response.

'So what we need now is a volunteer to undergo the crucial test.' He scanned the occupants of the desks but each one had acquired an interest in a fingernail or the cuff of a sleeve; in fact, anything at all that would keep her from meeting his gaze. 'Now, I wonder . . .' he said, and turned to look directly at Judith. She was not aware of reacting strongly, but something about her face must have given him pause for he passed quickly on to Gwen. 'I think I have the solution. What if our second

65

delivery girl here – such a lovely young woman of colour – were to offer herself so that we can conclude the purchase, wouldn't that just be so appropriate?'

There was a full second's silence and Judith could see Gwen trying to decide. Then she straightened up and said: 'OK. Right. So what is it I'm in for?'

'Oh, well done, darling. *C'est bien, n'est-ce pas, mes filles?* Just a little six of the best with our new friend here. Nothing to it. Of course, to simulate the conditions of its normal use, you will have to take your trousers down.' Gwen pursed her lips but did not demur. 'If that's agreed, then, just come over here with me.'

At the front of the room beside the large table was a tall teacher's desk. It stood on its own without an accompanying chair and as the purpose of it became clear Judith recalled in a rush the time she had seen its twin at Nemesis with Helen bent over it for a dose of Miss James's strap. That seemed an age ago, yet it was little more than a month. Then she had been horrified and bewildered. Now, observing Gwen being prepared for similar treatment, she was more excited than scared. When the black leggings were lowered to the top of her boots, Judith's pulse quickened some more. The bad girl's got no knickers on *again*, she thought, as Bozzy began to enthuse about what he had uncovered.

'Oh, I say. What a treat we have in store, girls! We have such a lovely bottom here for a demonstration of our new instrument. Now, *ma chérie*,' he carried on, running his hands over Gwen's posterior, 'spread your legs just a little more and go right forwards. That's it. Wonderful. Exactly as it should be – a charmingly *full* rear presentation.' It was indeed quite a sight, the rich rounds split by a dark furrow that ended in the black-frizzed fig of exposed cunt, and Judith felt proud that the behind which had so taken her fancy was the object of such unqualified admiration.

'Very good. Now *you*, darling –' here he turned to Judith '– if you'd be so good to come round the back – *c'est ça* – you can lean over and hold your young associate's waist. Not to restrain her, you understand, I'm sure she means to co-operate fully with us, but to give her the reassurance of your touch. A little moral support. *Parfait*. Now I think we can begin.'

As Judith watched, heart in mouth, the man took the broad, two-tailed tawse and brought it down across the whole breadth of the target. As the buttocks bounced she felt the body tense under her hands and there was a semi-stifled 'Fuck!' from beneath her. At the second stroke the hips jerked and the vocal response this time was loud and clear: 'Oh, fuck!'

Bozzy laid down the strap on the table, looking very angry. 'Now, I must insist, such language simply will not do. It is the one thing I cannot countenance, especially *that* word you used. I am going to start again from the beginning and this time I expect more self-control. *Qu'est-ce que tu dis à ça?*'

Later Judith wondered why they didn't just get up and walk out. However, at the time it seemed quite appropriate that Gwen should say, in an uncharacteris-tically small voice, 'I'm sorry,' and that the leathering should continue. Towards the end of what had become eight strokes, her legs kicked and she cried out, but there was no more swearing. When it was over, Gwen leaped up and clapped her hands to the injured parts but once again Bozzy was not impressed.

'Stop that and pull up your clothes!' he said sharply. 'We don't allow any rubbing, do we, girls?' The prompt reply was in unison and this time almost gleeful.

'No, Bozzy, we don't!' The would-be models' flushed faces and bright eyes made it clear that while none of them were keen to *be* strapped, they all found the spectacle rather pleasing. Seeing, too, the bulge in the director's satin pants, Judith wondered whether he was quite as queer as he made himself out to be. Perhaps, at least, there would be willing hands, or a mouth even, to bring about his detumescence.

These speculations were supported by the haste with which they were now escorted from the building, not in fact unwelcome since Judith was in the grip of needs of her own. 'Get on – quick,' she said, starting up the Vespa and with Gwen clinging very tightly to her body they careered down the drive out into the country lane. At the first gate they came to Judith pulled right off the road and stopped. Inside the field she removed her friend's belt, tugged the leggings down and kneeled behind her to kiss the hot cheeks. But when she moved to part them for a more intimate investigation with her tongue, she was rebuffed.

'Hey, I told you I'm not free,' said Gwen, pulling her up. 'Not yet, any road. Let's just do *this* for now.' And opening Judith's waistband and zip she pushed her fingers in under the matted pubic hair.

Half an hour later they emerged and, as she wheeled the machine back on to the tarmac, Judith was thinking it was as well there had been no passing traffic. Who knows what a driver might have done, eyes fixed on the sight of two young women, bare-arsed and kissing passionately, each with a hand between the other's legs. As she started up and Gwen climbed on at her back, she said over her shoulder, 'Well, girl, d'you remember you were dead keen at the weekend to see some imp-lem-ents? I'd say you found out a lot about one of them.'

'Too fucking right!' was the answer in her ear and, laughing, they sped off between the high hedgerows.

Judith opened her eyes and peered at the clock. 8.05; loads of time. She stretched luxuriously, wisps of a dream still clinging to her consciousness. Gwen was in it again, just as she'd featured every night since their adventure as delivery girls, though they had agreed not to meet in the flesh for another week yet. Judith snuggled into the bedding and tried to recover the image: there was a long T-shirt that she was trying to lift up, but each time Judith got close to exposing her delectable bum the girl twisted away with that laugh . . .

Oh, shit! She sat bolt upright, suddenly wide awake. Horribly awake. It was Monday morning and today was the day. After vacillating all week, on Friday afternoon she had written a note to Ms Morris and sealed it in a large envelope along with the video of the janny and his helper *in flagrante delicto*. The word Melissa had used for him brought her warning to mind: that the boss wasn't going to like it. And if the mysterious Liss, who swanned round Europe for Eumenides and was plainly an intimate of Ms Morris, told Judith to be careful, she should have listened. Fuck, what had she done?

The clothes she had put out the night before were on the bedside chair and Judith got out of bed with a heavy heart and began to dress. The crisp white blouse and black skirt that wasn't, for once, too short or too tight gave her image in the mirror a conventional smartness she normally eschewed, but this time it seemed appropriate. The condemned girl ate a hearty breakfast, she said to herself, buttering a piece of toast and stirring a strong mug of coffee, while thoughts of Mary Queen of Scots and the executioner's block floated into her head. Judith gulped down the steaming liquid looking at the clock and shook herself, almost angrily. Jee-sus girl, get a grip! The worst that can happen is that you'll be out of a job for the second time this summer. Big fucking deal!

Walking in, Judith's spirits lifted a bit. Maybe she had gone out on a limb, but something had to be done about that bastard Jennings. When he discovered she'd taken Gwen out last Tuesday he berated her for letting an outsider get information about the corporation's activities. He'd cornered her in the garage putting the bike away and threatened to tell the boss unless she'd accept correction from him there and then. He'd had the nerve to produce a cane and suggest that if she stretched across the bonnet of the van beside them and took a dozen of the best he would forget about the whole thing. Judith picked up a heavy spanner from the bench and told him that if he came a step nearer she'd lay him out cold. He'd fucked off pretty sharpish after that, but she regretted the action before he was out of the door. He'd never been well-disposed towards her, but now she had made a real enemy.

It was that incident that had really decided her to leave the tape for Ms Morris on the Friday night with a note that complained about Mr Jennings' other lapse of decorum in groping her behind at every opportunity that presented itself. As Judith crossed the quad, it occurred to her that maybe she was still deciding what to do and they wouldn't discuss it at all until later in the week. Then, climbing the stairs, she wondered if perhaps the boss hadn't even had a chance to see the tape yet. However, once she was through the outer door of the director's office, voices sounded clearly from within, and in a gut-wrenching instant she knew her thoughts for the idle wish-fulfilments they were. It was Mr Jennings and Mrs Butler, here in advance, and together with Ms Morris they formed a reception committee that was waiting just for her.

At the inner door, which stood very slightly ajar, Judith hesitated. If she turned round now she could come back in the afternoon when Ms Morris would be alone. Then, as she dithered on the threshold, her fate was sealed: the door opened and the director herself was right before her. Without a word she took hold of Judith's arm and drew her into the centre of the room.

When she turned to close the door, Judith saw with a pang of anxiety that she locked it and dropped the key into her jacket pocket.

'We have grave matters to deal with, and I wish to ensure we are not disturbed.' The superintendent and his assistant sat at opposite ends of the large sofa, and it gave the young woman standing in front of them no comfort to see them nodding keenly at Ms Morris's remark. Neither in fact looked the least bit grave, and the director had a high colour and a glint in her eyes that made Judith's nervousness grow. This was not at all how she had imagined the encounter that would result from the delivery of the video recording.

Then, as Ms Morris began to speak, it became clear that the contents of the tape were not her prime concern and Judith's heart sank. 'Now, I understand that last week you brought an outsider with you on your delivery round without seeking anyone's leave. Is that correct?' Judith began to attempt an explanation but was instantly silenced.

'Answer me, please. Yes or no.'

'Yes.'

'And yet you must have realised that this was a potential compromising of our clients' confidentiality?'

'Yes. I'm sorry, but you weren't here, and Gwen wouldn't –'

'Be quiet. I'll ask again: do you accept that you were wrong? Yes or no.'

'Yes.'

'In that case, when Mr Jennings offered you the opportunity of summary discipline to wipe the slate clean, you should have accepted, should you not? Instead of which, you threatened him with violence. I consider such behaviour quite outrageous!'

Judith was rendered speechless by the construction that the director had put on the events in question. That she could regard the leering groper with his cane

71

as an agent of on-the-spot justice was so at odds with the truth as to make her head spin and she gaped foolishly. However, Ms Morris was not looking for a reply.

'And what makes the whole thing ten times worse, in my view, is your effrontery in lodging a complaint against Mr Jennings of what is sexual harassment, no less. You, my girl, have been with us barely three weeks and you have the nerve to attempt to blacken my right-hand man's name in this way. Shame on you! I need hardly add that Mrs Butler confirms that no behaviour of the sort you allege has taken place in her presence.'

'But, but, but –' Judith was finding her voice '– but what about the video?' As soon as she'd said it, she realised her blunder: it was something that should have been raised only when she had the boss to herself. As it was, her question seemed to set the seal on the occasion and Judith stood aghast as Ms Morris's tirade reached a climax.

'When I received it, I called Mr Jennings and after we had spoken I gave it him to burn. The only fit end for such a thing. How dare you!' The lady's colour was now even higher than before and her eyes blazed. 'I am going to do something now that is obviously long overdue. I am going to put you over my knee and spank your bare bottom red raw.' The last words were said with a quiet venom that rooted Judith to the spot. She flinched as the director reached forward, grasped the hem of her skirt and yanked it up over her waist.

'Hold that!' she snapped and signalled to the couple on the couch who got up and lifted a long wooden chest into the middle of the floor. Then they returned to their seats, leaning forwards for a good view, as Ms Morris sat on its padded top and dragged the shocked girl across her lap. An elbow pressed the back of Judith's neck, forcing her face into the rough tweed of the cushion, and the forearm pinned her back while the

72

other hand tugged the knickers down round her thighs. Then began a series of hearty slaps at intervals that were measured to punctuate the stream of verbal censure.

'This (*smack*) is what little Judy (*smack*) should have had (*smack*) a good dose of (*smack*) when she was small (*smack*). Then (*smack*) we should have had (*smack*) less of the trouble (*smack*) that has earned her (*smack*) this spanking (*smack*). This is for disobedience (*smack! smack! smack! smack!*) and this for rudeness (*smack! smack! smack! smack!*); this is for spying and telling tales (*smack! smack! smack! smack!*) and this (*smack!! smack!! smack!! smack!!*) is for all Judy's naughtiness.'

The pace and intensity of the onslaught on her behind had moved up a notch, yet while she jerked with the pain of each blow, Judith lay unresisting. It was as if her mind, unable to rationalise the humiliation of a punishment that was being inflicted to the undisguised relish of the audience, had disengaged from the possibility of evasive action. For a minute or two the spanking continued without commentary, save for Judith's own gasps and cries; then there was a pause and Ms Morris spoke again.

'At last this *naughty* bottom is getting what it deserves, but I think we have some way to go yet. So what does bad little Judy have to say, now?' There was a further volley of slaps that made Judith yell in earnest, then: 'Is Judy sorry for her bad behaviour?'

Appalled, Judith heard herself say: 'I'm sorry.'

'I'm sorry, *ma'am*.'

'Sorry. I'm sorry – ma'am.'

'Not sorry enough yet, I see.' And the chastisement continued, now in a grim silence.

'Oh, please, please. Ma'am, I'm sorry. Ow! Ow! Ple-e-e-ease!'

The whole of Judith's posterior was now so tender that a touch would have been painful. But, if anything, the director's smacks were growing harder minute by minute and any remaining shreds of self-control vanished. Judith howled and pleaded for it to end, all without effect, and she slumped sobbing across the implacable lap. Then, through the tears and snot of a thoroughly spanked teenager, Judith became aware that something else was happening. Oh, God, she was wet. The hot throbbing hurt of her buttocks was matched by a pulsing in her loins that was growing with each new slap and making her hips thrust into the fine weave of the director's skirt.

Appalled, Judith realised that she was going to come. In thrall to the mounting sensations, she had a horrid certainty that the watchers had recognised her state, and through misty eyes she could see them both eagerly attentive. Then, as the spasms took hold of her and the spanking hand seemed to follow their rhythm, to a remote part of her mind there came the beginnings of knowledge. Ms Morris had intended this: somehow *she* had known what Judith herself did not. Then even these glimmerings of understanding were wiped out as the abject Judy, cringing under the leering gaze of Mr Jennings and Mrs Butler, convulsed in orgasm.

Afterwards, she slid off Ms Morris's lap on to her knees and held her bottom, snuffling. Dimly conscious that the couple were leaving, the next thing she knew was that Ms Morris was in front of her.

'Get up!' she said sharply. 'Get up, girl. Look at this.' Judith stood slowly and saw the damp stain that was indicated on the director's dress. 'Look what naughty Judy has done now. And, tell me child, what happens when Judy is naughty? Well?' The voice was raised and Judith felt panic.

'She – she gets spanked. Ma'am. But I've just been spanked and I'm so sore . . .' The tears started to flow in earnest once again.

'Stop that nonsense at once!' Ms Morris lifted her skirts and sat down again, patting her thighs. 'Over here. IMMEDIATELY!'

Judith jumped, heart fluttering with anxiety and obeyed. 'Please, ma'am, I'm sorry, I can't bear it –' she began as soon as the smacking started, but she was cut short.

'SILENCE! Any more of that, Judy, and I shall call Mr Jennings to come back, this time with his cane. A bad little girl like Judy would benefit from a real thrashing, don't you think?'

'Oh, no, ma'am, please, I'll be quiet.' Desperately Judith stifled her sobs and submitted to her fate. Now the spanking hand worked at the junction of buttocks and upper thighs, and once more Judith found herself lubricating freely. And as each blow connected with the wet, swollen lips of her cunt it was not long before she was again racked in the throes of her climax. When it was over she lay panting for the few moments granted before she was jerked roughly to her feet.

'Come with me.'

Judith stumbled weakly after the commanding figure who led the way through two doors into a small bedroom. On a tallboy was set out a glass of milk and a round of sandwiches.

'Stand here and eat. I shall return in five minutes.' As the key turned in the lock behind the departing director, Judith was suddenly ravenous. When she finished there was barely time to look round at the narrow bed against the wall before the door opened again.

'Strip and put this on.' Ms Morris held out a short, frilly nightdress. When Judith was re-attired the woman held up an oval of thick leather whose handle was bound in twine. 'The remedial treatment necessary in this case – which has only just begun – is beyond the capabilities of my own hand. So here is Judy's very own instrument, which will be kept by her bed when it is not in use. In the morning, she will warm it between her thighs so that it is good and supple for the first spanking of the day. But now it is time for the last. You will see that a pouffe has been placed by the side of the bed. Kneel on it and stretch across the covers.'

The last spark of resistance gone, Judith obeyed and as she took up position the baby doll garment rode up to the small of her back, leaving her posterior completely exposed. She felt tears coursing down her cheeks and heard a little wheedling voice that could only be her own.

'Please, ma'am, please, not too hard. Judy's bottom hurts so much . . .'

'It will be as hard as necessary to correct a naughty girl's misbehaviour. No more, no less.' The tone was dispassionate, without pity, and a hand explored the tenderised flesh on display. Then there were six resounding slaps, each of which wrenched an agonised shriek out of her, though she had no spirit left to take evasive action.

'Get up and get into bed. Remember my instructions for tomorrow.' Again the key was turned in the lock and Judith lay face down, unwilling to pull the covers over her inflamed, throbbing buttocks. Then, even as her brain tried feebly to encompass the enormity of what was happening to her, the blackness rolled up in a tidal wave and she knew no more.

BEAST

Wendy Swanscombe

Wendy Swanscombe has published three books with Nexus – *Disciplined Skin*, *Beast* and *Pale Pleasures*. All of them are equally full of twistedly inventive arcane fetish fiction. Three sisters – blonde Anna, redhead Beth and raven-haired Gwen – find themselves entombed in the Schloss of Herr Abraham Bärengelt – half-mad, half-genius artist and collector obsessed by the alabaster whiteness of their skin. Whether using them as orchid-beds collecting their menstrual blood for sausage-production, the devious, consensual torments to which Bärengelt subjects the girls makes Sade look like a social worker. In this extract from *Beast*, the three sisters are made to find inventive sexual uses for flora . . .

By way of a brief glossary of terms, note that, in the following extract, the following are used:

crinny: one of the narrow patches of skin exposed by the lifting of the breasts or the folding aside of the cunt-lips.

dreckle: (of sweat) to flow down the cleavage or the buttock cleft.

gluft: the female perineum.

yelm: sexual secretions from the cunt.

H er harness quivered and she realised they were descending. She lifted her feet a little, glancing over at Anna and Gwen, seeing if they'd realised the best way to land. Which was simultaneously, feet touching the floor all at once, so none of them fell over. But Anna's eyes were puffed and red, squeezed half-shut, and Gwen seemed blind with rage. At the injustice of the quiz. The way it had ended. Fuck. She watched their feet, trying to judge when best to put her own feet on the floor.

It came slowly up to meet them and she put her feet down, struggling to keep her balance as Anna and Gwen landed without co-ordination. The trildo twisted painfully in her cunt and she gasped. Fucking handcuffs. Fucking Bärengelt. Anna was about to fall over. Christ, that would wrench the fuck out of the trildo. Might give her and Gwen a hernia.

But Bärengelt was there, catching Anna by her shoulders, propping her back up.

'Come on, Annalein. Let's get you out.'

Snik. He'd unlocked Anna's handcuffs, lifted them away, tossed them on the floor.

'Now get yourself unstrapped, Annalein. Don't make me wait. Come on.'

Now he walked over to her. *Snik.* He'd unlocked her handcuffs. Christ, the fucking relief. She heard them clatter on the floor too.

'Unstrap yourself, Betchen. Come on, quick.'

She brought her hands from behind her back, rotating her wrists, rubbing at them, then began to unfasten the straps and slip out of the harness. Bärengelt's black cane tapped at her arm of the trildo.

'That too. Give Anna a hand when you're finished.'

She shrugged off the last of the harness, letting it hang in the air from the ceiling, and took hold of her arm of the trildo in both hands. She pulled it away from herself, feeling it slide free stickily. Her cunt was in a right state. The head of the trildo slipped from her cunt with a faint *shlop* and she stepped away from it, her legs feeling shaky for a moment, knees trembling. She heard the *snik* of Gwen's handcuffs being unlocked, then the clatter as they landed on the floor.

'Unstrap yourself, Gwenchen.'

Anna was still struggling with her straps, the trildo still up her cunt. Beth moved to her, still a little unsteady, feeling the arselight wobble between the cheeks of her arse. Anna's hands were shaking and she took hold of them soothingly, rubbing at them, rubbing at the red marks of the handcuffs on her wrists.

'Like this, Ansie,' she whispered.

She helped her undo the straps, slip the harness off, then uncork the trildo from her cunt. Gwen was out of her harness, tugging at her arm of the trildo, sliding it out. The head emerged between her cuntlips and fell free. *Shlop. Shlop.* Anna's came out too. They let the trildo fall but it was caught in the straps of the harnesses, hanging clear of the floor, its three arms shiny with yelm.

'Good girls. Now line up, and bend over. Over here.'

The cane pointed and they obeyed, lining up, bending over. She felt the arselight sitting solid in her arse, settled in firmly again. Anna gasped. He was pulling her arselight out. Gasped again. Groaned on a rising note that broke into a gasp and a *pop*. Then silence. It was out.

After a moment her arselight shifted in her arse. He had taken hold of it, was pulling it free, twisting it one way, then the other, as it came, to loosen it. Her mouth came open and she gasped silently: the pain was mounting, climbing back to what it had been as he inserted it, peaking for a moment, then suddenly shrinking to nothing. *Pop.* It was out.

He moved on to Gwen. No sound from her, nothing until the same faint *pop*, and hers was out. He walked out from behind them and stopped.

'Straighten. Look at me.'

She straightened and looked at him. He was holding the cane in one hand, the arselights in the other, fanned out like cards. All of the bulbs were streaked with come, but one more heavily. The one that had been up her arse.

'They're big, aren't they? Did you ever think you could get something that size up your arse before you came here? Anna?'

'No, master.'

'Gwen?'

'No, master.'

'Beth?'

'No, master.'

'Watch.'

He dropped his hand and then flicked it up, throwing the lights straight up in the air, tumbling end over end, up, up, pausing for an instant, beginning to fall . . . and they had gone. Just gone. She stared up where they had been.

'Master . . .? Where d–'

'Later, Betchen. Later. Much later. For now, we have some dressing to do.'

She looked down and at him. He had clothes over one arm now. Where had he got them from?

'Knickers,' his voices said. 'For you, first, Anna.'

He lifted something off his arm with his other hand and flicked it to Anna. She caught it.

'Put them on. Quick.'

She watched Anna climb into them, pull them up her slim legs. They were too small. Even for Anna. Schoolgirl's knickers.

'Bra.'

He tossed it to Anna, a white flutter of filmy cloth. Anna caught it, mouth twisting with dismay. It was too small too. Even for Anna.

'Put it on.'

She watched Anna strain to fit the cups over her breasts and close the strap. Nearly. Nearly. *Snik*. She'd done it.

'Shirt.'

Anna grabbed at it a moment too late and it had landed on her head and shoulders, veiling her. She tugged it off, the bra straining on her breasts as her arms and shoulders moved.

'Quick, come on.'

This was easier, but still too small. Anna had to leave some of the buttons undone, the white silk of the shirt taut over her small, bra-constrained breasts.

'No, all of the buttons. Do them all up.'

She struggled to obey, managing to button up the top one, the second-from-top, then as she tried to do up the third-from-top, directly over her breasts, the thread gave way and the button flew to the floor, landing with a faint click.

'Leave it. Skirt.'

Anna caught it, folded it open and around herself. Purple wool. Too small. Absurdly short and tight. Even for Anna. The zip rasped up, jammed, and Anna struggled with it, hands beginning to tremble again. Another rasp of the zip, cut short, Anna gasping in frustration, then *zzzzz*, the skirt was on and fastened.

'Stockings.'

They fluttered towards her simultaneously and she snatched at them, missing one, having to stoop to pick it up, the too-short skirt riding up high over her thighs, her breasts bulging provocatively beneath the too-small shirt. She put the right one on first, hopping on her left foot, then the left one, hopping on her right foot. White stockings, reaching above her knees. Stockings on a schoolgirl, socks for Anna. Even for Anna.

'Now boots, Anna.'

He was holding out a pair of shin-boots by their tops. White leather shin-boots. Too small. Even for Anna. As Anna herself saw.

'Master . . .'

'What's wrong?'

'They're too small, master.'

'No. Not too small. As you will see. Beth and Gwen will help you.'

He left go of them and they fell to the floor, landing upright on their soles with a simultaneous *clap*, the white leather too stiff to bend. The bastard. They were brand-new. Never worn. Too small even for Anna.

'Come on. Beth and Gwen, help her into them. Anna, sit on the floor.'

Anna sat down on the floor, looking miserable. Poor bitch. Beth walked over to the boots and picked one of them up. The left one. It was light but stiff. Brand-new, as she'd thought. Oddly smooth leather. Oddly light.

'Hold up your left foot, Anna. Straighten the toes.'

Anna held up her left foot and she took hold of it and guided it into the boot. The first bit was easy enough, but the boot narrowed further down and Anna's foot got stuck. Gwen took hold of the boot too, tugging, less careful of hurting Anna, who bit her lip and closed her eyes, lying back against the floor.

'Gently, Gwen. Anna will be running quite a distance in them, so let's not incapacitate her before she begins.'

Anna wailed. The boot was sliding on inch by inch.

'Help them, Anna. Don't be so passive in the face of fate. It's true that you can do nothing to forestall it but still, meet it with more spirit, girl.'

Anna struggled to sit up and then took hold of the top of the boot between their fingers, tugging at it reluctantly, wincing as it slid further on, half-inch by half-inch now. Her foot was in the foot of the boot now, nearly fully in.

'Nearly there. Stand up, Anna. Stamp it on.'

Anna obeyed him, standing up, stamping the boot at the floor, working her foot finally and firmly into the toe, looking unhappier than ever.

'Harder, Annalein. Harder. OK, good, that's it. Now the right.'

Anna sat down on the floor again, lifting her right foot into the air. Beth picked up the boot and guided Anna's foot into it again, tugging the boot up. Anna took hold of it too, tugging with her and Gwen.

'Good. You're getting the hang of it. OK, stand up and stamp it on again. It's nearly time for your run.'

What was the point of this? she thought as Anna stood up and stamped the right boot on. Making the poor bitch get into boots that were too tight for her and then making her run in them? The sick bastard. Sick. Bastard.

'Yes, you're almost ready. Almost. Just one thing. A scarf for you. Do you see it, over there?'

The cane flicked out, pointing behind them, to the hanging straps of the harnesses and the discarded trildo caught up in them. Looped around the arms of the trildo was a white, fluffy scarf.

'Get it, Annalein. Put it on.'

Anna walked cautiously over in the tight white boots and crouched to unloop the scarf. It seemed to come away endlessly, metre after metre, and when she stood up with it it was piled in her hands like a huge, loose snowball.

'Put it on, Annalein. Wind it tight.'

She began to wind it around her neck. Poor little bitch. She was going to swelter. Sweat like a pig. Sweat like a sow. A beautiful blonde sow. Even if she just stood there she would sweat, and Bärengelt had said she was going to run. Run, for fuck's sake. Poor little bitch. But Beth was glad it wasn't her.

'Good girl. Now, come back over here. I want to check that everything is just right.'

Anna walked back to him, tottering in her too tight, too small shin-boots, neck completely and shoulders almost completely hidden beneath the huge scarf, legs exposed absurdly beneath her tiny schoolgirl's skirt, breasts straining at the buttons of her tiny schoolgirl's shirt. She stopped in front of him and he bent to inspect her, tugging at the scarf, fingering the buttons of the shirt, tweaking at the hem of her skirt.

'OK. Turn round.'

Anna turned.

'Bend over.'

She bent over, the skirt riding up to expose her arse and the tiny triangle of her white knickers, the cloth cutting into her flesh, riding high into her gluft and arsecleft. Bärengelt flicked the hem of the skirt completely up with the cane, letting it lie on her back, and put a finger under the waistband of the knickers, tugging it up and letting it twang back into place. Anna gasped.

'Too tight, Annalein?'

'Yes, master.'

'Good. OK. Stand up. Turn round. Now, Annalein, tell me, how fast can you run?'

'I, uh, I don't know, master.'

'Well, can you run quite fast? Or very fast? Or not-so fast?'

'Uh, quite fast, master. I think.'

'You think, do you? Well, really, that's not good enough. I don't want you to think, I want you to *know*.'

His cane came up, pointing down the hothouse.

'Do you see that orchid there? With the purple flowers? A fine specimen of *Odontoglossum sapphica*. I want one of those flowers. Bring me one. As quick as you can, on the word go. OK?'

'OK, master.'

Anna was nodding, but tears were starting to shine in her eyes again. The bastard.

'OK, go. Go!'

Anna set off, trying to run, obviously in pain after a few strides, the boots too tight and too small, clacking against the marble floor, sliding and squeaking as she ran and slid and. skipped her way to the orchid Bärengelt had pointed out to her. She reached it and bent to pluck one of the flowers.

'A good one, Annalein. Or I will send you back. Now, hurry back.'

Anna straightened and started back, running, sliding, skipping, the pain of the boots visible in her face. One end of the scarf flew free, shaken loose by her exertions, and she nearly trod on it and tripped. She reached Bärengelt and stood to attention, gasping, face pink, sweat gleaming under the golden stubble of her scalp and starting to gather and trickle at her temples.

'Here, master.'

She held up a tiny purple flower.

'Thank you, Annalein. But that was far too slow. I'm sure you can do much better than that. Can't you? For me?'

'I h– I hope so, master.'

'You hope?'

'Yes, master.'

'No. You are sure. You are *sure* you can do better for me. Can't you?'

'Yes, master.'

'Good.'

He took the flower from her and held it up.

'A good specimen, but far from the best available.'

He dropped it, waiting for it to fall to the floor, rotating like an empty little purple parachute, and then put the toe of his right boot on top of it, casually grinding the toe left right left right and then lifting the boot to reveal the flower ground to pulp against the floor. A purple smear of something organic, unidentifiable now from what it had been.

'Get me another, Annalein. A better one. And let's see if we can't shave two seconds off your time, eh? On the word go. Ready?'

'Yes, master.'

Her breathing had scarcely slowed and the trickle of sweat at her temples had thickened.

'OK. Then go. Go!'

Anna was off again, moving faster, hopping and skipping, her gasps of pain and effort magnified between the walls of the hothouse. She reached the orchid and bent to it for the second time, skirt riding up to reveal her arse, the white triangle of her knickers lost against her white skin at this distance, so it seemed as though she was naked beneath the skirt. Then she had straightened, turned, and was coming back, her gasps of effort interwoven with gasps and squeaks of pain.

She stood to attention again in front of Bärengelt, gasping, trying to control her breathing.

'Here, master.'

She held up both hands this time, two flowers in one hand, a single flower in the other.

'Oh, dear, Annalein. What is this?'

'Flowers, master. Flowers for you.'

'How many flowers, Annalein?'

'Th- three, master.'

'But did I ask for three?'

Anna's head dropped, chin sinking into the fluffy white folds of the scarf.

'No, master.'

'Head up when you are talking to me, Annalein. You are right, I did not ask for three. I asked for one. So why did you bring me three?'

Anna drew a deep breath, still trying to control her breathing.

'Bec– because I thought if I brought three, there was a better chance that one would be good enough, master. Good enough for you.'

'Did you, Annalein? Did you think that? But you are not here to think, are you? You are here to obey. Give them to me.'

She put them on to the outstretched palm of his left hand, vivid purple against the black leather. He turned his hand over and they fluttered to the floor. As they landed he put the toe of his right boot on to one and ground left right left right.

'Do you understand, Anna?'

He lifted the boot away and put it on to another of the flowers, grinding left right left right.

'Yes, master.'

He lifted the boot away and put it on top of the third flower, grinding left right left right.

'Good, Annalein. Very good.'

He lifted the boot away. Four smears of purple organicity on the floor, of organic purpurity. Beth looked away, then looked back. A pattern. Emerging in the smears of the orchid flowers.

'Head up, Annalein. You have failed me twice: do not fail me again. Go and get me a single flower. Do you understand? A single flower. One flower. One perfect flower. That is all I ask. OK?'

'Yes, master.'

Tears were streaming silently down Anna's face, riding across her lips, so that when she spoke she must have tasted salt. Warm salt. Beth felt her cunt shift and ripple. She wanted to kiss Anna. Kiss the tears. Bite into her briny lips.

'Then go. Now! Go!'

Anna set off with a sob, hopping, sliding, skidding, gasping.

'Faster! Faster, you lazy bitch, or I'll warm your arse for you when you get back. Faster!'

Anna nearly tripped and fell as she tried to move faster. She was limping now, limping almost on both feet, proceeding by dot and carry, carry and dot. Poor bitch. Poor little bitch. She reached the orchid bush again and bent over.

'Hurry up! Pick me one and get back over here.'

Now she was on her way back, trying to move fast, limping again, tear-streaks glistening on her reddened face, her breath wheezing, bubbling, her blonde stubble wet and shining with sweat.

'Master.'

She could barely speak. Bärengelt held his hand out.

'Give it me.'

She put it on his hand. Silence, but for the gasp of Anna's breath. Then:

'Yes? Is that it?'

'Yes' – she choked, swallowed – 'Yes, master.'

'What did I ask for?'

'A flower, master. A – a single perfect flower.'

'And is this a single perfect flower?'

'Y – yes, master. It is.'

'Is it? Are you sure?'

'Yes, master.'

'Then why are you speaking so uncertainly? Is it what you say it is or not?'

'Yes, master.'

'Louder.'

'Yes, master.'

Silence again. Anna's tears were gathering at the point of her small chin and dripping on to her scarf. Drip. Drip. Sparkling as they fell.

'"Yes, master"?' Bärengelt mimicked. '"Yes, master"? Is that all you have to say?'

Anna tried to speak. A broken smile flickered on her face for a moment.

'Yes, master.'

'Lou–'

'Yes, master!' she shouted, before Bärengelt had finished the command.

'OK. You are right. This is a single perfect flower. You have chosen well and I am satisfied. Are you glad to hear that?'

'Yes, master.'

'Then smile for me, Annalein. Smile to show how happy you are that I am satisfied and will not send you to fetch flowers for me again. Eh?'

The cane came out and poked at Anna's stomach, tickling at her. The broken smile returned, staying longer, brightening, and the rhythm of her low sobs broke, stuttered, and began to fade.

'Good, Annalein. I am so pleased to see you happy that I am satisfied. But Beth is not. Not yet. She wants you to bring her a flower. *Fetch* her a flower. Don't you, Beth? So choose one for your little sister. A flower for her to fetch.'

'One of those, master.'

She pointed.

'Where? Those?'

The black cane came up.

'The white ones?'

'Yes, master.'

'Too close, Betchen. Far too close. I see you have not entered into the spirit of our little game, so you are disqualified. What about you, Gwen? What flowers would you like Anna to bring you?'

Gwen's arm came up without hesitation, pointing far down the aisle to a point high on one wall.

'One of those, master. The red ones.'

'Ah, an excellent choice. A special variety of *Paphiopedilum sanguineum*. Do you see them, Anna? No, keep your mouth shut. I am sick of the sound of your whining voice. Just nod. Do you see them?'

Anna nodded, fighting back renewed sobs. Bärengelt had played her so skilfully, pretending to take pity on her, then throwing her to Gwen, who never needed a second invitation to indulge in cruelty.

'Good. Then fetch one for your big sister Gwen. Can you do that? And without mistakes? One perfect flower for your big sister? Fast as can be?'

Anna didn't move. Then she shook her head a little, uncertainly.

'That was not a nod, Anna. Are you telling me you won't fetch a flower for your big sister?'

Anna shook her head again.

'Then what is it? Tell me.'

'I c–can't, master. It's not that I won't, it's because I can't.'

'Why not?'

'M–my feet, master.'

'Your *feet*, Annalein? But what on earth could be wrong with your feet?'

'They're blistered, master. Very badly.'

'Oh dear. Blistered feet. *Badly* blistered feet. *Very* badly blistered feet. Little Anna has very badly blistered feet and she thinks that is enough for her to cry off from fetching a flower for her big sister. But what does that big sister herself think? Gwen?'

'No, master. It's not enough. I want one. Now.'

'And quite right you are to want one too, Gwen. Your aesthetic sense cannot be faulted. But what of your moral sense? Anna has blistered feet. Still, whose fault is that?'

'Hers, master. For wearing such ridiculous boots.'

'Yes, I'm afraid you're right, Gwen. It is her own fault. So, Anna, I'm afraid you will have to fetch your sister a flower regardless. But I'll tell you what, I'll take pity on you and allow you to take, oh, half as long again as I would otherwise have allowed you. Isn't that good of me?'

'Y–' Anna started to say, then stopped and nodded her head.

'Good. But you mustn't blister those very badly blistered feet of yours any more, must you?'

Anna nodded.

'No, you mustn't. So you can crawl, you snivelling little bitch. Get down on the floor, Annalein. Hands and knees. Hurry up. And on the word of command *crawl* to fetch your big sister one of the flowers she has chosen. The red ones, over there. OK?'

Anna was on her hands and knees now, facing in the direction she would have to take. She nodded, sniffing, her tears dripping to the floor.

'Good. You have fifty-six seconds to get there and fifty-five seconds to get back. So go, you idle little slut. Go! *Go!*'

Anna was off, crawling fast towards the flowers Gwen had chosen, her knees slipping for a moment as she passed over the little puddle of her tears, the long scarf starting to unravel, trailing out behind her. And her skirt was constricting her: after a second or two she had to stop and tug it higher, exposing her thighs and the lower curve of her buttocks.

'Hurry up, you idle little slut. Forget about flaunting your backside at us and get that flower. Quick.'

She was already crawling again, leaving a trail of glistening tears behind her, little specks of light on the marble floor. Gwen watched her, eyes shining, face a little flushed. She was enjoying this. Enjoying the chance to dominate Anna, who had almost reached the hothouse wall below the red flowers Gwen had chosen.

'Faster. Faster. You are a second behind schedule and still have to climb for what your big sister wants.'

She reached the wall, stood up, and began to climb the wall, doll-like with distance, a little doll climbing a wall of orchids in white boots and tight clothing. She reached the flowers, hesitated for a moment, plucked one, began to climb down.

'Three seconds behind schedule now, Anna. You'll have to run back, despite your poor blistered feet. Otherwise I'll have to punish you hard. Very hard.'

Anna was still a long way up the wall, two or three metres up, but as Bärengelt's voices rumbled out along the hothouse she jumped, landing hard, the *clak* of her boots hitting the floor reaching Beth's ears with a fractional delay. She fell over, rolling on the floor for a moment, then she was up and running, limping, skipping.

'*Acht . . . sieben . . . sechs . . . fünf . . . vier . . . drei . . . zwei . . .*'

Anna was sprawling at his feet, holding up a single red flower. But it was imperfect, one of its red petals lolling brokenly, like a wounded limb or wing. She saw this as she held it up, and the eagerness in her face broke with disappointment and fear.

'Just in time, Annalein. But you paid for your extra speed with the quality of your harvest. Look at it. A beautiful flower. Perfect a minute ago; a little less than perfect now. And alas, Gwen will not accept anything less than perfection. Will you, Gwenchen? Even for your little sister's sake?'

'No, master. I'm afraid not.'

'See? So drop it, Anna. On the floor.'

Anna's hand trembled and opened and the flower fell to the floor. Bärengelt moved his right foot, the toe poised to descend on the flower.

'Stand up, Anna. Strip. Boots and socks first. I will deal with you properly later.'

The toe descended, ground left right left right, and lifted to reveal a fifth smear against the floor. Anna was sitting on the floor, struggling to take the boots off. Bärengelt grunted with annoyance.

'Lift your legs.'

The cane had vanished from his hand and as Anna lifted her legs he took hold of the soles of the boots, tugging harder, lifting Anna's hips and arse off the floor, her lower back, leaving only her shoulders and arms still touching it. He tugged and Anna left the floor for a moment almost entirely, just the back of her head and forearms touching it, landing back on it hard with a suppressed cry of pain. Christ, he was strong. He tugged again and Anna bounced free and back to the floor. The boots were starting to slide off her feet. Slowly. Another tug, another bounce, and they suddenly slid an inch at a time, two inches, three.

Bärengelt let go of her and her arse and legs hit the floor with a thump, breath knocked from her lungs.

'Get on with it. You can get them off yourself now.'

Anna sat up and tugged at the boots herself, absurd in her too large scarf and too small clothes. One came free with a *pop* and she put it to one side, tugging at the other. It came free too, *pop*, and she stood up, stooping to pull her stockings off, hopping on one foot, then the other.

'Stockings. I want them. Give them to me. I don't care about the scarf. Throw it to the floor. Hurry. Shirt next, then skirt and knickers and bra. Hurry.'

Anna handed him the stockings and he hung them over his left arm, white and moist, stretched with the weight of the sweat in them. Anna was unwinding the scarf, letting it fall to the floor. The last fold came free and she threw it aside, then began to undo the buttons of the white shirt with trembling fingers. Gwen was watching her with even brighter eyes now, her tongue passing along her lips. Like a hungry she-tiger watching a lamb. A fat white lamb.

'Yes. Give it to me.'

Anna handed him the shirt and he hung it over his arm next to the stockings.

'Hurry up. Faster.'

The zip came down and Anna stepped out of the skirt, picking it up and handing it to Bärengelt before beginning to pull the knickers down. With difficulty. They left red lines around her hips and on her buttocks, and her pubic hair was damp with sweat, plastered thinly against her *mons Veneris* and cunt. Bärengelt took them from her and she reached back to unclip the bra. The fastener clicked open and her breasts jerked and quivered, falling free from the bra's double-fisted grip.

She peeled the cups from her skin and handed it over to him.

'Thank you, Annalein.'

He hung it over his arm with the shirt and skirt and knickers. Anna was naked again, her face and body glistening with sweat, threads of it trickling downwards over her tits and arse, stomach and back, flanks and thighs, thicker threads dreckling downwards in her arsecleft and titcleft. Beth could smell it. Fresh Anna-sweat. Her cunt stirred again.

'You enjoyed that, didn't you, Gwen?'

Gwen blinked as though waking from sleep and looked towards him. The smile that had come over her lips as she watched Anna touched her lips again.

'Yes, master.'

'Good. As did I. But you are not here to enjoy yourself. Look at your little sister. She is deliciously drenched with sweat, is she not? *Mädchenschweiß*. Girl-sweat. I can savour her rich odour from here. So fresh, so strong. *Heißer Mädchenschweiß*. Hot girl-sweat. Delicious. To you, however, falls the privilege of licking her clean. You, Gwen. Every inch. Cunt, arse, tits. Every inch.'

Gwen blinked again.

'Master?'

'No, Gwen. No, no, no. No. I have spoken. You shall lick her clean. Every inch. But not now. She must

95

ripen first. She must allow her sweat to lie upon her white skin and ripen. Dermal bacteria are multiplying in it even as I speak. Gorging on its salts and proteins. The musk-notes of that heady female bouquet will strengthen and deepen, acquiring subtle variations of timbre on different parts of her body. You will detect different flavours as your tongue passes over different regions of her. Different flavours on the globes and in the crinnies of her breasts. Around her nipples. On the white plain of her belly and in the bowl of her omphalos. Down her back and in the cleft of her gorgeous arse. On and in her cunt. Around her cunt. In her swiff-paved gluft. Do you not feel your mouth begin to water at the prospect of it?'

'But Beth. I have been neglecting you. I shall now make it up to you. Knickers.'

The cane had moved up and lifted the knickers as they lay on his outstretched left arm. He flicked them to her and she caught them as they flew towards her. They were heavier now. Heavier with Anna's sweat. The thin cloth was warm and moist under her fingers as she held them.

'Put them on. Hurry up.'

She opened them and bent to step into them, drawing them up her legs with a shiver, feeling them smearing her legs with sweat as they dragged upwards against the skin. She had to tug hard to get them up her legs, to settle them around her hips and cunt, feeling Anna's moist, warm sweat kiss her into her. Cunnilingue her. They were tight, too tight, cutting into her crotch, pressing hard but insubstantially against her cunt and gluft, climbing uncomfortably into her arsecleft. She shifted from foot to foot, wanting to finger them loose, but enjoying the heat and moisture that were in them, heaviest around the crotch, where Anna had sweated as she ran to fetch the flowers.

'Bra.'

She caught the white flutter of cloth as it flew towards her. A bra. Filmy silk and lace. An expensive schoolgirl's bra. Warm and moist with Anna's effort and sweat. She held it open wonderingly, worried that it would tear if she pulled at it too hard.

'Put it on.'

She fitted the cups over her tits, shivering with pleasure at the odd mixture of warmth and moistness in them. Warm, sweaty bra and knickers, freshly stripped from Anna. She held the straps behind her back, her fingers struggling with the fastening of the bra, its cups tight and cruel on her breasts, barely covering them, its delicate cloth cutting into her shoulders and back. Nearly. Nearly. Then the fastening snapped shut and she tugged at the edge of the cups, adjusting them on her breasts.

'Shirt.'

She caught it as it billowed towards her. Warm, sweaty shirt. Silk too. A white sports-shirt. Too small for Anna, far too small for her. Schoolgirl's again. Soaked under the armpits. Almost wringing wet. She slipped her hand into a sleeve and drew it up her arm, then slipped her other hand into the other sleeve, beginning to draw it up her arm. It stretched taut across her back and the cuffs only reached as far as her forearms, riding higher as she tugged the shirt inadequately into place and began to button it up. Began trying to button it up. Too small. Far too small. And it was missing a button. A white pearl button. Third from the top. Where the schoolgirl's shirt strained over Anna's adult breasts.

'Roll the sleeves up.'

She gave up on the top two buttons and began to roll the left sleeve up carefully.

'Not like that. Not carefully. Carelessly. Verisimilitude, Betchen.'

She frowned a little, rolling the sleeve down, rolling it up again, carefully careless. For verisimilitude. What did he mean? Now the right sleeve. Carefully careless.

97

'Good. Skirt.'

She caught it. Light purple wool. Lamb's wool. With a crest in gold thread. *Anactoria*. Christ. She was starting to understand now. Light silver zip. She stepped into it and tried to zip it up. Too tight again. A schoolgirl's sports-skirt. She had to tug it higher, up over her thighs, before the zip began to work. Zzzzz. Zzzz. Like a sleepy bumblebee, testing its wings in spring. Zzzzzz. Zzzzp. And it was up, straining the skirt against her thighs and arse.

'Stockings.'

He tossed them to her one by one. White stockings. Not just moist: damp. Wet. Wringing. She shook them loose. Long white sports-stockings. Socks for Anna. Socks for her. She had to sit down on the floor to put the first on, pulling hard, already sweating into the sweaty clothes. The silk of the stocking slid hard against her skin as she pulled on it. Pulled hard. She adjusted the hem where it lay just above her knee. What a pervert Bärengelt was. Though not just a pervert. An *Über*-pervert. Not just making her wear a schoolgirl's sports uniform, but a schoolgirl's sports uniform her little sister had sweated into. Heavily. She put her other foot into the other stocking and started tugging it up her leg.

'No. Leave it rolled down. Around your shins. Yes . . . And loosen the other one. Not so well-adjusted . . . OK . . . Good. Now, go and get that.'

She looked where the black cane was pointing and her mouth quirked with amusement. A hockey stick. And ball. A hockey stick leaning against the wall, its handle hidden in the leaves and flowers of an orchid. Red and white/gold flowers.

She walked over to the stick, feeling the sweat in her socks squelch against the floor, and picked it out of the orchid, smelling creamy sweetness and a tickle of pollen. Hockey stick. Cloth handle fitting snugly into her hand. Snugly and somehow . . . familiarly.

'Juggle the ball.'

'Master . . . ?'

'Juggle the ball. Bounce it up and down on the stick.'

'Master, I can't. I've never played hockey.'

'Do it.'

She adjusted the stick in her hand and bent to pick up the ball. Squeezed it for a moment. Hard beneath her fingers but somehow . . . familiar. She tossed it into the air and tried to hit it up with the stick. Not that she could – she'd miss for sure, because she'd never pl–

'Good. Very good.'

It was bouncing up and down on the blade of the stick. No, *she* was bouncing it up and down on the blade of the stick. Controlling it easily and smoothly. Which was mad. Because she'd never played hockey before. Never even touched a stick or ball. But here she was juggling a ball expertly with one. Just like . . . Emily. Emily McFadden.

'*Wunderbar.* Wonderful. Now, boots. Come back over here.'

She turned (*still* juggling the ball) and walked towards him. He was holding a pair of boots in his left hand. By their laces. Hockey boots. She let the ball fall to the floor and trapped it dead with one crisp movement of the stick. How could she *do* this? She'd never touched a hockey stick before today. Before *now*.

She bent to put the stick on the floor beside the ball and stood up to take hold of the boots. He let go of the laces, letting them drop into her hands. They were too small too. Schoolgirl's hockey boots. She sat on the floor, feeling the fading bruises in her arse re-awaken, and began to put the left boot on. Pull it on. Fucking tug and wrench it on.

She stopped and looked up at him.

'Master, it's too small. They're too small.'

'Put them on.'

'I can't.'

'You can. Or you will suffer more than you would do by putting them on.'

She looked at the black cane in his hand and bent back to the boot. Tugged again at it, sliding it up over her heel a fraction of an inch at a time. Stood up cautiously to stamp her foot into it, balancing on her other foot. As though she were hammering it on. Christ, she would cripple herself if she tried to move in them. Stamp. Stamp.

It was on. She sat down to put the right boot on. Pull it on. Tug and wrench it fucking-well on. Christ. If she could take her sock off it would be easier. She looked up again, mouth beginning to open, but his helmet was already swinging side to side. *No*. She tugged at it, sliding it up over her heel a fraction of an inch at a time, then cautiously lifting herself, kneeling on her left leg while she stamped with her right, forcing the boot on. Stamp. Stamp. Nearly. Stamp.

Yes. They were on and she didn't like thinking about getting them off again. She tied the laces, her hands moving smoothly and expertly, looping the laces twice under the sole of the left boot, three times under the sole of the right boot (why?), and stood up slowly.

'Take a few steps.'

She obeyed him. (Why? Because that was what Emily had done. For luck.) The studs clicked on the floor. She'd never heard that sound before but it was somehow . . . familiar. Again. Clashing studs on a hard surface. Sweating schoolgirls coming in off the hockey field.

'Pick up the stick. Dribble the ball.'

She bent and picked up the stick and tapped at the ball. Tapped left, tapped right. Left right left right. Dribbling it. Expertly. Walking towards the wall and turning back again. In a body that wasn't her body. It knew things that she didn't know. That she'd never learned. She dribbled the ball towards him, trapped it, stood in front of him.

'Very good, Beth. Now, do you think you can run in those boots?'

'No, master.'

'Sure?'

'Yes, master. Not on this floor. Especially not on this floor.'

'OK. Take them off.'

Fuck it. She dropped her head as she sat down on the floor again, hiding a scowl. What the fuck was he playing at? She untied the laces of the right boot, hands and fingers moving smoothly and expertly again, and began to slide it off. Jesus. It wasn't . . . coming. Oh, fuck. She strained again. No use.

'Stop. Hold your foot up.'

She lifted her right foot. He walked to her, took hold of the boot, and tugged.

'Ow,' she said.

'Did it loosen?'

'Yes, master. A little bit.'

'Lie back hard. Arms wide.'

She obeyed him.

'Now, on the count of three, pull away as I tug. One . . . two . . . three!'

She pulled away as he tugged, her whole leg lifting into the air, her arms sliding on the marble as she swam them frantically, trying to keep herself from being lifted bodily into the air. Then she fell back, her arse hitting the floor hard, her bruises giving up pain like the juice from crushed grapes, and the boot was in his hand, off.

'Thank you, master.'

He let the boot drop to the floor. It bounced and lay on its side. Five studs in an odd, irregular pattern.

'A pleasure, Betchen.'

And it had been: he had an erection. She could see it bulging behind the black leather of his bodysuit, a thick white cudgel concealed behind a silver zip. She looked away and down at her left boot, unlacing it, setting her teeth and tugging at it. Hard. Hard.

'No good?'

She gave up and let go.

'No good, master.'

'Raise your leg. As before, on the count of three.'

She lifted her leg, lying back against the floor, arms spread wide, and he took hold of the boot.

'One . . . two . . . three!'

He tugged, she pulled, leg stretching upwards, arse leaving the floor, arms sprawling wide to hold her down, then thump, she'd fallen back, arse hitting the floor again, fresh pain pressed from the wine-purple and grape-yellow-and-green bruises beneath her tight white knickers, and the boot was in his hand, off.

'Thank you, master.'

He dropped this boot too. It landed, bounced, but stayed upright on its sole next to the first. Left boot and right boot.

'A pleasure again, Betchen.'

She glanced covertly at his crotch. The erection was still there.

'Yes, Betchen. It's time again.'

His hand dropped to his crotch, unzipped it, and helped his cock out, absently thumbing back the foreskin.

'Take your socks off.'

She sat down on the floor, holding back a sigh, and pulled her socks down one by one, rolling each into a ball as it came off, taking them in her hand and standing up.

'Here they are, master.'

'No. Unroll one of them.'

She unrolled one of them. A silk sock, damp and warm with Anna's sweat. And her sweat, now.

'Here, master.'

He took them from her, dropping the one still rolled to the floor with the boots, then folding the other in half, in half again, and taking hold of an end in each hand.

'Stand with your head up, mouth open.'

She was puzzled. What was he going to do? Whip her face? Her mouth?

'Stick your tongue out.'

Whip her tongue? She stuck it out. No, not that. It wasn't that. He held the twice-doubled sock over her mouth.

'Drink. Drink it all.'

And he wrang it. Wrang it out over her mouth and protruding tongue so that a thin trickle of sweat fell from it. Straight on to her tongue. Straight into her mouth. Warm, salty sweat.

'*Mädchenschweiß*, Betchen. *Annaschweiß. Deinschweiß.*'

It was still trickling into her mouth. Christ, his hands were strong, to twist the sock like that. Keep the sweat flowing from it. He shifted the sock suddenly, allowing the trickle of sweat to hit her lip, then her nostrils. She snorted and choked, not able to keep her mouth open any longer. He relaxed his hands on the sock and moved it away, holding it above his cock, twisting it again, hard, so a final trickle of sweat fell on to his cockhead.

'*Mädchenschweiß.*'

He let go of one end of the sock and flicked it out, swinging it, his freed hand dropping on to his cockhead and rubbing Anna's sweat into it. Her sweat into it. Making it gleam rich purple, like a huge heavy gem.

'Knickers off, Betchen.'

103

CAGED!

Yolanda Celbridge

Yolanda Celbridge has written the most novels for us of any of our authors, and her work has encompassed settings as diverse as a nineteenth-century English school, an SM fantasy island, the wide-open spaces of the USA, and a North African army unit of a very specialised nature! In *Caged!*, the novel excerpted here, Yolanda Celbridge turns up the satire *and* the Sadean torment. Though an anglophile (as you can tell from her early pastiches of Edwardian erotica!), Yolanda's currently turning her attention to her native North America, with books such as *The Taming of Trudi* and *Belle Submission*. But in the following extract from *Caged!*, Lady Pollecutt gets a nasty shock . . .

There are two worlds, the cold and the hot. In the hot world, a wench's lust must be tamed, and in the cold world, it must be kindled. The instruments of both taming and kindling are the same: rod on bare arse, and tarse in coynte, or better, her nether hole most secret and sublime.

Sir George Pollecutt, *Universall Travels*

'Fan harder, you wretch,' drawled the woman, reclining on her divan.

The male continued to wave the garland of goose feathers, his exertion as placid as his gaze, at the woman's half-dressed body, was stern.

'Bah! You don't understand a word,' she sighed. 'How I hate Tangier! The babble, the stink and fools who cannot speak the King's English. How I wish His Majesty had never gotten this place, nor given Pollecutt his post. Sometimes, I wonder if Dodd's tropic whippings weren't better than Pollecutt's neglect – at least I got regular swiving from him, with a tarse not so damnably big as to hurt my pouch.'

The windows were open on the balcony; below them, the noise of afternoon in the souk: donkeys, carts clattering, voices in Spanish, Berber and Arabic. The woman loosened an eyelet of the brocade corselet, which was all that covered her upper body, and allowed her maid and two male servants to view her white breast, straining against the heavy fabric. The ripe pears of her bottom were sheathed only in a voile negligée shift, its sweat-damp fabric clinging to the rippling contours of buttock and thigh, which were naked under the film of cloth. Her stockinged feet waggled the air, their curled Moroccan slippers discarded on the carpet beneath.

A second male filled her glass with mint tea, and proffered a dish of marshmallow. Both servants were muscular dark youths, Berber tribesmen, of the lady's own age, slightly over the twentieth year; like her, they were clothed for the heat, their upper bodies bare, with loose blue ankle-robes draped at their loins. Despite their ebony bodies, the young men had blue eyes. The barefoot, besmocked maidservant kneeled by her mistress's feet, bathing her toes in scented water. Though tanned by the sun, she was European, of the same young age, ripe body and tresses as her lady. The lady sighed.

'So hot . . .' she gasped. 'Well, you are but heathens . . .'

She unfastened her corselet completely, allowing her bare breasts to spring free, with the strawberry nipples jutting and firmed. She shook her head, waving her long blonde mane, so that its hairs caressed her nipples.

'*That's* better,' she murmured, sipping her mint tea.

'Yes, you damned hussy,' whispered a male, concealed behind a spyhole in a false wall, on the shaded side of the boudoir. His shirt was clinging wet to his torso, above cotton breeches and calfskin boots, with a brace of pistols, rope, donkey-crop and rapier at his belt. 'Messalina, Jezebel, the temptress Eve herself, were lambs compared to you!'

The lounging woman pulled up her negligée, baring her buttocks and pubis completely; her bush of tangled, golden pubic hair glistened with her sweat. She began to fan her loins with the voile negligée, parting her thighs, to show the rich ruby lips of her vulva and the wet, shining pouch within. The male servants continued at their tasks, each with a growing bulge at his crotch, while the maid lifted her smock and fanned her lady's feet, showing her own bare arse and loins, and a pubic jungle massive on the lithe, muscled basin of her quim.

'So,' said the lady, 'you are heathens, but men for all that! How I wish Sir George recognised my charms! I so rarely see him – prancing in the desert, in search of treasure, or, more like, goats to swive!'

'Foul harlot!' hissed the spying male.

'When he serves me, his tarse swives me so ill, I can scarcely move for the pain of it! More a horse's than an Englishman's, and too often put in the place unintended by nature! You have no English, so cannot understand my woman's plaints ... but serve me well, and I shall reward you well.'

'Ah ...' groaned the male. 'Calumny upon vileness!'

'Perhaps *this* you may understand,' she continued, licking her teeth and placing her fingers on the lips of her vulva.

She drew her lips back, and thrust three, then a fourth, finger inside her pouch, now gushing with copious juice.

'You see? My purse needs good meat for the filling – just as yours needs silver. Peruvian pieces, fresh snatched from the king of Spain ... *piezas de plata peruviana!* – one for each of you, if you obey.'

She rose, casting off her negligée, and placed her hands upon her head, standing with one leg bent and raised, with the heel wedged in her open slit.

'I am as helpless,' she moaned, 'as a slave in your marketplace. The captain is away until tomorrow, and I have no one to protect me from your tools I see so monstrous, you lustful brutes.'

The two males had fully erect cocks, clearly outlined as they strained against the fabric of their robes. Her teeth and eyes sparkled in the shadowed chamber; a shaft of sunlight fell on her nipples, fully hardened and erect, like plums. Juice trickled from her quim down her thighs to the sole of her raised foot; her thigh trembled as it supported her. The two servants let fall their robes and the lady gasped, licking her lips. She reached out and touched each of the swollen, shiny helmets on the peehole.

'Your foreskins cut! Smooth horns, both, to give my husband horns! Truly, you are heathens, so I can commit no sin . . .'

'Knowing nothing else, you count sin as virtue, damned trollop!' snarled the watching male.

He continued to watch, as the lady took a marshmallow from her mouth and moistened it inside her wet quim. She bit the sweetmeat in half and put a piece in each of the servants' mouths; stretching herself belly down on the couch, she raised and parted her taut bare arse-melons. Both males chewed and swallowed their juiced sweetmeats. One stood at each end of the couch, while the maidservant drew up her smock, revealing her own naked loins and her tangled quim-hairs glistening. She mounted her lady like a pony, sitting on the small of her back, and began to rock back and forth.

'Ride me, Ghislaine, ride me . . .!' groaned her mistress.

The lady fastened her lips over the male's cock, and her tongue began to dance on the glans while her lips pressed and tickled the helmet's base, and her fingers dripped with her juice, as she frotted her swollen nubbin. She gasped as the second male's cock nuzzled the open lips of her gash, and grunted when the dark tool penetrated her wet crimson folds, right to the balls. Her mouth fastened completely on the cock at her lips, taking the whole shaft right to her throat. Her head bobbed up and down as she sucked one cock, while the second rammed her quim. The maidservant's own cunt was bared, seeping copious oil. She masturbated her swollen nubbin as she rode her mistress's back, slapping the lady's bare buttocks, quivering under the black tool's thrusts.

After several minutes of vigorous swiving and sucking, the lady moaned and gestured. Ghislaine remained in saddle; the males switched places, and she began to suck the cock slimed with her own cunt-juice, while its fellow penetrated her womb, fucking her vigorously for several seconds, before she grasped the member and transferred it to her opened anal pucker.

'Oh! I am the weaker vessel! Take me where you will!'

The cock sank deep into her arse-passage and she sighed, growling in her breast, and masturbated hard, using both hands to frot her clitoris and erect nipples, as the naked servant vigorously buggered her. She squealed, drooling, as she sucked, and her buttocks writhed under buggery, with the male's hips and belly slapping her bare arse-flesh.

'Do your worst, you Vandals!' growled the watcher.

Both males spunked in unison; she swallowed the sperm creaming her mouth, while the bugger's spunk bubbled at her jerking anus bud, and the lady masturbated her clitoris to a loud, long spasm. The maidservant's panting breath indicated that she, too, had masturbated to climax, attested by the stream of come flowing down her mistress's writhing bare back, Ghislaine's bucking mount.

'Ah – ah – *ahh* . . .' the lady squealed, her cries dying away to a sated gasp: '*Mmm* . . .'

The spy quit his cubbyhole. Moments later, he burst through the door of the chamber, clutching his pistols.

'You vile beasts!' he cried.

'George!' shrieked the lady, groping for her negligée.

The maidservant Ghislaine pushed down the front of her smock and curled herself in the corner of the room;

the two males seized their robes and vaulted over the balustrade, to disappear into the throng a few feet below.

'Oh, Captain,' sobbed the buggered woman, clutching her bum-cleft. 'How thankful I am! You have rescued me from shame and agony! I gave those damned beggars a few coins, and they refused to leave me until they had earned my charity! Little did I know . . .'

Whap! Whap! Whap!

Her husband slapped her face three times.

'*Oh!*' she squealed, bursting into tears as he ripped her negligée from her, and wound her hair in his fist.

Holding her on tiptoe by her hair, he began to slap her naked breasts, until her strawberry nipples were bruised blue. She shrieked, sobbing, her mouth drooling spunk and her quim and bumhole dribbling. Her heavy teats shook under the slaps; her bare feet flapped helplessly, trying to kick her husband's calfskin boots; her bottom still glowed pink from her maidservant's spanks.

'You lie, slut!' he hissed. 'I saw you buggered. Your holes are still full of another's spunk! Little Ghislaine, your bawd, got those whelps to serve you.'

The maidservant emerged from the shadows.

'No, Sir George!' sobbed the lady.

'Though mute, Ghislaine speaks to me,' said her husband.

'Ghislaine!' shrieked the lady.

Ghislaine smiled coquettishly, and nodded. She expressed in swift, impish sign language the entire transaction: her procuring the males, and her mistress's promise of silver from the captain's treasure. Without command, she accepted the rope, uncoiled from the captain's belt, and bound her mistress by her wrists. The captain ripped her negligée in half and wound it around her ankles. Trussed, the lady was pushed on

112

her belly, on the floor. The captain slid the point of his rapier under her pubic mound and touched her clitoris, obliging her to raise her buttocks and cunt basin; Ghislaine held the sword, while the captain unbuckled his belt. The lady sobbed, her sob turning to a scream as Sir George's cock penetrated her still-slimed anus, and began to bugger her, with hard, slamming thrusts.

'Take that, ma'am! And that!' he roared. 'Damn you for a strumpet!'

'*Ahh . . .!*' shrieked his wife.

'High office I have won, yet am still bound to a whore!'

'How *dare* you, sir!' she shrieked, her arse-globes writhing under her husband's buggery. 'God! The shame! *Oh! It hurts!* To be Lady Pollecutt, an *English* lady, *twice* ravished in the foul sin of buggery! *Ah! Ah!*'

'You were nothing but a bonded slut when Dodd sold you in the mart of Hispaniola, with your coynte the best travelled road in the Caribees, and the widest. Why, a man could get his camel to fill your chasm, and have room for himself and a squadron of hussars! Before your bondage, slut, you were Molly Coker, a whore from the alehouses of Hartlepool . . . my faithful Ghislaine, though heathen, is more a lady than you! Wait . . . yes . . . ah! A dirty job, but must be done! You'll have your punishment . . . ah!'

Sir George Pollecutt grunted as he spunked in her anus, his jet frothing over the lips of her squirming anal pucker, already slimed with arse-grease. His wife sobbed, quivering helplessly, as Ghislaine fixed her roped wrists to a pulley, which she drew up, until Lady Pollecutt hung naked, with her bare feet wriggling inches from the floor. His member breeched, Sir George reclined on the couch, lit a cigar and accepted the bottle of port wine which barefooted Ghislaine nimbly served. While she poured the wine, her master's fingers slipped under the girl's smock and began to play

113

between her legs. He grinned at his trussed and suspended wife, who sobbed, staring aghast at Ghislaine's face of pleasure and the bouncing of her pert bubbies, as her loins swayed to Sir George's fingering. Leering at his helpless wife, the male withdrew his fingers from Ghislaine's basin, and showed them, oiled with her fluid. He licked his fingers, one after the other, of her come. His port wine drained and his lips and fingers well slimed by the pretty young maid, Sir George's cock was stiff.

'The tarse you affect to despise, dear,' he said to Lady Pollecutt, 'inspires your further chastisement.'

'No! Please! I beg you!' she squealed. 'I'm so sore! Oh, no, please!'

Sir George rose, and took his *tap*, the Berber crop of heavy braided leather used on the hides of asses and camels. Ghislaine knelt once more at her mistress's feet, this time to hold them still, pulling and stretching Lady Pollecutt's body, to present the quivering bare buttocks as a ripe, fleshy target for her husband's crop.

'No, sir! Please! Don't *flog* me!' she squealed.

'Whipping is the only language your whore's arse understands. Many's the time you were hauled and strung, to be lashed naked, as a bondservant.'

Vip! Vip! Vip!

His wife's bare buttocks clenched and squirmed as the crop bit her trembling skin.

'No!' she shrieked. 'It hurts so! *Oh, please, no!*'

Vip! Vip! Vip!

'*Ahh . . .!* You'll ruin my fesses!'

'On the contrary, madam! A pink arse is the tastiest.'

Vip! Vip! Vip!

'*Ahh! Ahh!*'

Her ankles firmly held by Ghislaine, Lady Pollecutt shuddered, wriggling, as the *tap* bruised the bare expanse of her fesses with livid stripes of crimson, darkening to purple. Sir George thrashed every exposed inch of her naked croup, from her haunches, which were soon black with welts, to the fleshy, quivering mid-fesse and the inner thighs below the croup, where the tip of the crop caught the jutting, swollen cunt lips amid her wet pubic jungle.

Vip! Vip! Vip!

'Ah! Ah! Ahh . . .!'

Vip! Vip! Vip!

'OH! Stop . . .! Please stop . . .!'

When Lady Pollecutt's flogged buttocks were a blotched, puffy mass of crimson and purple welts, her husband laid down his *tap*. The ridges, wealed in her thrashed bum-flans, were etched in shadow by the lowering sun.

'Now, dear lady, you shall see *real* pleasure,' said Sir George. 'I warn you – if you avert your gaze, your flogging shall begin anew.'

Sobbing and trembling, the trussed woman watched, as Ghislaine lifted her smock to reveal her heavily juicing slit and tangle of pube-hairs, exceeding her mistress's in richness; flat, muscled belly and hard, conic bare breasts, with domed nipples already stiff with excitement, as Sir George's cock penetrated her. Ghislaine lay beneath her dangling mistress, with her thighs wrapped around Sir George's back, clutching him to her, as he fucked the maid's copiously juicing cunt.

'I fuck in your arse for your pain, milady,' he panted, 'but in sweet Ghislaine's coynte, to give her pleasure! She is a true whore, as pure as the desert sands. Your lusts are cold and joyless, and only your arsehole has sentiment. You cannot feel pleasure without suffering pain, to remind you that pleasure is wrong.'

'Mm! Mm! Mm!' Ghislaine cried, rocking back and forth, as her belly threshed under the male's pounding.

Sir George began to fuck her very slowly, withdrawing his cock to its full length from the wet, squeezing gash, before plunging into her again, each stroke right to the hilt.

'See how Ghislaine enjoys, my dear! As she will enjoy our bed tonight, while *you* hang, to meditate on your sins.'

'*No . . .!*' wailed Lady Pollecutt.

'There are many like Ghislaine here in Barbary,' said Sir George. 'Pity a slut like you cannot share my philosophical interests. What can *you* understand of the goddess *Flagella*, worshipped by Roman and barbarian alike? Nature repeats herself, in strange harmonies and strange places. How many tribes have seeded the desert sands! Greeks, Goths, Romans – Vandals, like Ghislaine here, blue of eye and blond of tress. Our English race itself is nourished by divers roots. I feel it my duty as an Englishman to reacquaint *these* beauties with the joys of an unskinned tarse . . . and a well-pickled rod for their fesses!'

'*Ah! Ah . . .!*' shrieked Ghislaine, her body lathered in sweat and her cunt pouring come, as Sir George, fucking vigorously, spunked at the neck of her womb; his cream spurted from her gash flaps, over her thighs, and the maid writhed in whimpering orgasm. '*Mm! Mm! Mmm . . .*'

As the room dimmed, with the setting sun's rays a departing red glow, Sir George Pollecutt followed Ghislaine downstairs, where the two blue-robed youths waited in the shadows of the courtyard. Sir George handed each a silver coin.

'Guiseric and Alaric . . . fine names, my lusties,' Sir George said, clapping the backs of both the males who had served his wife.

He reascended the stairs, and took port wine and biscuits as he watched Ghislaine at her toilet. The lithe brown girl stripped naked, then pissed and stooled into a rose-tapterned English chamber pot, which she emptied into the street. She wiped and perfumed her loins with her fingers, before climbing into his four-poster bed. Sir George crept into the salon, where his trussed wife hung, snuffling and sobbing. He picked up her brocade corselet from the floor.

'An English lady mustn't catch cold, my dear,' he said, pressing the brocade to her bare bottom.

The brocade stuck.

Afternoon wind breathed softly across the baked rock of the desert, bathed in pink light from the lowering sun. Not a shrub, nor blade of grass, shivered under the azure sky; whorls of dust spurted briefly, to float, glittering in the haze, beneath jagged red mountains, with the fort and its cluster of humans no more than shards in the moonscape. A pennant of pink brocade fluttered atop the ochre fort, topping clusters of bougainvillea, honeysuckle, date palms and hibiscus fringing a limpid oasis pool.

Tears streamed down the fair girl's cheeks, as her body jolted against the bars of her cage. Her T-shirt, once white, was smudged and ripped, as were the filthy panties wrenched to her crotch and scarcely covering her bare tan thighs. Ragged and sweat-soaked fronds of pubic hair glistened beneath the fabric, riding up over their tufts, and her shirt, translucent with moisture, clung to the massive breasts, their nipples stiff, squashed against her ribcage by her jolting. Her head was bent, and her back and buttocks pressed against the rusty cage bars, better for an animal smaller than a woman. Her eyes were wide and frightened, yet she did not emit any sound of protest other than a whimper. The toes of her left foot were jammed into her mouth, held there by a rope, which bound her right ankle around her neck, parting her thighs and extruding the glistening lips of her quim from her panties.

Metal cuffs, looped to a pin-studded rubber punishment corselet under her breasts, clamped her wrists high up her back. Her mane of yellow hair was plastered to her skull, dripping with sweat that sparkled in the sun. A garland of honeysuckle in her hair shaded her brow. Her eyes were wide, as her two male bearers, each swathed in sky-blue robes, padded on bare feet across the rocks, towards the flogging-frame. They held the cage on poles, balanced on their shoulders, so that the girl's shame was fully exposed to the audience of captives.

Nine sullen, fearful, wide-eyed European girls crouched barefoot on the desert rock, their wrists cuffed at the small of the back, and shackled to a chain, whose end rested with a third blue-robed guard, his free hand holding a coiled leather whip. The chained girls were nude. They crouched with their bellies positioned over spikes driven into the rock, the points almost touching their pubic mounds and keeping their bottoms high in the air. All wore pairs of nipple clamps, each pair of clamps threaded by a short chain to a spike driven into the rock, obliging the girls to hold their heads as high as their croups. The girls were bare-headed under the sun's glare, broken only by the shadow of the ochre fortress and by human figures, stark against the desert, and by the gaunt oblong of the flogging-frame. Eddies of sand blew over their foot-prints from the fort to flogging-frame. From the oasis pool, beside the fort, a single track snaked through a pass in the jagged mountain; in the far heat haze, the same high peaks ringed the fortress, adding nature's confinement to that fashioned by humans.

The blue-robed guards were ebony; two Europeans were present at the scene of punishment, and both dressed in white. One, a young, hard-muscled male, sweated in a cotton suit, with his striped silk tie tight beneath his jaw, shaded by a panama hat. The second, a woman his junior, stood with arms folded, holding two coiled whips. She wore a thin cotton *peplos*, hanging to just below her vulva from two knotted shoulder-strings, and cut deep at the breasts, rippling on her body free of underclothing. Her long brown legs were roped in high sandals that covered her calves. The tip of a slender cane, worn on a leather thong at her waist, slapped the ribbons of her sandals. The contours of her proudly jutting breasts and full, taut buttocks were plainly visible to the guards and audience alike, with the crimson plums of her nipples already erect in excitement as she watched the caged girl advance to her. She was bare-headed, like the other females, but with her long honey tresses smooth and a parasol held over them by another blue-robed guard. The guards approached her, stopped and, without a sound, dropped the cage with the girl inside it.

The woman in the white skirtlet walked around the cage, inspecting her prisoner. The dozen chained girls stared at the caged girl and at the woman, who smiled as her prisoner sobbed. She nodded and the blue-robed guards unlocked the cage door, dragged the girl out and untied the rope that gagged her with her toes. They wrenched her erect and forced her to stand, wailing in a choked sob, her wrists straining against the cuffs that furrowed them. Her head hung low in shame. The woman kicked her legs apart, revealing yellow liquid streaking her inner thighs.

'Frightened, Edwige?' she said softly.

Sniffling, but without looking up, the girl nodded.

'Yes, Mistress,' she sobbed.

'Your bottom is no stranger to my cane, Edwige,' said the blonde woman. 'But this is your first proper whipping.'

Edwige snuffled.

Without letting go of her whips, the blonde woman cracked her palm full across Edwige's cheek.

'Oh . . .!'

'*Isn't* it, Edwige? Your first flogging?'

119

'Yes, Mistress . . .'

'So – this time, not dusted a few dozen stingers with my dainty woman's cane on your bottom, but flogged by the strongest of *males*, on the bare back, in front of your comrades in filth . . . what you *really* came here for. Isn't it?'

'Oh! No, Miss Habren, I swear!'

Habren slapped her face twice more, then her bare breasts, several times, so hard that the nipples slapped one against the other.

'Miss Edwige Joule, so prim and proper and submissive!' she spat. 'Is this honestly your first real flogging?'

'You *know* it is! I've never taken a back-whipping before, only bare-bum caning! *Oh, God . . .!*'

She stooped suddenly, parting her thighs, and a jet of golden fluid hissed from her crotch, splashing her feet and the rock between them. The domina turned to her crouching prisoners.

'Edwige disgusts me. You *all* disgust me,' she spat. 'Girls who should be the decent property of their males, allowed to roam Africa, in search of forbidden, or fancied, excitements. And you end up here, in the women's prison. The Berber are a proud and pure people. By your immodesty, you have forfeited the right to be considered human, and are chained like bitches. Every single one of you has screamed as her bottom reddens under my cane, and *still* you will not learn! Perhaps Edwige's whipping, and loss of remission, shall be a lesson. You, Edwige, shall serve your full year. It shall go easier, if you explain why you are to be flogged.'

'I looked through the bars, Mistress, and watched a male bathing in the oasis at night,' stammered the girl.

'Knowing full well that a Berber male may not be seen disrobed by any woman not his wife. That was the crime that sent you to the women's cage, wasn't it? The male found with you went unpunished, of course – to the Berbers, the female is the temptress, the lustful beast, who must be tamed by corporal punishment. That is why canings on the bare are part of all your sentences. Any objections?'

It was not a question.

'N-none, Mistress.'

'Go on. Why do you merit whipping?'

'It was the heat ... this dreadful, scorching heat, night and day ... I couldn't help myself! I ... I masturbated as I watched.'

'I have caned you on the bare, several times for masturbating, Edwige. What is the tariff?'

'Twenty-one strokes for solitary pleasure, forty-two each for girls caught together, or sixty-three each for triads ...' Edwige blurted. 'But this *heat* ...!'

'On four occasions, you and two companions have taken sixty-three strokes on the naked buttocks,' said Miss Habren crisply. 'This time, your eyes gleamed at your cell window, and were observed by the guard, who shall now flog your back to the bone. It shall hurt much more, and much longer, and you shall bear your stripes home – if your perverse nature ever lets me release you.'

'*Oh ... no! Please!*' Edwige wailed, convulsing in sobs.

At a nod from Habren, the guards ripped her T-shirt and shorts from her, and she stood revealed in her nudity, breasts and belly trembling, and with her massive pubic bush drenched in her sweat and the pee, which still dribbled from her shining red gash. They undid her corselet and handcuffs, showing her tan flesh bruised from the studs inside the corselet. The flogging-frame was a simple wooden oblong, embedded in a basalt plinth, with cuffs for the wrists and ankles at each of its corners. The cuffs hung on cords, adjustable to the victim's height. Dangling from the centre of the crossbar was a headcage of metal strips: a brank, or scold's bridle, with a tongue depressor. One berobed guard cuffed Edwige's wrists and the other her ankles, taking only seconds as her height made no adjustment necessary.

When her naked body was stretched, hanging in a cross, between the posts of the frame, each guard disrobed and stood nude, save for a blue loin-thong. One held the girl's head, while the other fitted her into the brank, with the tongue depressor clamped in her mouth. Although the chain was left slack, the wide collar of the brank would oblige its occupant to hold her head high throughout her punishment. Edwige faced her sister prisoners, whose eyes fixed on her nude body, already trembling and with pee dribbling from her bush. Habren handed a whip to each of the guards.

'*Two* males shall whip you, Edwige –' she said.

'*Two*, Mistress? Oh . . .!'

'– and naked, for their greater comfort and power. There is no taboo broken, for chained women are mere animals. They shall feast on every shudder of your whipped body, and every tear that falls from your eyes, and, when your whipping is complete, you shall not dress, so that your welts may urge your sister sluts to behave.'

She murmured in Berber dialect and both males raised their whips behind the naked prisoner. The young European male in the panama hat stared, licking his lips, at the nude body of Edwige, glazed with her sweat.

'Satisfied?' said Habren, and he nodded.

'I don't expect you to stay still, Edwige,' said Habren, 'or to be silent. Your brank should help muffle your screams and save you from total shame, but, I warn you, I shall extend your tariff if you blub overmuch. As it stands, your tariff is one hundred lashes. As for you, young ladies, you saw Edwige at the dormitory window, and your complicity in her crime has earned each of you a dozen strokes from my cane. You are not branked, so that if there is the slightest squeal from any girl, her set shall be repeated right from the first stroke. If it happens that I have not completed your canings by the end of Edwige's flogging, then Edwige shall be whipped on, until your canings are complete.'

She murmured again, in Berber, and leather flashed.

Crack! Crack!

Each whip lashed Edwige's naked back, the first striping the shoulders and the second her mid-back. Edwige's nude body shuddered violently, her face twisted, and her gorge trembled.

Crack! Crack!

'Mmm . . .!'

Habren strolled to the first of the nine pegged girls and raised her cane.

Vap!

The girl shivered, as a pink weal appeared on her bare bum-flesh.

Vap! Vap! Vap! Vap!

Her buttocks began to clench as Habren's strokes became faster. The dry tapping of the cane was drowned by the crack of the two whips on Edwige's naked back, the strokes now slamming her body against her restraints, as her head bobbed in its metal prison. There was no pause between the strokes, the whips dancing like twin pistons.

Crack! Crack! Crack! Crack!

'Mmm! Mmm! . . . Mmm . . .' came Edwige's gurgling cry, her body shaken like a doll's.

Habren completed the dozen strokes to the shivering jellies of her victim's bare buttocks, red as her face, straining not to blub under punishment. As Habren delivered the last stroke, the girl shook desperately and a stream of pee flooded her clamped thighs. Habren smiled, lifted her skirt well above the jungle of her

123

pubis, and looked at the young man in the panama hat, sitting forward in his chair, with his eyes darting from the flogged girl in her brank to the shuddering bare bum caned by the sandalled woman, her flimsy *peplos* swirling as she caned. His crotch bulged in erection as he fanned himself with a newspaper. Habren's eyes flitted to the naked whippers, and her smile widened as she looked on their own bulging cocks beneath their blue loinstrings.

Habren raised her cane above the tensed buttocks of the second crouching girl, and placed her fingers at the wet slit under her pubic jungle. The girl's clitoris peeped hard and swollen from the moist folds of her labia. Habren brushed her hair back from her brow, and looked at the guard who held her parasol. His robe bulged at the crotch and Habren flicked his erection with her cane tip, pursing her lips in a pout of mock surprise. She nodded and the guard grasped the hem of her dress, raising it over her swollen nipples and holding it at her collarbone, but without touching her skin. Habren placed her free hand at the jutting peach of her croup and slipped her fingers into her bum-cleft. She lifted her right leg and placed it on her left calf, widening her cunt basin, so that her palm and fingers could embrace both anus and vulva.

Vip!

As she caned her second girl, Habren began to masturbate. She reached between her thighs, stroking her wet vulva and thumbing the bud of her anus pucker as she applied even strokes of her cane to the girl's bare.

Vip! Vip! Vip!

'*Ahh . . .!*' the girl moaned.

'Blubbing! We begin again,' hissed Habren, her fingers probing deep into her dripping slit.

The girl stifled a sob as Habren reapplied the cane to her fresh welts, deepening them to crimson and making

124

the buttocks clench white around the dark red stripes. Each stroke slammed the girl's clamped nipples against their fastening and jerked her belly close to the raised spike, close beneath her opened buttocks. Habren took her to her dozen; the girl's body quivered helplessly, her face red and her buttocks squirming, clenching flans of crimson. Come dripped on the spike, inches below her moist gash flaps.

As she caned the next girl, Habren's eyes fixed on the whip-jolted body of Edwige, flogged on her bare back and jerking in the frame as each lash of the twin thongs scarred her. Habren's aim to the buttocks, bared below her, was swift and accurate, and no sound accompanied the caning, save for her victim's faster and faster panting and the slam of her nipple-clamps against their tethering spike. Habren's fingers were slopped with juice from her own swollen red gash and, without pausing in her caning, she slid her hand from her anal cleft, to lick her fingers clean.

Crack! Crack! Crack!

Edwige's body dripped tears and sweat, as each whipstroke sliced her. Deep in her throat, a harsh gurgling whimper vibrated, her clamped tongue unable to form words. Her whippers glistened with sweat, their muscles rippling over their massively swollen loin-pouches, as they striped Edwige's writhing golden back, her ribs pulsing into relief at each shuddering breath between strokes. Her breasts bounced like balls beneath the collar of her brank at each crack of leather on spine and shoulders. As Habren caned the last girl, Edwige's gurgle of agony was a long, single mewl. Her vulva dribbled pee without ceasing, yet the yellow fluid glistened with pouch-oil. Whipped so hard, the girl was juicing at her gash.

Habren paused as the last girl raised her bottom a fraction and parted the cheeks, to show the hairy wet mass of her pouch and perineum. Her auburn hair was cropped to sleek fleece but her mound boasted a jungle rivalling Habren's; the breasts, massive as Habren's own, pressed around their spike, unstrained by the nipple-clamps, and her pencil waist ripened into tan buttocks like bursting calfskin, lined with cane marks, with her cunt dripping come over the menacing belly-spike.

'One would think your bottom invited my cane,' Habren murmured. 'And your gash, too, so insolently displayed. English, aren't you? Susan Race . . . cheeky bitch.'

The girl did not respond but stared at Edwige's squirming body.

Vip!

Habren slashed her cane hard between the arse-cheeks, deep in Susan's befurred slit. Susan shuddered but did not squeal.

Vip! Vip! Vip!

Habren lashed her again on the open vulva, and twice more. Her fingernails were a blur as she masturbated.

'Those strokes don't count to your caning,' she panted, and Susan nodded, smiling as she gasped.

Vip!

The cane lashed Susan's bared buttocks full in mid-fesse. The hard, muscled flesh quivered as a pink weal appeared amid the hardened dark skin of previous canings.

Vip! Vip!

Two strokes took her on the tender skin of the upper fesses.

Vip! Vip!

Two more followed, one to each haunch, raising livid welts. Susan's cheeks began to clench, rapidly and involuntarily, as the wood reddened her skin. Her back remained straight and her breasts quivered only slightly at each impact. Juice flowed from her swollen pouch flaps. Suddenly, Edwige's mewling became a muffled

126

howl. The whips continued to stroke her back, but she threw herself against the flogging-frame, instead of allowing the whips to jolt her, and began to jerk her branked head from side to side, her eyes wide, staring at Habren. Habren paused in caning Susan's bare.

'*Mm! Mm! Mm!*' moaned Edwige, shaking her head frantically.

'How many strokes left?' Habren barked.

'Sixteen, Mistress,' said the first whipper.

'*Mm! Mm!*' sobbed the flogged girl, shaking her head.

'Can't take it, Edwige?' said Habren. 'Had enough?' Edwige nodded yes, her moans fainter.

'Give the girl her sixteen, and continue to whip her until I have finished this one,' Habren rapped, and recommenced her caning of Susan.

Crack! Crack!

The whips streaked across Edwige's writhing bare back.

Vip! Vip! Vip! Vip!

Four strokes bruised Susan right on the softest skin of her top buttocks, and her back and buttocks began to shudder.

Vip! Vip! Vip! Vip!

'*Ahh . . .!*'

After four strokes to her gash, Susan yelped, and Habren murmured that she must begin her dozen over again. Susan's punishment was continued three times, while Edwige's body stiffened and jerked at each whiplash, carrying her well past her hundred. When Susan Race's bare fesses were two puffy crimson gourds, Habren delivered a final cut to the arse-cleft and vulval lips, and her thumb pressed her own stiff clitoris into her pubic bone.

'*Ah! Ahh . . .*'

Habren sighed in climax as her come flowed down her quivering thighs, puddling the rock beneath her and staining her sandal-leather.

'Enough,' she ordered. 'Cut her down.'

'*Ohh . . .*'

Edwige collapsed, sobbing, on the sand at Habren's feet; she ripped the honeysuckle garland from her mane and threw it to Habren's juiced pubis.

'*You bitch!*' she wailed. '*You fucking bitch!* I begged you to stop . . .! *I couldn't take it!*'

'But you did,' said Habren, 'and deserved it, too, you submissive bitch.'

She lifted Edwige on to the chair beside the young male, and began to bathe the wounds of her back with scented salve. Habren stood at the chair back, leaning over, so that her nipples brushed Edwige's forehead. Her fingers ran up and down the girl's spine, covering every inch of her flogged skin, then descended into the buttock cleft and massaged Edwige's anus. Edwige moaned. Habren parted her legs and Edwige lifted her head.

Hesitantly, her tongue slipped out of her slack lips and penetrated the swollen folds of Habren's gash. As Habren rubbed her anus, twisting to get her fingers in the flogged girl's quim, Edwige began to press Habren's erect clitoris with her teeth, then penetrated the slit with her whole tongue, swallowing the juices that seeped from the swollen cunt. The young male watched, face red and crotch bulging, but he did not move. When Edwige's scarred back was thick with salve, Habren ordered her to kneel while continuing to tongue her mistress's gash. With the blonde girl kneeling and her mouth slopped in Habren's come as she nosed and tongued the proffered vulva, the girl masturbated her own clitoris and her come juices joined her mistress's in an oily pool on the rock. The first whipping-guard lowered his loinstring and stood nude behind Habren's buttocks.

She lifted her left thigh and, at once, he reached to her vulva to retrieve a palmful of her come oil. With her own fluid, he lubricated her anal pucker and his shaft, putting an index finger in, while oiling the bulb of his own giant cock, before nuzzling her exposed anus with his peehole. A swift jerk of his loins and his massive black tool was halfway embedded; a second and he impaled her anus, right to his balls. The young man in the panama hat gazed, transfixed.

With Edwige still licking her clitoris, Habren began to respond to the black tool's thrusts as it buggered her vigorously, withdrawing to the crest of the glans before each new penetration and soon slimed with Habren's arse-grease as well as the come from her slit. The black guard buggered Habren for several minutes before he groaned, and bubbles of sperm frothed at her anal mouth, stretched by the cock to many times its pucker.

His place was at once taken by the second whipper, his cock as massive as the first and his buggery as hard. The guard who had shaded Habren laid down his parasol and grasped Edwige by the belly. He pushed aside her masturbating fingers and took her from behind, thrusting his cock into her wet vulva and tooling her at the crouch, with his belly slapping her squirming buttocks, while she continued to tongue Habren's clit. Habren's fresh bugger gasped as he spunked in her anus and his sperm dripped to a creamy pudding on her thighs.

The guard, holding the shackle of the nine caned girls, dropped the chain and removed his own robe. Four guards were now nude; the two already spunked put their cocks turnabout in Habren's mouth while she tongued the helmets, raising the cocks to new stiffness. Grunting, the male fucking Edwige spermed in her cunt, and at once presented his slimed cock for sucking by his mistress, while she climbed on to the chair, parted her buttocks, and was anally impaled by the first guard who had buggered her, his cock sucked to new hardness. She pushed the chair away, and swayed, her full weight taken by his impaling cock, with her feet cradling her face, and calves squashing her breasts, so that her erect nipples jutted like pears.

The second guard thrust his own erect tool into her soaked gash. Both men fucked her, one anally and the other in the cunt, squeezing her slippery body between them, while Edwige, masturbating her clitty, clawed Habren's exposed nipples, and Habren's mouth took the cocks of the other two guards turnabout, sucking them to orgasm, swallowing their spurts and licking her lips clean of their copious creamy spunks. She moaned in constant orgasm, and the dripped come under her loins grew to a pool. When the males were gasping and spunked dry, Habren turned to the rear of the scene where a film camera whirred.

'Cut and print!' she cried. 'I only meant it as a rehearsal, but I think it's good enough to use.'

The guards released the tethered girls from their fastenings; all, rubbing their caned bums, clustered around Habren.

'You didn't have to leave us trussed quite so long, Mistress!'

'Nor cane us quite so hard!'

'Verisimilitude, my dears,' said Habren. 'I make a film about caned sluts in a Moroccan prison fort, *in* a Moroccan prison fort.'

'I begged you to *stop*!' Edwige wailed. 'Shaking my head was a *sign*! I really meant it, Habren! God, that whipping hurt!'

'When does *acted* penance become *real* penance? You are glad it didn't stop,' purred Habren, staring Edwige down.

'Yes,' sobbed Edwige. 'I deserved it. I've never hurt so hard, or come so much . . .'

Habren slapped a square of pink brocade into Edwige's bum-cleft, and it clung to the bruised skin. Edwige patted her flogged bottom and smiled.

'Any girl who tires of being paid to do what she *likes* doing, is free to go back to Marrakesh,' said Habren.

She turned to the gaping male in the panama hat, his crotch still bulging, as he ogled the nude, fully suntanned girls rubbing their flogged bottoms.

'Have you no shame?' Habren snapped. 'You're stiff, you dirty little creep. How can a husband watch, drooling like a pervert, as his *own wife* is abused?'

'But, darling – you *know* I am your *most* devoted fan. That is how we met – oh, the glory that you noticed me! – and ... and let me produce your films! I *love* your acting!'

'A girl buggered is *never* acting, dear Joss. As for producing my very money-making films, you still haven't the nerve to sell them in your beastly supermarkets.'

'But Abby, you know ... the uninformed public might think them lewd,' he blurted.

'Miss Habren, to you,' she drawled. 'Lewd, eh? Not like the big tits on your checkout girls.'

'Darling Abby – I mean, Miss Habren –'

'No, I think, "Mistress" ...'

'Mistress, you know I've nothing to do with actual hiring at Gauntco ... I merely approve.'

'And afterwards?'

Joss Gaunt squirmed in his chair.

'We have already established your regime of correction,' she said. 'How lucky you are that I permitted you to marry me, before you wasted all Papa's money on filthiness.'

'Am I to be caned, for watching you *act*?'

'Why, yes,' she murmured.

'How many, Mistress?'

'A good three dozen. No, four.'

'On the bare?'

'Of course.'

'Oh, Habren ... Mistress ...'

131

'Not *yet* . . . you must wait.'
'*Ohh!* You are *awfully* cruel,' he gasped.
'Yes,' said Habren.

WHIP HAND

G. C. Scott

G. C. Scott is an acute observer of games of submission and domination, especially those involving restraint, total enclosure, and the kinky feel of rubber and PVC. The first novels for Nexus featured male submission almost exclusively, but since then they've broadened to include more switching, although you'll still find an imperious female domina master- (or mistress- !) minding the action. In the following extract, Richard, central character of *House Rules* and *Whipping Boy*, finds his mother-in-law in rather a compromised situation . . .

THE PASSIVE VOICE
HIS MISTRESS'S VOICE
AGONY AUNT
A MATTER OF POSSESSION
HOUSE RULES
WHIPPING BOY

It was early afternoon when Richard arrived to find Ingrid's shop closed. Odd, he thought. She normally opened during business hours. Her assistant at least should have been there, but was not. He went around to the back entrance, where deliveries were made in the enclosed yard. The gate was closed, and the door was locked.

He let himself into the rear hallway with the key she had given him. Since the shutters in the shop windows were closed, there was little light in the hallway. He looked around in the dimness at the place where he had taken the first steps towards becoming Pamela Rogers. He had practised walking up and down these stairs in his high-heeled shoes. Ingrid had helped him choose the first dresses and underwear in the darkened shop, and upstairs she had helped him with the details of his transformation.

He recalled his transformation with a thrill of excitement as he climbed the familiar stairs to her flat. The door at the top led to the well-remembered sitting room overlooking the street. It too was dark. There he found Ingrid, but someone else had found her first. Margaret, he guessed.

Ingrid was shackled into a rigid frame that resembled a cross with two short cross bars, one near the top and the other at the bottom. The device forced her to stand upright with her hands held out to each side of her at shoulder height. Her elbows were bent and her wrists were shackled in irons welded to the upper cross bar. Her ankles were shackled to the ends of the lower cross bar. A steel collar encircled her neck. Another went around her waist. Both were welded to the frame, keeping her neck and head and waist back against the steel bar that formed a kind of backbone.

Naked, she stood near the window. She would have been visible to anyone passing by in daylight. The drapes were wide open, left so deliberately, he guessed, by Margaret, the more to humiliate and embarrass Ingrid, who could not move from her strained position. Richard wondered how she had been able to maintain her balance. Then he saw the chain attached to the steel backbone of Ingrid's frame. It led to a stout hook in the ceiling that had not been there on his last visit. She could not fall no matter how strained or tired she might become.

The strain of standing for long hours showed in her face. The possibility of being seen was also part of the ordeal. Ingrid's relief when he called her name showed plainly.

'Oh, Richard, I am so glad it is you who found me. Anyone could have come upon me – and done whatever they wished to me.' She was shaking with relief and strain.

Richard went to her, intending to free her from her restraints, but she stopped him.

'Kiss me,' she said. 'I have been thinking of you all afternoon. I was hoping you would come. Margaret said that you were coming to her weekend party. I knew you'd come to see me too.'

They kissed lingeringly. Richard embraced Ingrid, his arms around the steel bar that held her rigid from neck to heels. Unable to touch him, Ingrid nevertheless made him welcome with her lips and tongue. She sighed when the kiss ended. When he drew back she almost lost her balance, and would have fallen but for his arm and the chain that held her frame upright.

A close examination of her restraints revealed that they were locked on to her. When he asked about keys, she replied that Margaret had taken them away with her.

'How long have you been here?' he asked.

'Hours and hours,' she replied.

'And has anyone . . .?'

'If you mean, has anyone come to check on me, the answer is no. If you mean, did anyone see me, I would imagine that several people did. I could not move from this place.'

'And you mean that no one came to investigate – or called the police or the fire brigade?'

'Do you think anyone in England would interfere in such a situation?'

'Probably not. At least not for a long time, anyway. Too embarrassing. And suppose it – you – turned out to be a cardboard cut-out, or merely a photograph stuck to the inside of the window?'

'Exactly,' Ingrid replied, 'although there was one man who looked at me for a long time. I don't think he believed I was a photograph. I was afraid he'd break in.'

'But he didn't, probably because that's not the sort of thing one does either – at least not in broad daylight.'

'Still, I am glad that you are here now,' Ingrid said.

'Do you need to go to the toilet?' he asked, looking for a bucket to hold under her while she peed.

'Margaret took care of that,' Ingrid replied. 'Look.'

Richard noticed then that a catheter had been inserted into her urethra and led to plastic bag now nearly full of her urine. 'What would happen if the bag filled up?' he asked.

'Then I would have a very uncomfortable time,' Ingrid replied matter-of-factly. 'Nothing can be done until Margaret returns with the keys.'

'She's gone too far this time.'

'Margaret has indeed gone too far this time. She is in Dresden on business, and won't be back until tomorrow morning. But I am sure that there is someone at the house who has been told to look after me, because . . .' She stopped speaking abruptly, and a curious look of distress crossed her face. 'Oh!' she said suddenly.

'What is it?' he asked sharply.

Ingrid did not reply. Her attention was focused on internal matters. Richard looked at her closely, and noticed again something he had not seen before. Along with the tube of the catheter which disappeared between Ingrid's thighs, there were wires leading to her cunt and anus. More of Margaret's subtle torture, he guessed at once. There had to be dildoes inside her, and they were connected to the telephone socket via a black box which had to be the control device. Clever, he thought, simply dial your victim's number and the control box dispensed judgement for you.

'Does she shock you with electricity?' he asked, thinking of Margaret's fondness for hooking her victims' genitals up to batteries.

'What?' Ingrid asked vaguely. 'Oh . . . yes. Sometimes. But there are . . . other things . . . she does as well. She makes me want to . . . come. That is the worst. She always stops me before I can reach a climax. I don't know how she does it, but that has been happening all afternoon. I sometimes think I will make it this time, and I shudder and cry out – and she stops me again. Now – oh, God – she is doing it again!' Her voice rose and her body tensed as if she were on the verge of orgasm. 'I can't stand it any longer. I have to come! Please!' she cried desperately to her absent torturess.

She shuddered in her restraints as the signals came down the telephone line and into her body via her two orifices. Richard could see her arousal. Ingrid arched her back; her nipples grew taut and her breath became ragged. She moaned with desire and frustration, twisting as far as she could in her heavy irons. She swayed on her feet, the chain alone holding her up as her knees went weak. Ingrid was trying hard to reach orgasm, her need plain on her face.

Richard could see her taut belly as she clenched her vaginal muscles in anticipation. The cords in her neck stood out with the intensity of her effort. And suddenly the terrible tension left her, and she groaned. 'Oh, God! I can't come. She won't let me! Please help me, Richard. Touch me. Make me come! Please make me come!'

He kneeled in front of the tortured woman and buried his face between her thighs. He kissed her labia as she writhed in her need. Ingrid was warm and wet. He could smell the musk of her arousal. The clean salty taste of her was in his mouth as he teased her clitoris with his tongue and teeth. And he could feel something hard buried inside her – the dildo which had brought her to the brink of orgasm and then stopped her. But there was no stopping Richard. As he kissed Ingrid's labia and bit her clitoris, she moaned loudly, shuddering as she came once more to the brink of orgasm. He took her over the edge while she cried out with pleasure, jerking in her irons. She had forgotten her exposed position by the window, her restraints, her long afternoon's sexual frustration.

'Oh, yes!' Ingrid cried as the waves of her orgasm swept through her, tautening her belly and making her knees buckle. 'Oh, yes! Oh, God, yes!'

When he broke off momentarily to ensure that Ingrid would not fall, she became frantic.

'Oh, God, Richard, please don't stop now!'

'Just a moment.'

He looked around for a safer place for Ingrid. He finally decided that the floor would have to do. He unhooked the chain that held her upright from the ceiling and caught her beneath the arms from behind. She cried out in alarm as she felt herself tilting backwards.

'Shh! I've got you. Don't worry.' He kissed the back of her neck, just above the steel collar. She stopped fighting as he laid her on the floor on her back. 'Is that all right?'

Ingrid nodded. Spread open like a starfish in the heavy irons, she looked incredibly desirable. And desirous. 'Oh, Richard, make me come again! It has been so long.'

He kneeled between her thighs and once again used his lips and tongue and teeth to arouse her. Unable to move in her restraints, Ingrid nevertheless managed to signal her pleasure by a tautening of her muscles and a continuous low moan as she came, the sound rising and falling in time with her orgasms. The muscles in her thighs and stomach stood out in relief as she came. Her hands opened and closed convulsively in the heavy iron bracelets, and her toes curled.

Richard, looking up momentarily from his position between her thighs, saw a sudden flood of urine pass down the tube and into the bag as she came. Ingrid, until then only moaning, screamed in ecstasy at the double release. The bag filled rapidly as she screamed in pleasure.

When she went limp, Richard realised that she had passed out. He checked her over anyway. She seemed all right. He unclipped the bag and took it into the bathroom, where he emptied it into the toilet. Back in the front room, he reattached the bag to Ingrid's catheter and paused to examine the arrangement. He had never seen a woman with a catheter.

He spread her labia and saw the tube disappearing inside her, but he soon lost sight of it as it passed up the urethra. He tugged on it, feeling resistance. He let go of it. So long as Ingrid was locked into her restraints, it was best to leave the tube in place.

In any case, Margaret would know all about it. That idea excited him too. How would a catheter feel? Margaret would no doubt enlighten Pamela if she only asked. There would no doubt be a practical demonstration as well. Pamela knew she was going to ask.

In the meantime there was Ingrid. He sat beside her, studying the contrast between her smooth skin and the unyielding irons that held her prisoner. This was what bondage was all about. And why he liked it so much.

Ingrid opened her eyes and looked contentedly at him. That's what sex is all about, he thought – making a woman look at you like that. Helena did it too. Could Margaret be taught the trick? Would she want to learn?

'I feel like a stranded turtle, Richard. I must look like one too. But a satisfied stranded turtle. It was wonderful, what you did to me. I thought I would go crazy from frustration. You know, before we met I could go for weeks without thinking about sex. Now I think about it – and you – all the time. Not bad for an older woman, is it?'

'All right, I know when I'm being provoked. I promise to spank you as soon as I can get you out of these irons.' He spoke lightly, but he was glad to know how Ingrid felt. Knowing that he was loved and appreciated by Helena and her foster-mother made him proud and happy. He bent to kiss Ingrid. She opened her mouth to him again as she had opened her body.

They sat quietly for a time, Richard leaning back against the front of the sofa, Ingrid in her stranded-turtle position on the floor. It was Ingrid who spoke first.

'You know, I was right about Margaret. She is definitely after you. And she is quite jealous of anyone who seems like a rival.'

'Do you mean yourself?'

141

'Yes. She knew about my visit to you and Helena. And she knew – or guessed – that we did not spend a great deal of time going around the village or the local attractions. She thinks that we spent most of the time in bed – or at least in some form of sexual play. Which is what we did.' Ingrid smiled fondly in recollection.

Richard smiled too. 'When did Margaret do all this?' he asked, gesturing at her irons.

'Early this morning,' Ingrid said. 'I have been here all day.'

'Until I came, and then you came.'

'And then I came. Thank you again.'

'Ingrid . . . do you think you could come again?'

'Yes, if you will help me. Gladly.' Her nipples were growing erect at the prospect.

'I meant . . . the two of us,' he said. 'I want to come inside you.' His voice was tense with excitement.

'I cannot stop you,' Ingrid said with a smile. 'As you see, I am helpless. But, of course, I want you to enter me. There is only the small matter of the plug . . . and the catheter.'

'I can get the plug out. I'm afraid the catheter will have to stay, but I'll be careful not to hurt you.' Richard grasped the base of Ingrid's dildo and pulled the long, thick plug from her cunt. He laid it on the floor beside her supine body.

'I cannot open my legs any further,' Ingrid said apologetically. 'The irons . . .' With a small motion of her head, she indicated the rigid bar between her ankles.'

Richard stood to remove his clothes. His cock sprang free of his shorts, and Ingrid gasped in anticipation.

'I do that to you?' she asked wonderingly.

'Of course you do. You know that. As Margaret says, it's the sincerest compliment a man can pay a woman. She always says that just before she refuses to accept it in the place where a woman is meant to.'

He lay down on top of her pinioned body, guiding himself into her with one hand and supporting his upper body with the other. Ingrid, unable to move, nevertheless managed to welcome the penetration with a small squeeze of her vaginal muscles. When he was fully inside her, she sighed happily. The catheter was an unfamiliar pressure on his cock. He clamped down hard to keep himself from coming too soon.

Ingrid sensed his excitement. 'Dear Richard, come now if you want to.'

'Not yet,' he said through gritted teeth. 'I want you to come too.' He lay still on top of her as her vaginal muscles clamped his cock. He could feel her growing warmer and wetter as he lay on her. When she moaned he felt the first rippling spasm of her cunt as she had a small climax.

'Oh!' she sighed. 'That feels so good.'

Richard risked a small withdrawal and return, testing his control and her arousal. He was excited by Ingrid's restraints. Making love to a beautiful woman who could not move was one of his favourite fantasies.

Ingrid clenched her fists in the shackles as she came again. He felt the spasms as her body tensed and relaxed, tensed and relaxed. As Ingrid fought the unyielding restraints, he fought the desire to lose himself in a wild climax of his own. Her body was totally motionless below him, but her internal muscles, unrestrained, responded to his movements.

Ingrid moaned again with her climax. She was panting and her cheeks were flushed – like Margaret's when she was aroused, or angry. 'Oh, Richard! Oh, yes!' she moaned.

He knew that if she were not locked into the rigid steel frame that her body would be moving against his own. As he imagined all that energy being restrained he lost control. Her helplessness and immobility were too much for him. He came in sharp spasms, spending himself in her while her muscles clamped his cock, milking him as she groaned with her own climax.

He lay on top of her only briefly, even though he would have liked to remain longer. It must be terribly uncomfortable to be locked into those unyielding restraints. Lying beside her on the carpet, he listened as her breathing slowed. He reached to clasp one of her manacled hands, feeling her fingers close over his own and squeeze hard.

'I would like to lie in your arms, if I could,' Ingrid said.

'Take the wish for the deed. We'll do it soon enough. In the meantime, what shall we talk about?' They exchanged news of everything that had happened since her visit, the banal conversation seeming bizarre in the circumstances.

It was Ingrid who got them back to the main subject. 'Richard, I am getting excited again,' she admitted. 'I have never worn such severe restraints as these. Do you think you could manage another . . . fuck?'

He nodded. 'Even if it kills me but, this time, you get on top.'

'Oh, Richard, do not laugh at me. You know I cannot move.'

'You can if I do the work.' He bent over her rigidly confined body, raising her with his hands beneath her shoulders until she was nearly vertical. Then he rotated her and laid her down on the floor on her stomach. 'Stranded turtle, back view,' he commented.

'Would you like to enter the stranded turtle by the back passage?' Ingrid asked.

'I know lady turtles prefer it that way, but they don't usually wear chastity belts like yours. I'm afraid we'll have to use the front entrance again. Try not to be bored, will you?' He chuckled.

Richard kneeled beside Ingrid to kiss the back of her neck. She tried to turn her face, her mouth, to him, but she could not. He kissed her hair and the lobe of her ear, inhaling her fragrance as he moved over her. His lips moved over her shoulders and down her back. He kissed the backs of her thighs and the hollows behind her knees, moving down to brush her ankle bones and the soles of her feet with kisses. She sighed with happiness.

He lay beside her and reached across to pull Ingrid and her crucifix on top of his body. She could not assist in any way, so the operation took time. Eventually she lay on top of him in her iron frame. He guided his cock into her, and found her ready.

Ingrid lay looking down at him, her head held rigidly back against the steel bar by the collar around her neck, her hands raised to her shoulders as if in surrender, held by the steel bands around her wrists.

Once again he felt the unaccustomed pressure of the catheter against his cock as he moved for both of them. It was more difficult this time with her weight and that of her restraints bearing down, but the look on Ingrid's face was reward enough as he rocked his hips, moving his cock inside her in slow slidings and pressures. He raised his head and their lips met in a long kiss, Ingrid breathing out into his mouth in contented sighs as he moved within the tight sheath of her cunt.

Her breasts were flattened against his chest, and since she could not move or lift her body he had to forgo the pleasure of teasing her nipples. Ingrid did not seem to mind.

He felt her climax as a tightening of vaginal muscles around his cock. It was a ripple compared with the storms that had shaken her earlier, but her face showed pleasure as it passed through her.

And so they rocked gently together, giving and taking pleasure in one another's bodies despite Margaret's attempt to make it impossible. Richard was still excited by the novelty of the catheter and of making love to a woman who was unable to move any part of her body except those supremely important internal muscles. Ingrid relished her helpless immobility as she was thoroughly fucked.

She reached several smaller climaxes, gradually building in intensity to the point where her whole body stiffened and she cried out in release. He felt the catheter swell against his cock as Ingrid urinated at the moment of climax. He felt he could relax his own control after that, and so when he came a few moments later Ingrid was able to match him with a more sighing gentle climax.

This time, with Richard taking her weight, they were able to lie joined for some considerable time. From time to time he raised his head to kiss her lips and eyes and cheeks while he stroked her back and bottom, touching the steel that imprisoned her. When he slid out from under her at last, he admired the back view of the woman he had just pleasured lying imprisoned in her steel frame.

Finally he turned her over on to her back once more. More to admire that way, he thought as Ingrid smiled up at him. Her face was relaxed and more beautiful after the long pleasure of their multiple couplings. He remembered thinking the same thing about Margaret after she had finally stopped trying to dominate *their* coupling. He kneeled to kiss Ingrid once more.

'Richard, would you please clamp the catheter and empty the bag once more? And thank you for the fucking. It was wonderful.'

Pleased that she was pleased, he did as she asked, returned with the empty bag and reattached it to the tube that disappeared inside her.

'OK, now what?' he asked with a grin. 'Shall we speak of science and art and the possibility of life on Mars? Make the beast with two backs again?'

'Truthfully, I don't think I can come again after what you did to me. So let's talk now. You will have to leave me here, but I would like company for a while.'

146

'I don't mind talking to you, but I am not going to leave you here like this.'

'What else can you do?' she asked.

'Either bring the keys here, or take you to the keys. I'll have to call Helena to decide which course to take.'

When he finally reached her at Margaret's country estate, he described Ingrid's predicament and told her about the loose stone in the fireplace where Margaret had once hidden her keys. 'Go look,' he suggested.

She returned with the news that the hiding place was empty. Helena thought that her aunt would have taken the keys away with her. 'What now?' she asked. 'We can't leave her there like that.'

He suggested that she choose the vehicle with the most luggage space and drive into the back entrance of Ingrid's shop. There they would load Ingrid aboard and transport her to Margaret's estate.

Helena agreed that that was the best solution. She would leave immediately. 'Expect me in about thirty minutes,' she said.

She hung up and Richard went to sit beside Ingrid once more. 'We are going to transport you to Margaret's estate, where we can look after you until Margaret gets back with the keys. Helena will be here shortly.'

'But ... but,' spluttered Ingrid, 'what if someone from the village sees me? It will be all over town in minutes. Please just leave me here.'

He shook his head. 'It's nearly dark outside. By the time Helena gets here there will be no one about. Helena is going to back the car up through the gates at the back and it's only a short distance from the door to the car. We will load you into the back, and away we'll drive over hill and dale. You just relax and enjoy the ride.'

Ingrid still objected, afraid of being seen.

'Shut up. You're coming with us. Leave everything to Helena and me. We'll cover your face so no one will recognise you,' he said, thinking of ostriches in sandy country. He smiled at her.

Ingrid failed to see the joke. 'And who will they think is being taken from my shop in irons if not me?'

'Shut up,' he said again. 'Let's talk about something else. Tell me what you would do if we left you here and some intruder did manage to get in and find you.'

'I would lie back,' Ingrid retorted, 'and think of . . . Germany. Or I would pretend it was you.'

'Flattery will only get you another fucking,' he told her.

When Helena arrived, they had both run out of things to say and were sitting in companionable silence. They both heard the back door open, and the sound of her feet on the stairs. She came into the room and went straight to her foster-mother.

'Did Richard make you come, *Mutti*?'

After a startled silence Ingrid smiled. 'Yes, he did. Many times.'

'Then you are luckier than me. I have been waiting for him to come back and fuck me for hours and hours,' she said. 'And all that time he has been here fucking you.'

Turning to Richard, she demanded, 'Aren't you ashamed of yourself?'

'No,' he replied.

'Good. I would have been ashamed of you if you had been ashamed of giving *Mutti* pleasure, shameless woman that she is.' Practicality returned. 'How are we going to move her, Richard?'

Ingrid started to protest again.

'You don't get a vote in this. And you can't stop us. So be quiet,' Richard said again.

To Helena he said, 'You take her feet and I'll take her shoulders. The stairs will be the tricky bit, but if we're careful we'll manage.'

Helena laid the urinal bag on her foster-mother's stomach and coiled the catheter so that it would not snag on anything. 'Is it uncomfortable, *Mutti*?' she asked.

'Ask Richard,' Ingrid replied. 'It makes fucking more exciting on this end.'

'On this end also,' he said. 'But let's get you under way.'

Helena grasped the spreader bar between Ingrid's ankles while Richard lifted her by the spreader bar that held her wrists apart. On his signal they lifted the helpless woman in her iron frame and carried her towards the door.

'Was there anyone about when you drove up?' Richard asked Helena. 'Ingrid is afraid of being seen by the neighbours. I told her we would cover her face so that she would not be recognised.'

Helena too failed to see the joke. She replied seriously, 'We will need to cover her with something when we get her into the car. It has grown cold outside. We may get snow later.'

Together they carried the immobilised woman down the stairs. The big Land Rover was backed up to the rear door of the shop, its own rear doors propped open to receive their cargo. Ingrid in her iron frame just fitted into the rear space. Helena spread a car rug over her naked body and indicated that Richard should ride in the back.

'I know the way best,' she said. 'You sit with *Mutti* while I drive. And if you choose to keep her happy on the way, I won't mind very much. You might try feeling her up. We all know how much she likes that. But whatever you do keep her quiet.'

Ingrid gave a scandalised gasp which Helena ignored as she got into the driving seat.

They drove through the silent streets of the town and out into the country, Ingrid fearful the whole time of being stopped by the police. 'How will you explain me?' she asked.

149

Helena told her they would say she was a statue they had stolen from a church.

'Be careful,' Ingrid warned. 'I don't know what we would say if there were an accident.'

'I do,' Helena replied. 'We will tell the police that you always travel this way. Your version of seat belts.' To Richard she went on, 'Can't you do something to make her shut up? Try biting her clitoris or something.'

'Helena!' Ingrid protested.

'Go on, you know you love that. I would bet you've never been had while driving through the countryside. Do you think you could do her now, Richard? I'll drive slowly if you'd like to try.'

Ingrid made more dissenting noises.

The car turned into the gates of Margaret's estate. Now that they were on a private road, Ingrid was less anxious, but still worried about 'people' seeing her.

As they drew up outside the front entrance Helena hopped out and said she was going to fetch some of the slaves to help carry Ingrid.

Ingrid was not in favour of that either.

'Well, at least Heidi and Bruno,' she said with a grin as she and Richard lifted Ingrid from the back of the car. 'And we could use some more light out here.'

'Stop teasing her, Helena,' Richard finally said. 'It's cold out here. Let's get her inside.'

Helena used one hand to ring the door bell. Ingrid scolded and protested as they waited to be admitted, but they had to wait.

The woman who opened the front door to the bizarre trio did not seem surprised. She looked over the burden they bore before stepping aside to admit them. 'Hello, Frau Wagner,' Heidi said. 'Will you be staying with us tonight as well?'

'I thought we could put her in the barn, Heidi,' Helena said to the beautiful blonde servant. 'She has been making too much noise. She needs to be where she won't be heard.'

Heidi smiled. 'You know your mother would not like the barn. Come. We will take her up to the bedroom I have prepared for you.' To Ingrid she said, 'You will be comfortable there. I will look after you.'

Ingrid went scarlet with embarrassment and protested that she would be all right on her own, that she did not want to be a nuisance. As she spoke the bag of urine slid to the floor. Ingrid flushed more brightly as Heidi picked it up and laid it on her stomach once more.

'Someone will need to help you until we can get you free of your shackles,' she observed.

'Don't worry, Heidi. We'll stay with her,' Richard said. 'But maybe you can help us get her up to the room. We'll use the lift.'

Heidi led them to the lift and opened the doors for them. There was room for only three people inside. When they had manoeuvred Ingrid into the lift and leaned her against the back wall, there was only room for two. Heidi stepped inside.

'We will meet you on the second floor,' Helena said.

The doors closed and Ingrid began her journey upwards.

Upstairs they reversed the process, carrying Ingrid to the bedroom and laying her on the bed. She was still scarlet with embarrassment. Heidi bent to kiss her cheek. 'Do not be embarrassed. Everyone here is accustomed to bondage of one type or another. Look.' She lifted her skirt to show Ingrid her chastity belt. 'I wear it all the time, but,' she said with a smile, 'Richard managed to get around it on one memorable occasion.'

Ingrid looked less uncomfortable. 'He manages to get around most things in time.'

'He even got around *Mutti*'s iron frame and catheter today,' Helena remarked.

151

Ingrid's blush returned full strength. 'Helena!' she scolded.

'And they spent the whole afternoon fucking,' Helena went on as if she hadn't heard. 'Just look at her. She should be worn out by the non-stop sex, but she was trying to seduce him again on the way over here. Once she is free of the rack, she'll give him no rest. All I get is what she's left.'

'Speaking of racks, do you know if Margaret took the keys for this one?' Richard asked Heidi.

'I do not know.'

'We'll go have a look.' Richard beckoned for Helena to follow him. To Ingrid he said, 'We're going to look for the keys. Heidi will entertain you until we get back.' To Heidi he said, 'She likes to have her clitoris licked and bitten, but be gentle. She's had a long day.'

Ingrid flushed with renewed embarrassment. 'Don't you dare!' she said to Heidi.

'Pay no attention,' Richard said. 'Once she feels your tongue she'll change her mind.'

Heidi climbed on to the bed and settled herself between Ingrid's parted thighs. She wet her lips and bent down to Ingrid's cunt.

Ingrid thrashed futilely in her irons, unable to move away from the descending mouth. Her protests followed them down the hallway.

ANGEL

Lindsay Gordon

Lindsay Gordon is, by the standards of any genre, an excellent writer. Her erotic fiction encompasses just about every fetish in the canon of perversion, always written with a compelling, reflective and ultimately arousing quality. *Forum* said of *The Bond*, Lindsay's third Nexus novel, that it 'rescues the vampire novel from the lush clutches of Anne Rice'. The following extract is from *Angel*, a dystopic erotic tale featuring an Orwellian nightmare world in which the privileged exploit the underprivileged for sexual gain, and always press their advantage – until the tables are turned. It's some of the most original erotic fiction you're frankly likely to read anywhere.

Also by Lindsay Gordon in Nexus:

RITES OF OBEDIENCE
THE SUBMISSION GALLERY
THE BOND
SEE-THROUGH

Alone inside the gents' bathroom, Angel threw water on his face. Straightening up, he adjusted his tie – he could almost complete a Windsor knot now. He smoothed his hair back and took a mint from a small dish beside the white facecloths. Inside the third cubicle, he locked the door behind him, lowered the toilet seat and then climbed up to feel the top of the cistern. His reaching hands touched paper. Carefully, he withdrew the padded envelope from the plumbing. As he brought the weight of it against his chest and stepped down from the toilet seat, he heard the jingle of chains inside the envelope. His stomach turned over. What was the fascination with these strange bindings?

He checked the time: three minutes remained until his appointment was due to commence. Leaving the gents', he walked down a plushly carpeted hall of red. Still was the air, sombre the atmosphere. It was as if he walked on hallowed ground. The walls on either side of him were wood-panelled. It had been designed to look unlike a medical facility and made him wonder where the operations were carried out. On this floor the powerful surgeons, the transformers and lengtheners of life, gave consultations. Somewhere behind one of the oak doors he passed, a man cleared his throat. And then a drawer was closed on the other side of the corridor. The sounds were incongruously sharp.

On the door of number thirty-eight, a small brass plaque at eye-level was inscribed with the title of *Dr M. Sutton*. Outside the door, he smelled a trace of perfume. Had she prepared herself for him? The thought made him shiver with excitement. There could be no error this time. One woman, one room, a locked door and closed blinds; there was little risk. And a doctor; an educated woman. Already, he fantasised about other illicit trysts with this woman and her powerful mind. A lover and mentor who could tell him where he fitted into the scheme of things. His ignorance and clumsiness would vanish and he too could stake a claim in her society.

He held the door handle. It was cold in the palm of his hand. For a moment he paused and inhaled the distilled air of power – sharp with brass, tangy with wood – and told himself he could not have found a better occupation in more spectacular surroundings. For the first time as a companion he truly recognised his own love and devotion for the corporate world. He willingly offered himself as a sacrifice.

Sensing a desire for surprise, he never announced himself with a knock. The office was vast. It was big enough and sufficiently grand to be part of a palace with its porcelain, bronzes, aspidistras, oils, chandeliers and fireplace. Besides the heavy desk there was little to suggest that any work took place in here. But he only allowed himself a fraction of a second to take in the opulence, because a greater prize than the furnishings waited for him. Behind the desk, facing the window, was the figure of a woman. Tall with long red hair, she stood with her back to him and smoked a cigarette – a habit that had returned to fashion since synthetic tobaccos had been made beneficial to respiratory health. She never turned around. Besides what he thought to be a tensing of her shoulders at the sound of the door, she never moved. Angel walked to the front of her desk. The envelope in his hands felt heavy, and he with it suddenly ridiculous.

At last, she turned to face him. Though pale and thin-faced, there was something eminently handsome about her, like the woman who watched a polo match from beneath the wide brim of a hat on the label of a vodka brand he had seen on the subway sidings. The crimson of her painted lips was startling, but the way her mouth thinned in response to his welcoming smile made her seem troubled.

She looked away from him and drew on her cigarette. It was fitted into a black holder. 'So you came,' she said, after exhaling the smoke she held inside her chest for what seemed a long time. 'I never doubted you would, but . . .' She paused and smiled sadly. 'But then, don't you think there is too great a distance between what you dream of and the moment when, supposedly, it arrives?'

He wanted to say something, but the buzzing in his head and the hot wash of self-consciousness kept him mute. The moment was lost. The trace of a melancholy smile remained though, in the creases that deepened at the side of her mouth. It was as if, through his hesitation and silence, he had actually said something naive.

'This is it, then,' she said to herself.

Angel hadn't expected this. His ideas of what to expect were never clear. How foolish he was to think of some connection. She was older, supremely intelligent, a separate species from those left in the townships.

'You know . . .' she began to say, but then stopped again and filled her lungs with smoke instead. To break the silence and the thickness of the air that seemed to be forever dropping slowly to the floor around them, Angel tore open the envelope. She flinched at the ripping sound. He swallowed. Refusing to look at what he poured, silvery and twisting, on to the desk top, she looked into his eyes. The sound of the chains and the wide cuffs, rattling against the wood, seemed unnecessarily loud, as if this inanimate thing were against them.

'I really don't think this can be done,' she then said, her smile nervous. 'Maybe if this is done to me. Then something will start that should never be seen. If . . .' Her sentences were breaking apart like the thoughts that created them, but abandoned them and then made other thoughts jostle forward in a kind of confused crowd.

He understood her doubts and walked back to the door. She never made a sound. It was as if he had felt her freeze behind his back. He imagined the smoke from the cigarette still moving across that intensity in her eyes. Yes, despite her sudden display of reticence, there was something uncompromising about her face. And it was as if she was afraid of just that – afraid of herself. He reached for the handle and then locked the door. Behind him, he heard a quick inhalation from the doctor. He turned around and walked to the window where she stood, still watching him. He kept his face angled down. If their eyes met, he thought, it would be terrible.

Slowly, he drew the blinds and the room darkened. Only a smoky vanilla light from the desk lamp, with a green scallop shade and a brass stem, gave any shape or definition to the furniture or the occupants. It was beginning to be too much for him: this having to assume the power, to dim the lights and turn a room to a prison cell. Inside himself, he seemed to bend like a sapling stripped of bark and made white. Even when he turned to her, his shoulders seemed to dip of their own accord, as if he were prepared to bow. But she never seemed affected by him being crushed by her pressure. In fact, it was as if the opposite dynamic had occurred. She stubbed out her cigarette, her face still stiff with anxiety, and then moved away from him to stand on the rug before her desk. She gave the impression that she was suddenly following orders. She bowed her head and crossed her hands over her stomach, as if commanded into submission.

Between them, their positions reversed, the cuffs developed a special hue in the umbra; greenish – like treasure glimpsed in the depths, suddenly within reach after a long excavation, but only now to be surrounded by unseen hazards and curses.

Angel followed her to the rug, wondering if her strange reaction to him was part of the scenario she desired – this assumption of his control and her reticent compliance. Their eyes locked once he stood before her and, even in the dark, each of them suffered from the glare of the other's stare. A frown creased her forehead. A shiver ran up one side of her face and he felt its ripple inside him too. It made her blink the eye on that side of her face.

'Oh, God,' she said. The colour of her eye make-up was charcoal and matched the faint soot of rouge on her sharp cheekbones. There were some fine lines on her skin that he could see more clearly now, but the beauty and vulnerability of her expression was stronger for them. He liked this face, so close to him, and wanted to see it stirred.

He reached for her hand. Her fingers were limp and cool but had closed in on the palm. So his touch made but the briefest impression on her softness, he held her wrist between the finger and thumb of his right hand. She closed her eyes. Her breath came in quick gusts from her thin nose and broke against his mouth. He could smell mint.

'You mustn't ... Mustn't get into this,' she whispered, and he never knew whether she said it for herself or for him. 'Can I have him? Can I do it? Can I have another one?' she said excitedly, and he felt the question was intended for someone else in the room.

Confused but curious, Angel continued with his assignment, operating on an instinctive level now, unable to think quickly enough. He moved her hand out before her, so her fingertips touched the front of his shirt, by his navel. The hand retained a rigidity inside its delicate bones. He coaxed her left hand out also and placed it against her right hand. Then he grasped them both, suddenly and tightly, by the wrists.

'Oh, God,' she said again. Her eyes opened. 'You must –' she tried to say, but Angel stopped her by resting his lips against her mouth.

Just to touch the slippery, red cosmetic, more than to kiss her. Closing his eyes, he then drew away from her mouth, but only slightly so she could watch him tentatively touch his lips with the tip of his tongue – to savour her taste, and take it inside.

Then, determined to soften her, he kissed her fully. But still, her mouth did not relent. The lips remained parted and soft, but unresponsive. From her chin, he kissed her cheek, her jaw, and then nuzzled the hair off her ear with the end of his nose.

'Oh, God,' she whispered again.

Down her neck, he left the impression of his mouth and then kissed her collarbone. Feeling dizzy and strangely weightless as his arousal was released to flow and then thicken through him, he pushed his face into the angle of her shoulder and throat where it was warm. She could hear his air and feel the rise and fall of his chest against her as he breathed.

It was when he clenched his fist even tighter that he heard her breathing quicken. Immediately, his kisses became harder. Through the angle of her head, falling backwards, and in the tremble of the fine membrane of her eyelids, he could see she had begun to fall into the urgency and insistence of his attentions. With one hand in the small of her back, he squashed her against the pronounced edges of his body. Against her long thighs

160

his longer thighs were firm. Into her breasts went the hard ridge of his chest. Along her flat belly, so soft with a promise of wet depths and a tight, nervous clinch, stretched his thick sex. Feeling the significance of his greater breadth, height and strength, she became utterly precious to him. Fragile, guarded, elegant, civilised – he sensed these qualities slowly surrendering their hold on her.

Down to the floor they went; she under him, protected from the hard boards by his hand and then his elbow. She clung to him, her need for a firm touch plainly revealed the moment his hand ventured inside her flimsy blouse. 'Oh, yes. Yes. Be hard there,' she said, her lips lavishing passionate kisses against the side of his face as she spoke.

And after seven days of abstinence he felt imbued with a curious power; his strength seemed to have no limits and she felt weightless in his hands; the hard floor offered no discomfort, and his co-ordination was slick despite the incongruous angles of this new body at his disposal. As his stubbly cheeks writhed in her hair, he pressed his hand against her breasts. Such a pressure against so intimate a place eased the remaining rigidity from out of her porcelain, designer body. When he sought her lips again and kissed her, his hand firmly kneading below, she responded and he felt a stranger's tongue inside his mouth.

Releasing her wrists, he placed a hand under her buttocks and one behind her coiffured head and then pulled her in tight against him. Blind to everything but his lust, he suddenly wanted to consume her, to devour and digest every scrap of her – the long bones and smooth flesh, the lavender and musk, the shiny hair, the long doctor fingers and the wedding ring. All of her. She let him spread her thighs with his knee, like he'd once done to a girlfriend on a staircase in Binton, and then, with a frown, she eyed the thick lump inside his trousers that he tugged her towards, her bottom slipping along the floor.

Her skirt and slip ruffled under her buttocks and displayed her panties. He felt he might explode at the sight of the little gauzy black triangle over a clipped mound. And when his face hovered over her dark brown stocking-tops he saw a peppering of freckles on her inner thighs. Lowering his face, he kissed the freckles on the warm skin and all about his head he could hear the rustle of disturbed silk as she relaxed, offering herself. Pushing his face further under her skirt, he inhaled the doctor's musk. It smelled of soap and hormones. And so rich was her perfume, it made him squint. The salted damp patch at the front of her dark briefs was studied and then placed under the lap of his tongue. Through the thin fabric, he could feel the shape of her lips. Moving her panties to one side, by hooking a finger through the leg, he then plunged his mouth into the heavy sap on her sex. And while he sucked and lapped, he thought of the dark red hole, so close to his face, that he would soon fill and stretch and push through until she wrapped all around him like a pretty anemone in a coral pool. And he stayed between her thighs and ate until his jaw ached, and until she bit her knuckles to stifle her own cries. When finally he sat back to breathe, she moaned and wriggled her buttocks for more.

Driven by this sudden display of her appreciation and this need she possessed to be pleasured during the working day, he was overcome by a need to be free of his tangling, hot clothes. He wanted to writhe naked down there. So off came his jacket, stripped from his arms with the haste of a medic in a roadside emergency. Off came his tie and shirt and trousers and underwear, all of which were thrown aside while she watched, her eyes wide, her fingers busy between her legs until his mouth or cock were ready to continue. Nostrils broad, he dipped his head back between the

162

length of her smooth thighs. Her nylons made slippery sounds against the side of his head, and a full blare of her seasoned sex, peppered and gamey, clouded about his face once more.

His hunger for this rare food made him groan. Under her shiny gusset he lapped, his tongue wide and outstretched again. Screwing up her features, she shielded her eyes with both hands and then uttered a series of quick, feminine sounds, more like whimpers than moans. Pulling her panties across her sex and then stretching them completely out of his way, he un-covered more of her soft down, and all of her wrinkled, dew-plastered lips. Pressing his tongue harder against her teeny red clit-tendon, upon which mere draughts of his breath made her body seize up, he caressed her with a more circular action using the tip of his tongue. Her groans deepened. Pursing his lips, he then pulled this part of her into his mouth and she began to roll her head about on the rug. And, as he sucked so fastidious-ly, he reached up her body, with his shoulders packed behind her thighs, and seized her breasts.

Her feet rose from the floor and she slid her legs over his back. With the indent of her nipples in the palms of his hands, he gently and slowly massaged her breasts. When his hands and tongue found the rhythm that other lovers had liked, her breathing stuttered. And it seemed as if she were stuck for something to do with her arms; she raised them from across her face into the air and then dropped them back down so she could smother her moans with her forearms. Skating his tongue over the little bead between her legs, or flicking it left and right across this nucleus of nerves he associated with the very tip of his penis, all of her body gradually softened as if something had drained out from beneath her suit.

'Bastard. Dirty, common bastard,' she whispered, surprising him.

Tongue replaced by the pads of his fingers, Angel tickled and then pushed her clit. Moving up her body, but leaving that one hand behind and busy in her wet fur, he dropped his sticky lips, odoriferous with the fragrance she knew to be her own, on to the doctor's open, hot and blaspheming mouth. Alive to the kiss, with all reticence gone now, she licked her own brine from around his mouth. She took all of it away and then let her head drop back to the rug. She squeezed her eyes shut and then groaned as if the muscles of her womb were pushing something out. Fingernails, red and long and lacquered stronger, dug into his triceps and shoulders, leaving small half-moons of bruising on his brown skin. Angel clenched his teeth on the discomfort and watched her face as the intense feeling passed over it and through her body too; a momentary paralysis, mixed with a sweet pain. It seemed to rise through her and then last for so long, if her screwed-up features were any indication, until the peak then jolted through her muscles, little volts that made her shudder, until they died away too and left her face dreamy and lost.

Angel kissed her neck, before disentangling himself from her arms, to sit back on his ankles and stroke her legs. Remembering his instructions, he reached for the cuffs on the desktop. He slipped his hands under her knees. Perspiration had dampened the stockings and made them cling to her ligaments. He raised her legs and drew her ankles together. After knocking her sling-back heels off, he then placed the heels of her feet on his chest. The doctor stared up at him, her eyes wide and intense now, the expectation in them almost unnerving. Around each ankle, he closed the curved steel bands of the cuffs. They felt so cold in his hands and the sudden embrace of something so hard and confining on her ankles prompted her to prop herself up on her elbows. The clasps in the bracelets locked and the chain between them shook loose.

She snarled at him. He was surprised again. The shock must have been evident on his face, but she never relaxed the hard grimace from her beautiful features. To Angel, she looked like a savage. It pleased him.

Smoothing his hands down her legs, from ankle to thigh, he felt her stockings ripple and tug around the contours of her legs. 'Open your mouth,' he whispered at her wild, staring face. She rocked her tousled head back and opened her jaws. He moved around her legs and took the blue, chiffon scarf from around her neck, hanging loose like a sling. A cloud of perfume dispersed from it. Angel put it under his nose and briefly inhaled. Then he stared hard into her eyes and slipped the scarf between her lips. There was no resistance. She even angled her head forwards so he could tie the scarf behind it. Cuffed and now gagged too, she closed those watchful eyes at last. Resting back on the rug, she placed both of her hands on her stomach and waited, wanting neither her frank stare nor raking hands to interfere with his work.

Angel unbuttoned her blouse and helped himself to her breasts. Pinky-tipped but so soft, it was almost impossible to grasp them in the palm of his hand and to feel their shape. He put his face into them. Tweaking her nipples with his fingers he rubbed his face in her scented cleavage. With flicks of his tongue, he then tasted her nipples – hard now, the size of pebbles – with just a twist of soap and salt on the puckered skin. Squashing her breasts down into her body, before gently pulling them back out, with her nipples held lightly between the inside of his fingers, he moulded and adored her pliant breast-flesh. And as the action of his kneading hands became firmer, his desire to enter the doctor increased.

'I'm going to have you,' he said to her, in a voice that was low, but firm with intent. 'I'm really going to take you now.' She moved her bottom on the floor, in small rotary rubbings of anticipation. 'Excuse me if I'm rough, Doctor. But I've had to wait for you for a long time.'

She cried out. He heard the word, 'Yes,' muffled into her gag.

He was more excited than he could ever remember now. The front of his underwear was wet with dew and the back of his head tingled cold. Up inside the ruffle of her skirt and creamy underskirt, his fingers rediscovered her now soiled panties, and drew them down her legs to leave them hanging by her cuffed ankles. Her breath suddenly quickened and sounded noisy in her thin nose. Hastily, Angel stroked his cock. It pulsed upwards in his hand, as if pulling back on invisible reins. He smiled. A flicker of something he thought cruel went cold in his mind, as if a shadow had fallen. 'Watch it, Doctor. Watch it go inside you. Then you can see yourself being taken by a servant. By a common bastard.' She was propped up on her elbows before he even finished speaking.

With one hand, he held her legs before his body, and gripped the stem of his girth with the other. The doctor moved her head to the side of her knees so she could watch. Angel moved forwards into position between her raised thighs. When the tip of his cock touched her sex – a gentle skim – they moaned together in the most exquisite moment of all. And then an impatience showed on each face – a need to commence with the quenching of so many basic needs.

Ready for the intrusion of a hired stranger's cock, her sex produced so much moisture that a trickle of her fluid made the cleft of her buttocks sticky. Slowly, Angel pushed the head in, shivering as her floss tickled his purple and sensitised skin. A moment of resistance. More pressure. A stretching of her sex, that almost felt to each of them as if something had been gently torn, and then the smooth slide of his entire length inside her

166

followed. Red in the face, teeth clamped on the chiffon gag, she rubbed the side of her face into the rug.

Inching forwards on his knees, so his hips pressed into the bottom of her thighs, Angel squeezed another small measure of penetration into her womb. Leaning forwards, he snatched her wrists together and pulled her upper body a few inches off the rug and then pressed his face into her ankles. Squeezing her wrists tight, he stroked her silky legs with his free hand, and kept his cock still inside her until the desperate temptation to ejaculate passed. When his sex felt less sensitive in the wonderful flesh of its surround, he began to thrust into her, delivering long and deep strokes, never breaking his rhythm. The doctor bit into her scarf and her nose became all pinched up and her eyes screwy and wrinkled.

'This is what you want?' he asked her, breathless, his pounding relentless. She never replied; she seemed unable.

'Maybe harder,' he muttered, and then rearranged himself so they lay on the rugs, his body behind her, both curled into an S shape with tangled legs, his cock never relinquishing its deep foundation inside her body. The side of her face was hot and her eyes seemed darker to him. 'Now it can be harder.' He clenched his teeth. 'Put your hands on your ... On your tits, Doctor.'

'Oh, you bastard.' Her voice was louder, sibilating around the gag. Her hands stayed still.

'Do it.' He slapped her thigh, hard. She squealed. Her eyes went wild and she grabbed her breasts, hanging free inside her blouse, and began to twist them with her fingers. 'That's it, feel them,' he whispered into her ear as he licked around its rim. Issuing a groan every time his groin slapped against her buttocks, she plucked and then rubbed at her nipples. He watched her fingers, delighted, but also keen to learn how she wanted them touched if she ever hired him again. 'Go on, harder, Doctor,' he said, and began to bang his pointy hips into her soft buttocks, increasing the speed of his thrusts.

With her ankles locked together, her legs were closed at the thigh and her sex especially tight around his cock. The friction was wonderful. One week of desperation and fevered dreams, when even the sheets of his bed had felt like a woman's hand, boiled inside him. Like an animal, he licked the side of her face, smearing and then eating the make-up off her skin.

'I'm going to put you on your tummy and come in you,' he said, his hands leaving her hips and joining her own fingers on her breasts.

Her breathing was loud in the heat and madness around and inside his head. 'Yes, yes. Anything you want, take it,' she said quickly, in a thick voice that seeped around the gag, now a thin dark strap that pulled the sides of her mouth wide.

Angel kissed her, his mouth aggressive, lingering. Right inside her ear, he whispered, 'You dressed for me.'

'Yes,' she said, her voice urgent.

'You dressed so this would happen right here in your office.'

'Yes. I did. I did.'

This confession made him thrust into her so hard he felt the first ominous pulse at the root of his cock. 'To make me do this. To make me wild for you. To make me want you so much.'

She closed her eyes and squeezed his fingers with her hands and then pressed them into her bosom. 'Yes. You know I did.'

'To make me fuck you on the floor.'

'Yes!'

He rolled her under his weight and began to ram his hips into her from behind. His hands were trapped

168

inside hers now, under the weight of her jolting body, and he could feel the jelly of her breasts on his knuckles and wrists. He powered himself from his thighs and lower back. His exposed stomach and groin made a slapping sound so loudly against her naked buttocks and back, it began to sound like a hand was administering discipline in the doctor's office.

She was crying out, too; every time his sex packed and stuffed itself through her most intimate place, she yelled, 'Oh!' And then the doctor began to mutter to herself in between the deep groans that followed. He pulled the scarf from her smeared mouth so he could hear her say, 'Handle me. Fuck me. Take me. Handle me.' Her eyes had closed and her monologue remained continuous until she came. As she climaxed, she pushed her backside into the thrusts from his hips, grinding herself in tight to increase the friction of their coupling.

He pulled the doctor's hands out from beneath her, and then clutched them in the small of her back with one hand. 'Hard in here,' he said, his face wet with sweat. 'And then much harder in the other place. To teach you what happens when you do this for me.'

'No, no, you bastard!' she shrieked.

'Yes!' he cried out. And with her squashed flat, cuffed and hand-held beneath him, on the rug in her fine office, Angel ground himself inside another of the beautiful creatures that never ceased to haunt his dreams. 'Ready for me? Ready for my come? There is so much.'

'Oh, oh, oh,' she said into the rug, face-down, muffled again.

Out it pulsed and shot; a stream, a gush, a continuous scalding of his pipes. 'There. Oh, yes. There it is. All of it inside you.' Flooded, spread, splayed, squashed, used by the degenerate needs of a savage, the doctor wept, lost in the ecstasy of being handled.

THE LAST STRAW

Christina Shelly

Christina Shelly is a relatively new author to Nexus, and we hope she's going to stick around for a while to come. Her stories of extreme male submission, featuring initiations into the worlds of transvestism, spanking, adult babies and mummification – in fact just about every possible way to humiliate the male – are drenched in a compelling sense of erotic arousal. It's plain from the following extract just how much Christina enjoys her writing!

Also from Christina Shelly in Nexus:

SILKEN SLAVERY

D enis watched Helen, his beautiful, sad-eyed wife, prepare for work. Sitting nervously on the edge of the large bed that dominated their bedroom, he beheld her with a mixture of despair and desire. There had been yet another argument, this time during lunch, and the last fifteen minutes had passed in painful silence. The argument had been tediously familiar, tired ground worn down another few inches. An argument about money and work. An argument about him. Weak, pathetic Denis: unemployed for two years now following a nervous breakdown; a pale, frail, vaguely feminine man who, at thirty, was perhaps unemployable; an intense neurotic whose anxieties and fears had left him virtually housebound. Yet even in the closed environment of the house he was useless.

'I can't take much more of this,' Helen said, her first words since the bitter exchange over vegetable soup and French bread.

He nodded weakly, relieved that at least she was talking again. His sad, pale-blue eyes met her own dark-brown orbs of fierce contempt through the full-length wardrobe mirror she faced while combing her lovely coal-black hair.

'I know, I'm sorry,' he mumbled.

She sighed wearily. 'You're always sorry. But nothing ever happens. You still just sit there all day, biting your fingernails and doing nothing. No cleaning, no cooking, no effort. Just worry, anxiety, inertia. I can't take it any more. I can't work *and* be the perfect housewife. Particularly with my job. You should understand that by now, Denis. You have to help!'

He nodded again, knowing this would change nothing, knowing this was merely the prelude to another wasted day watching rubbish television and eating junk food. He nodded and felt the stark truth of his utter humiliation before the woman he loved, a humiliation he appeared powerless to overcome. He stared helplessly at Helen and realised he was on the verge of throwing his marriage away. But it seemed he could do nothing: he was frozen by a strange, dark fear and a remorseless self-pity.

Helen, near to tears, threw down the hairbrush and moved to the large mahogany dressing table to fix her make-up. She was dressed in only a white silk bra, matching panties and black, seamed tights. He swallowed hard and tried somewhat hypocritically to resist the inevitable arousal this lovely spectacle inspired. Guilt and desire indulged in a brief tug of war that left guilt rolling in the mud and Denis with a violent erection.

His wife, his wonderful wife, just two weeks past her twenty-fourth birthday. His junior by six years. A tall, slim, athletic brunette with a shapely and carefully trained figure, the highlights of which were a pair of exquisitely ample breasts and the longest, sexiest legs imaginable, legs now wrapped in the scented embrace of the sheer black nylon tights and beautifully accentuated by their impressively straight seams.

He watched hungrily as she crossed her legs impatiently and began applying a little blusher to the golden flesh of her perfect cheeks. His eyes were drawn to the strips of darker nylon that covered her cherry-red toenails. Briefly, he recalled the sensual feel of this second skin against her warm thighs. Nylon on flesh:

the interaction of artifice and nature. He also remembered clandestine trips to this room during so many bored, lacklustre afternoons, afternoons in which he had found himself exploring her private drawers, caressing the soft nylons, the electric silks, the tingling satins, to find in the tactile experience of her most intimate garments a substitute for her body, the body denied him for nearly six weeks.

'No work, no sex,' she had said to him, the first sign that his helpless laziness was a real threat to their marriage. A practical response from a practical woman from a particularly practical family. And so the terrible tension that had built up between them had been heightened by a deeper, more physical frustration. And his own response had been to withdraw deeper into the inert world of petty neurosis that now so completely dominated his life.

He watched. He could only watch. Watch and remember, watch and indulge an increasingly fetishistic sexuality, a substitute sexuality. Yet he was vaguely aware that in this fetishism there was something more than the recent sting of sexual denial. In some way he felt that fetishism had always been in him, a part of his sexuality, but denied, repressed, sublimated in the joys of a superbly physical partner.

'And it's not just me, Denis,' his wife continued. 'It's Mummy, too.'

Denis felt himself physically shrink at the mention of Helen's mother. Her terrible mother: a beautiful but grimly threatening sword that hung so eagerly over his head. The woman who seemed to have bought shares in their marriage and had tried to manage it ever since they stepped out of the register office. The woman whose considerable personal fortune, inherited from a long-dead, older husband, had purchased the house they lived in and paid the larger bills that Helen's small National Health Service salary could not meet. The woman who had effectively replaced Denis as the breadwinner, who had taken over the role of financial manager with a disturbing enthusiasm, and who made no secret of her contempt for Denis.

'She won't put up with this much longer,' Helen said, tears filling her beautiful eyes. 'You know how she feels about you. You know she wants me to divorce you. Either that or –'

'Or what?' he snapped, gripped by a sudden, rare anger.

Once again he found himself staring at her reflection as she faced his, her eyes glistening with a deep-rooted annoyance, her cherry lips quivering, her lovely face red with shame and bitterness. We are miles apart, he thought, unable to touch, unable to face each other except through the mediation of a mirror.

'Or what?' he repeated.

There was no reply. Helen wiped her eyes and rose from the seat. He stared at her perfect back as she rushed to the wardrobe and pulled out her blue nurse's uniform. Helen Mann, his lovely wife, a senior ward sister. She hurriedly stepped into the uniform, zipping up the back with a single impatient gesture, and then slipped on her sensible black leather shoes. In less than a minute, she had pinned back her thick, black hair, grabbed her overcoat and rushed from the room. As she did so, he pulled himself off the bed and followed her out on to the landing, shouting that same question 'Or what?' over and over. Reaching the bottom of the stairs, she turned to face him, tears pouring down her cheeks.

'I tried, Denis, I really bloody tried with you. But there's nothing I can do now. You've brought this on yourself. You've got nobody else to blame. Remember that!'

With this, she swept her handbag from the hall table and rushed out of the front door, slamming it loudly and leaving him staring into a familiar but now slightly altered abyss.

He descended the stairs wearily, walked into the living room and found himself staring at his pathetic reflection in the blank screen of the television set. He felt tears well up in his own sad, defeated eyes. He tried not to listen to the sound of Helen's car pulling out of the driveway. It was just after 1.30 p.m.: she would be out until at least eleven, maybe later. Until then he had only his dark, oppressive thoughts and the television to keep him company.

At first Helen had been wonderful: caring, sympathetic, a professional helper doing her bit to relieve another's suffering. After the breakdown, she had encouraged him to resign, to seek a new life. She often worked extra hours at the hospital and he had agreed to help out more at home until he found something else, something less stressful. But even her patience had been stretched and eventually snapped by the enthusiasm with which he had rolled up into a ball and blocked out the world. And as her understanding had disintegrated, the presence of Helen's mother became increasingly apparent. Samantha, as beautiful in her way as her daughter, another tall, statuesque brunette, a woman who had never liked Denis. His mental collapse had confirmed all her jibes about his weakness, his inability to cope and, worst of all, his effeminacy.

Now, facing this grim, blank screen, he felt the familiar knot of humiliation as Samantha's acidic comments were recalled. She had even begun to call him 'Denise', to tease him about his 'utter failure as a man', and to suggest the possibility of 'a change of gender'. The last time she had visited, she unleashed a series of brutal remarks about buying him a dress! But Helen had intervened and Samantha retreated. Yet in this humiliation there had been something else, something less unpleasant, something he still refused to think about. But even as he fought this ambivalent emotion, he found himself remembering the lovely Samantha, her long black hair, her body in superb condition for her 44 years. He remembered her in this very room less than a fortnight ago, in a trim blue suit, black sweater, black hose and high heels, her long legs crossed as she reclined in the leather armchair. He remembered trying to avoid staring at her impressive form, particularly her legs and the gleaming patent leather stilettos to which they led.

'A nice pink number, I think,' she had teased, her eyes filled with contempt. 'Yes. Very *you*. Pink with plenty of frills. Short as well, so we can see those shapely legs of yours. White tights for those legs. White tights and red high heels.'

He tried to cast the strange feelings inspired by this memory out of his mind. He walked to the living-room window and stared out at the world he so deeply feared. Almost the first thing he saw was the lovely Wendy – Wendy Parsons, the eighteen-year-old only daughter of Mrs Adele Parsons, their attractive if somewhat haughty next-door neighbour, a cool-eyed widow who had recently arrived in the close after returning from a long period in the United States, and whose contempt for Denis now matched that of Samantha's. Yet Wendy, in her beautiful, fresh, almost naive manner, had only a mildly curious, polite smile for the unfortunate Denis Mann, her gorgeous eyes forgiving, understanding, helplessly girlish. And now, as usual, his eyes drank her up with greedy, gulping looks of desire. She was simply stunning, a tall, athletic blonde brought up since her early teens in America and now with a very American outlook. A champion swimmer, whose firm, subtle body was today encased in a tight black sweater, a very short, pleated tartan skirt, very sheer black tights and a pair of provocatively high-heeled shoes. A young woman returning to her sixth-form college after lunch at home.

He watched as she disappeared out of the close, then found himself staring into the oblivion of his frustrations and inertia. He took up the TV remote control, pointed it at the empty square of green glass and pressed the 'on' button. At the exact moment the ugly face of a well-known comedian filled the screen, the doorbell rang.

He sighed, flicked off the TV and walked sluggishly out into the hallway. The bell rang again, longer, impatiently. He mumbled an angry 'all right, I'm coming'. As he approached the door he could make out the figure of a woman through the frosted glass, a vaguely familiar figure. He opened the door. Before him was Samantha, a dark smile lighting up her beautiful face, a large leather travel bag at her side. He gasped in surprise.

'You look shocked, Denise,' she sneered, strolling past him into the house, a fog of powerful perfume engulfing his reddening face.

Taken off guard, he could only close the door and follow her into the living room, a sense of deep unease spreading over him.

'Well,' she exclaimed, turning to face her son-in-law while placing the large bag on the carpet, 'doing nothing, I see. How unusual.'

'What do you want?' he snapped back, trying to sound contemptuous, but only managing worried and uncertain. Her lovely brown eyes lit up, the cruel smile broadened. He found it difficult to hold her fierce, merciless gaze.

'A little chat to begin with,' she replied.

He was angered by his utter sense of helplessness before this beautiful woman, an anger made worse by the physical attraction that stirred within him every time she appeared.

She lowered herself on to the sofa next to his well-worn armchair, adjusting her short skirt around her knees, her eyes never leaving his. She was dressed in a short, tight but perfectly tailored red suit with a crisp white blouse, plus black hose and heeled shoes. His eyes wandered over this gorgeous display and rested on the shoes, stunning black patent-leather stilettos with five-inch heels, sado-erotic footwear for the dominant female. She crossed her legs, causing the skirt to ride up her marvellous thighs. He swallowed hard, but didn't move an inch. He was a rabbit trapped in the hypnotic powers of this woman's exquisite, sex snake form, a particularly frustrated rabbit.

'Like the shoes?' she teased, stretching out her lovely, nylon-sheathed legs. 'They do great things for my legs. Don't you agree?'

His gulping, high-pitched 'yes' broadened her bitter smile.

'Sit down, Denise. I really do need to talk to you.'

He moved towards the armchair, but she gestured for him to sit by her, on the sofa. He obeyed, never taking his eyes off her legs, riddled with desire and the fear of facing those splendid eyes. Suddenly they were inches apart, her sweet perfume washing over him, the rosy smell of her hair teasing his nostrils. He was overwhelmed by an intense sexual arousal, and no amount of fear or distrust could save him now.

'You know how I feel about you,' she continued. 'And I know how you feel about me. There's no getting away from the fact that we don't get on. But that doesn't change the fact that you're my son-in-law, that you're married to my daughter, and that your current behaviour is making both her and myself very unhappy. You've turned poor Helen's life into a nightmare, Denise. You've ruined her whole existence with your silly anxieties. We've tried to help you, but you seem to be beyond normal help. You just don't seem to be up to the role required of you; you can't behave like a man. So maybe we have to stop treating you like one.'

His eyes finally met hers. 'What on earth do you mean?'

'Look. If it weren't for me, you'd be out on your backside. I pay the mortgage, the bills. I keep you in trousers, trousers I don't think you deserve, or, *more accurately*, feel comfortable with. I've put up with you because Helen says she loves you. Well, now Helen has finally seen sense. This morning she phoned and told me to go ahead with a little plan, a plan we should have implemented ages ago, a plan designed to shake you up a bit, to give you a role that you'll feel more comfortable with, and which will hopefully result in you behaving more like an active human being.'

'Look, never mind the lecture, just tell me the bad news. You want me out. And now Helen's finally had enough and she agrees. OK. I understand. But where can I go, you just –'

'No, no. We don't want you out. We want you *in*. In skirts, to be precise.'

The last sentence took a few seconds to sink in. 'In skirts! What the –'

The slap to his face was hard and fast. Stunned, amazed, he felt a burning spread over his right cheek and tears fill his startled eyes.

'Shut up, Denise!' Samantha snapped. 'I'm talking. You're listening. Do you understand?'

The ironic tone had gone, replaced by a cool, brutal authority. He was speechless, yet outraged, appalled. But still he could only nod, rubbing his cheek, trying not to cry.

'If you can't behave like a man, then it's time you started to behave like the sissy you seem to be, a particularly submissive and extremely girlish type of sissy. Put simply, we've decided to feminise you. A complete transformation. And if you don't agree, then you are indeed welcome to leave. But as you will have nothing except what I've bought for you, including your now redundant underpants, I think this latter option may prove difficult.'

'You can't be serious!' he blubbered, feeling the tears begin to trickle from his eyes and the humiliation burn into him like an inescapable, all consuming fire.

'Of course I am! Deadly serious. I've watched you, Denise. Watched you roll up into a ball of self-pity and surrender to the void of fear and neurosis. And I know what your problem is: you can't stand being a man, you can't live with the pressures that rest so uneasily on most of your sex. Deep down, you want to be a more feminine being. You want to be controlled, dominated, overwhelmed. You want to be a slave, to have all decisions taken for you. And they will be – *completely*. You'll become Helen's personal housemaid and general servant. On the surface utterly unrecognisable as a man, but beneath your panties still biologically male.'

There were no words left to protest with. He suddenly knew he was doomed to whatever fate Samantha had dreamed up for him. To leave, to walk out on Helen and face the real world, with all its awful threats, was too much to ask. His only option was no option at all: tearful acceptance. So he burst into tears.

'You cry very convincingly,' Samantha continued, her voice full of teasing sarcasm. 'Just like a little girl. Can I assume from this typically pathetic outburst that you assent to your new role?'

Amazed at himself, wiping the flood of tears from his burning cheeks, he nodded.

'Right. Let's get on with it. Helen will try to be back by eleven. That gives us eight hours to get you dolled up and the house spotlessly clean. On your feet and follow me.'

He obeyed her without hesitation, amazed by the ease with which he was accepting this bizarre turn of events. Yes, it was all too simple. Secretly, he knew why. Samantha smiled: he could see she was pleased, even surprised, by his speedy capitulation. She grabbed the leather bag and led him out of the lounge, up the stairs and into the main bedroom. He followed her shakily, unable to keep his tear-stained eyes off her shapely, black nylon-sheathed calves and thighs, his sex rock hard and leading him almost as surely as his beautiful mother-in-law to a strange, new life.

Once in the bedroom, Samantha put the bag on the floor and faced him. 'First things first. From now on you call me Mummy. No other form of address will be acceptable. Helen will be addressed *at all times* as either Mistress Helen or Mistress. And you, of course, will be Denise. Understand?'

He nodded, on the surface quite appalled, but deeper down there was something else, a much more ambivalent feeling. Samantha stepped forward and slapped him again.

'When I ask you a question, Denise, I expect an answer! Now, *do you understand*?'

'Yes.'

'Yes *what*?'

'Yes, Mummy,' he mumbled, feeling his face burn the darkest crimson imaginable. He was so embarrassed, so utterly humiliated, yet far too frightened to resist.

She nodded, satisfied. 'Now the names are sorted out, it's time for you to undress.'

His hesitation inspired another hard slap. '*Get on with it!*' Samantha shouted.

So he undressed, struggling out of his jumper, nervously unbuttoning his shirt to reveal his particularly unimpressive chest, peeling off the shirt and placing it, together with the jumper, on the bed.

'And the trousers,' Samantha insisted, '*and* the underpants. *Everything!*'

Her words cut into him. The tears returned. Sobbing helplessly, he unbuckled his belt and unzipped the grey slacks. As they dropped around his ankles, he begged the room to swallow him. But worse was to come: after stepping out of the trousers and feebly removing his socks, he was faced with the appalling prospect of his underpants.

Samantha's beautiful, dark-brown eyes bored into him as he fiddled with the elastic waistband.

'*And* the underpants, Denise. *Now!*'

With one swift, desperate tug, he obeyed, pulling the underpants down over his shaking knees and virtually staggering out of them. Then he faced her, hands instinctively covering his genitals, utterly defeated, his face a deep cherry-red. She laughed, her lovely eyes full of sadistic malice. She leaned forward and unzipped the leather bag. From inside, she took a pink toiletries bag. She then ordered him to follow her into the bathroom.

Her heels clicked viciously against the tiled floor of the bathroom, percussive whip cracks that sent new flinches of fear and worry through Denis's exposed body. She placed the bulging toiletries bag in the wash basin situated beneath the mirrored medicine cabinet. From the bag she retrieved a silver razor and a can of shaving cream.

'Luckily, you're not very hairy,' she sneered. 'But even the slightest speck of body hair is unsightly on a young lady.'

She shook the can vigorously. 'Hands behind your back and feet apart,' she snapped, approaching him, the can aimed revolver-like at his chest. 'Don't move an inch.'

He obeyed and cringed as a jet of thick white foam struck his chest and upper stomach. Samantha used her free hand to rub the foam into a thick lather spreading from his neck down to the tips of his pubic hair. Then, to his horror, she proceeded to squirt a fresh dollop over his entire pubic region. Smiling cruelly, she repeated the energetic massage around his genitals, covering his pubic hair and thighs in a thick, white slick of foam. Eyes closed tightly, he fought a losing battle against the inevitable arousal her hands inspired, an arousal which soon resulted in a blatant visual testament.

'Well,' she jeered, 'at least that part of you is working.'

Within a few minutes, she had covered his torso, arms and legs in the foam. He was shrouded in a soft, damp suit of white lather, and, thanks to her teasing application, very excited. Suddenly, all thought of humiliation had disappeared, as had the tears of despair. In their place was desire, desire fuelled by the strangest, darkest thoughts about this beautiful woman. His eyes travelled over the generous curves of her body, paying particular attention to the exquisitely streamlined shape of her breasts as they pressed against the tight material of the jacket and the splendidly erotic lines of her legs sealed in the sensual embrace of sheer black nylon.

Samantha ran the razor across his chest, leaving a trail of pale, perfectly smooth skin. Using the shower to rinse the razor, she set to work with expert precision, quickly removing the hair on his chest and stomach. His arms followed. Then, inevitably, his pubic region. He gasped with a tantalising mixture of fear and excitement as she quickly whipped off the thick, black hair around his genitals and thighs, then stripped the finer, lighter hair from the rest of his legs.

Within thirty minutes of walking into the bathroom, Samantha managed to remove every visible hair on his body, leaving him feeling more naked and vulnerable than at any other point in his adult life. His skin tingled fiercely yet not unpleasantly. It was as if he had been sealed in a stocking of the finest silk imaginable. He looked down at his body and was amazed. What he saw was the body of a baby, a grown mutant baby, a man plunged into a helpless babified state by a beautiful, dominant and utterly merciless woman.

Samantha, this dark angel who had now taken over his life, stood back and admired her handiwork, a satisfied smile on her face. As he studied his smooth, vaguely feminine body, she returned to the washbasin and produced a bar of pink soap.

'Use this to give yourself a thorough wash,' she commanded. 'And use Helen's shampoo to do your hair. You've got fifteen minutes.'

With this sharp command, she walked out of the bathroom. As the sharp click of her heels echoed around him, he walked to the shower. Once satisfied the water was predictably warm, he stepped under the mild, refreshing spray and allowed it to soak his freshly shaven body. The physical experience of warm water on smooth skin was quite startling. It was like feeling for the first time, as if his sense of touch had suddenly been returned to a long denied level of intensity. Initially this was unsettling, but gradually the soft caress of water against his pink, exposed skin became rather pleasant. He found himself soaping his body with a new curiosity, examining each shaven section and pondering how just the removal of a few pieces of hair could make a male body seem so distinctly feminine.

He washed himself thoroughly, as ordered. The scent of the soap was a delicate rose and his body was quickly engulfed in this sweet, girlish aroma, an aroma that remained strong even after he had rinsed himself with an equal precision and set to work washing his thick, blond hair with his wife's shampoo.

By the time Samantha returned, Denis had stepped from the shower and was drying himself. His mother-in-law's entrance was announced by the now familiar click of heels, but as he stood with his back to her on the edge of a cloud of damp steam, he didn't actually see her enter the room.

'Good!' she snapped. 'You're showing a bit of initiative – who would have thought it was possible.'

He turned and a helpless gasp of astonishment escaped his lips, for she had removed the jacket and dress and was now standing before him in a stunning black satin panelled basque, black stockings and high heels, her marvellous figure displayed in all its mature but undeniably shapely glory. Her eyes burned with a black comic cruelty and her wicked smile broadened as his own eyes widened with shock and desire.

'Is there anything wrong, Denis?' she teased. 'I thought I'd slip out of those rather stuffy clothes. I'm sure you don't mind. After all, we're just two girls together.'

He nodded, dumbstruck, his arousal once again embarrassingly obvious. She marched past him to the washbasin and took a tin of talcum powder and a slender bottle of body spray from the toiletries bag. She quickly covered his already scented body in the pungent powder and then added to this a cloud of the powerfully scented feminine spray, concentrating on his armpits, chest and genitals. Soaped, powdered, perfumed, he struggled against the overwhelming odours of femininity and the fierce excitement inspired by the intimate presence of Samantha's luscious, semi-clad form.

She insisted he dry his hair more thoroughly. He obeyed with evident ill temper. When finally satisfied, she led him from the bathroom back to the bedroom. Here, the first thing he noticed was that the leather bag had disappeared and in its place on the bed was a startling array of feminine undergarments, together with a beautiful pink dress. The dress was incredibly intricate. Made from satin, it had a high, white lace-frilled neck, long, lace-frilled sleeves and, around its short hem, layers of thick lace petticoating. A dress for a little girl, a deliberately babyish but also incredibly sexy garment made for only one purpose: his humiliating feminisation.

He found himself staring at the lovely, delicate dress with something approaching desire. Yet not just a desire born out of an attraction to a sexually arousing garment: deep down he knew this was a desire *to wear* the garment, a sudden, shocking need that was quickly cast out of his mind by what remained of his masculine identity, a defence mechanism created by years of careful, but not entirely successful socialisation.

Denis was intensely aware of Samantha watching his reaction to the dress.

'Gorgeous, isn't it?' she said quietly, casually.

'Yes,' he murmured in reply. 'Very.'

'It'll look great on you.'

These words clawed him back from the brink: his eyes widened in humiliated disbelief and he stepped away from the bed.

'There's no point in resisting it, Denise. I know you can't wait to put it on.'

'That's not true!' he exclaimed. 'You know I've got no choice!'

She laughed bitterly, stepped closer to the bed and took up a white pantie-girdle, an ornately decorated, thick elastane panelled undergarment with a very high waist. 'Put this on first – it will cover your so-called manhood.'

His eyes filled with a mixture of anger and uncertainty. His face beetroot red with embarrassment, he took the garment from her and stared at it in total disbelief.

'Come on!' she snapped. 'I haven't got all day – there's work to be done!'

So he stepped into the soft, thick pantie-girdle, pulled it up his smooth legs and over his shapely thighs.

After a few minutes of wiggling (which clearly amused Samantha), he managed to pull the undergarment up over his genitals and position its sturdy, rubber-reinforced waist section around his stomach. The girdle was a perfect fit, gripping his waist snugly and completely enveloping his genitals and lower torso in taut, smooth elastane. He stared down at this fetishistic smothering and sighed with defeat, his face coated with a film of humiliation.

'It's you, Denise,' Samantha joked. 'Now stand still while I add the corset.'

He watched with some trepidation as his lovely tormentress took up a black, lace-trimmed garment from the bed and held it before him. It was a mini-corset made from satin and leather, with a series of silver hooks and eyes sewn into its curved back panels. Samantha made him raise his arms above his head and then wrapped the corset around his waist. He gasped as she pulled the two ends together in the middle of his back, forcing the air from his lungs and pushing his already insignificant stomach even further inwards. This had the effect of exaggerating the width of his chest and forcing him to stand more upright. Suddenly the lazy slouch which had characterised his helpless submission to fear and anxiety was gone. He stood tall, braced and stiffened, a new 'man'.

'Now that's much better,' Samantha exclaimed. 'A vast improvement in your posture. I should have done this months ago.'

He felt the combined restraining power of the girdle and the corset overwhelm his weak, under-exercised body and tried once again to repress a sense of disturbing excitement. Samantha's accusations spun in his mind as the arousal caused by this restraint increased. Perhaps she's right, he thought.

'I chose the tights especially: the most feminine pair I could find.'

She was holding a pair of white, patterned tights before him now, gossamer thin, yet firm enough to hold an intricate design of beautiful white roses. Tights designed to add to the theme of this dressing, the theme she had teased him with on more than one occasion, and which had been much more than hinted at during the preparations for this transformation: the sissy girl, the ultra-feminine, dainty, yet appallingly sexy adult baby boy-girl; a strange mixture of submissiveness and sweet, helpless femininity.

He took the tights from her. He took them and was immediately returned to those lonely afternoons spent secretly dipping into Helen's clothing drawers, caressing pair after pair of sheer black nylon hose and remembering how wonderful they had felt against her warm, firm, willing skin. A sickening, ecstatic fetishism, a fetishism he thought was rooted in his wife's absence, but now –

'Sit on the bed if you find it difficult. Roll them up and slip in one foot at a time, then draw the tights up your legs. Quickly, Denise – don't just stand there like a half-wit!'

He sat on the bed, feeling the corset and pantie-girdle tighten around his body as his backside sank into the soft mattress and silky sheets, a far from unpleasant sensation. He rolled the delicate legs of the tights into two soft, white nylon bowls and placed a foot in each one. Then he nervously drew the tights over his feet and ankles, one leg at a time. The feel of the sheer, ultra-soft fabric against his freshly shaven skin was almost overwhelming. He fought an audible gasp of pleasure as he guided the hose up over his shins and knees; he was plunged into an erotic realm of feminine softness and beauty and could not believe the intensity of the arousal this film of delicate, gentle nylon inspired. As he drew the tights over his thighs, he felt his sex strain desperately against its pantie-girdle imprisonment. Any doubts he might have had about his reaction to this feminisation disintegrated under the startling pleasure imparted by the heavenly caress of this gorgeous fabric.

'It's rather – nice,' he mumbled.

Samantha laughed. 'Yes, no doubt. But it's rather nice, *what*?'

He looked up at her as he stretched the tights over his upper thighs and pantie-girdled torso. 'It's rather nice, Mummy,' he said hesitantly, yet without resistance, without the embarrassment this word, this confession of utter submission, had previously inspired.

He positioned the tights around his waist and rose from the bed to examine his legs in more detail. The tights were a perfect fit. They also revealed the surprisingly shapely lines of his long legs to perfection.

'Well,' Samantha teased, 'you seem to have a very feminine pair of legs. Most women would envy you.'

He blushed, but, to his amazement, it was more out of pride than embarrassment. He ran his hands over the sheer fabric enveloping his shaven skin. It felt wonderful! There was no escaping this simple fact.

'And I thought this was going to be difficult,' Samantha said, taking a pair of spectacularly frilly lace and silk knickers from the bed. 'But I should have realised, Denise: you're a born she-male. This is *you*, what *you* really are. You've just been waiting for the right person, and it seems *I'm* the right person.'

She handed him the knickers. Without command or instruction, he drew them over his beautifully hosed legs and positioned them around his waist expertly. There followed a moment of exquisite hesitation as Samantha kneeled down and took from beneath the bed a pair of gleaming, red patent-leather court shoes with mountainous five-inch heels and a lovely diamond butterfly positioned on each sharply pointed leather toe.

'The pièce de résistance as far as those splendid legs are concerned, I think.'

She placed the shoes at his feet. He stared at them in utter wonderment. How often had he watched Helen slip into heeled shoes and admired the erotically enhancing effect on her own superb legs? And, maybe not so subconsciously, how often had he secretly envied her the pleasure of this enhancement?

He stepped forward and, with a feminine tentativeness, placed his right foot into the corresponding shoe. The second followed quickly. Like everything else Samantha had prepared, the shoes were a perfect fit. He felt exquisitely elevated, made obviously taller, but also more graceful, more of himself and the world, more complete. Yet this was his first time in heels and his untrained balance produced a few precarious wobbles. He gasped, reached out instinctively for support. Samantha grabbed his arms and steadied him.

'Just relax,' she whispered. 'Find your centre of gravity and calm down. Let the shoes become part of you.'

He followed her advice and tried to dispel the natural trepidation the heels produced. It was difficult, but he felt that was part of the pleasure. A look of fearful concentration lighting up his face, he took a tentative step forward. Then another. Then he was walking in the heels, or rather carefully mincing, as the shoes seemed to demand. Samantha watched each step, a smile on her full, red lips, a knowing sparkle in her golden-brown eyes. And as he minced before her, he found himself becoming even more aroused by the idea of parading in such a carefully feminised state before this beautiful, dominant woman. Now Denis realised how intensely attracted he was to Samantha, how he had always been attracted to her, even during the darkest moments of mockery and contempt. And with this realisation came a strangely unreal guilt, a feeling of betrayal, an automatic response, a programmed reaction. Yet he felt it wasn't so bad to desire this woman, his mother-in-law, and that this desire was itself part of her plan for him, therefore surely acceptable to his equally beautiful wife!

Once he had demonstrated an ability to walk in the heels, Samantha led him to Helen's dressing table.

He stared at his reflection, especially at his naked, shaven chest and the corset which so effectively imprisoned his stomach.

'First, we'll need to fix your hair,' Samantha said, her voice cooler, more businesslike.

Taking one of Helen's hairbrushes from the table, she worked quickly, with a combination of grace and speed, needing only a few minutes to transform his hair into a carefully shaped ornament of blond curls that highlighted the naturally feminine curves of his face.

'Not perfect, by any means,' she said, 'but it'll do until we can get you to a good hairdresser.'

He found her self-criticism harsh, and was about to tell her so when she produced a pot of foundation cream and poured a little of the light tan liquid on to her elegant fingers. 'Now, keep very still while I apply this.'

She covered the whole of his face and upper neck in the lightly scented cream, her fingers cool, careful, gentle. He watched the few masculine lines of his facial structure disappear. His face was softened, toned down, made even more effeminate. Soon he could see what she was seeing: the beginnings of a rather pretty girl.

After the foundation cream came the wonderful experience of Samantha applying a blood-red lipstick to his lips. As she guided the soft red tip of the stick over these once embarrassingly feminine lips, her own face was only an inch or so from his. He fought the urge to reach out and touch her.

The lipstick was followed by a peach eyeshadow, black eyebrow and eyelash highlighter and the slightest touch of peach blusher. Then Samantha stood back to study her work and Denis found himself facing someone else: an attractive woman.

Samantha's initial smile of satisfaction seemed to have changed to a smile of surprise. She was taken aback by the success of this crucial part of Denis's feminisation. But not as much as Denis! For him, this lovely creature was a fundamental challenge to his already badly dented sense of masculinity. Suddenly, the thing deep within him, the thing that had always secretly worried and, at some unconscious level, excited him, was fully exposed; the thing that Samantha had seen so clearly in his breakdown and subsequent descent into utter neurotic apathy: the woman in him.

'You look very convincing,' Samantha whispered. 'I'm very impressed. This is far more –'

Her voice trailed off. She told him to get up and come back to the bedside. He carefully raised himself to his high-heeled feet, grabbed one last look at 'his' new face, and then carefully minced over to the bed.

He found it difficult to walk in the heels without swinging his hips. His steps were short, dainty, as Samantha had instructed, but they were also helplessly provocative. At first this made him feel vaguely ridiculous, but then he thought of the pretty face in the mirror, the she-male he had so easily become, and embarrassment faded into a strange pleasure in his own natural femininity.

He stood before his mistress, his mother-in-law, his 'Mummy', his head lowered in a fetching imitation of feminine modesty, his penis straining against the tight layers of nylon, satin and elastane, a rock-hard manifestation of a distinctly ambivalent masculinity.

Samantha took up the splendid pink satin dress. She held it out before him, displaying it, revealing pearl button fastenings that stretched from the bottom of the full skirt right up the very tip of the high, lace befrilled neck. She held the dress out and smiled encouragingly. He swallowed hard, gripped by fear and apprehension, heart pounding, and then stepped into it, willingly plunging himself into the inescapable embrace of true femininity. As Samantha drew the dress over his scented, powdered, corseted body, Denis was truly lost and Denise was most certainly found.

Samantha carefully positioned the dress around his girlish form and began to button up the back. The dress was a perfect fit, its bodice section grasping his already corseted waist snugly and adding another layer of restriction. The layers of petticoating sewn into the skirt made it impossible for him to see either his hosed legs or the high heels.

When the dress was secured, Samantha took a large, lace-trimmed pinafore of white silk from the bed. This she carefully slid over his head and around his waist, tying it in place with a fat bow at the base of his spine. Then she stepped back to take further stock of her creation, her smile now almost envious. Then she was back by the bed, taking up a long length of pink silk ribbon. This she wrapped beneath his long, curled hair and drew up to just above his forehead, securing it with another large bow at the front of his hair.

'Gorgeous,' she whispered, her voice thick with what could only be described as arousal.

She took his hand and led him to the wardrobe mirror, the same mirror that, only a few hours before, his wife had stood before. Now 'he' was presented to himself. Revealed. Denise, in all *her* glory, unveiled to Denis.

He could say nothing, he couldn't even move. His breathing was constricted, his heart hammering with surprise and pride, his hosed legs weak. Before him was a truly beautiful, ultra-feminine girl, a pretty, sexy, baby maid, a sensuous blonde she-male indistinguishable from a real girl. A startling transformation. He was so aroused by the sight that he nearly passed out. Denise. Sweet Denise. So innocent in the intricate pink dress, yet also so erotic. Her long, shapely legs superbly complemented by the lovely patterned tights and dainty high heels, her expertly painted face framed by the pretty pink ribbon, her slender body perfectly enhanced by the tight folds of the wonderful dress.

'I can't believe it,' he mumbled, transfixed by this beautiful image, this feminine creature who had suddenly been revealed to the world.

'No. I've never truly realised just how feminine you are,' Samantha whispered.

Her words echoed in his head. He felt as if every drop of his masculinity had evaporated in the intense heat of a powerfully luminous feminine persona. My self is trickling away, he found himself thinking. But there was no fear, no horror. For this was the loss of a hated self, a despised, weak, helpless, anxious self that had left him a nervous wreck, useless to himself, to his wife, to life. Now, out of the initial inertia of amazement, he felt a new energy begin to flow within him, *her* energy, *her* vitality, the power that he had spent all his masculine energy trying to suppress.

'I feel alive. I feel awake. For the first time in ages.'

'Yes!' she replied. 'That's exactly it. Rebirth. But this is only the beginning, Denise: there's still a great deal of work to be done.'

He turned to her, smiled a sweet, sexy smile and nodded. 'Yes. I understand, Mummy.'

SLAVE ACTS

Jennifer Jane Pope

Jennifer Jane Pope is a very popular woman, with a following here and in the USA, and a thriving website (*www.avid-diva.demon.co.uk*). In Jenny's books, erotic fiction melds with science fiction. Set on a remote Scottish isle, the *Slave* series tells the story of the mysterious Healthglow Corporation, whose activities take human equestrianism well beyond the confines of formula, to include genetic re-engineering! The following extract features the voice of Sassie, a particularly alluring and demure pony girl, expounding on her interests . . .

Also by JJ Pope in Nexus:

SLAVE GENESIS
SLAVE EXODUS
SLAVE REVELATIONS

The best way I can explain it would be as some sort of a personal extension of mass hysteria, if that makes any sense. No? Well, I know what I mean – at least, I think I do.

Everything that happened at that race track was like a kind of madness; I was swept up in it and seemed completely to lose myself. Sara was another person altogether, left in some other world that was no longer anything to do with me. I was just Sassie the pony-girl, that's all, and whatever personality I now had was utterly subservient, yet really strong in that I knew exactly what it was I wanted.

That weird rubber face mask that Celia put on me at first – that started it all. That wasn't me, was it? That was some exotic female from . . . well, I don't know – name any one of a few dozen eastern countries and you could be right. I just looked at myself and saw someone else, and it was like throwing a switch. Anything I did now, especially as I was quickly cuffed under that cape, was outside my own responsibility.

And Celia knew what she was doing all right, as we already knew from that visit to her own place. As we were being blindfolded to pass through into that underground monorail system, she leaned close to me and whispered in my ear so nobody else could hear. Well, I don't think anyone else could hear, anyway.

'This is the only true freedom for a slave, Sassie,' she said. 'Now you have abandoned free will, choice, and your own needs, and given them willingly into the hands of your masters and mistresses.'

There was just one moment of doubt after that, during that rail journey itself, when I wondered just what the hell I was doing. I was completely naked under that cape and helpless to protect myself. Before the blindfold hood came off I felt hands under the material, hands fondling my boobs, playing with my nipples. It could have been Celia and probably was her on one occasion, but there were other hands, too.

They seemed to be evaluating me and it felt so impersonal – as if I was just another piece of livestock. Then another hand went down between my thighs, and fingers began to probe me. I heard a man sigh – just a sort of grunt, I suppose – when he discovered I was already aroused and wet and then he just patted me, like you would a dog, only you wouldn't pat a dog there, for sure.

As I say, I very nearly lost it about then and it was all I could do to stop myself from shouting out that I'd changed my mind and wanted to go back, but I knew the danger that I was likely to place the rest of you in, so I kept my mouth shut and thought I'd wait until I could say something quietly at the other end. I didn't realise I wouldn't get the opportunity again.

The stables were awesome. To think that someone could build a complex like that, and underground, too. The atmosphere just took my breath away. I could smell leather and sweat and rubber and all manner of other things I couldn't quite identify and suddenly I was back to being Sassie again and the scary feelings were going away.

Then, of course, I was handed over to the grooms and my last chance to back out swept away, especially when they fitted that thing across my back teeth and over my tongue. Even before they put the bit on me I was deprived of speech and the way they handled me was all so calculated. At the time it seemed so impersonal and offhanded, but I realise now it was far from that. Everything they did, everything they said, was intended to reinforce my status as a pony-girl and something inside me just responded automatically.

I stood there so obediently as they harnessed and bridled me and fitted those hooves and my tail and then all those various bells, and when they led me out I felt like I was walking on air. That other mask, the horse-snout shaped thing, and the blinkers, meant that I couldn't see very much at all, except for straight ahead. The collar kept my head up anyway, but even without it I know I would have walked proudly.

No, 'walk' isn't right at all – I pranced and everyone saw me, but I knew I was now just one pretty pony-girl among a whole string and there were some beautiful girls there. I didn't expect to win anything, to be honest, but there was a fire burning in me now that made me determined to give my all. When I ran, that was something else.

My boobs bounced so much it should have hurt, yet there was no pain now, simply a craving for victory, for admiration and, above all, for final fulfilment. I lost count of the number of times I came. There were proper orgasms and there were little mini ones and then there were multiple ones that just went on and on and I just carried on running throughout them.

The whip flicking my shoulders and back just added to it all and I remember wishing Celia would use it properly on me instead of just as a sort of symbolic action. I wanted her to thrash me, to show me and everyone else that I was her pony-girl; that I was the sort of animal who would do anything for the right mistress or master. Of course she wouldn't have done anything that would have left me permanently marked.

After the racing had finished, after I had won and when all the excitement was subsiding, then I should probably have felt deflated and the reality should have come back again. And yet it didn't. The moment that young groom took my reins and started checking to make sure my girth was still tight I knew what was going to happen. Everyone else was going to go off to whatever celebrations were planned back inside and I was simply going to be left to the hired help, the way a horse might be after the hunt is over. Except that real horses don't get handed over to grooms who intend to fuck them as soon as they get the chance.

His name was Jonas and he seemed to be the youngest of the grooms apart from maybe the one called Sol, but he'd apparently gone off somewhere else. I got the impression, from snatches of conversation I managed to pick up among the other grooms, that Sol was in some sort of trouble. Apparently he'd taken a pony-girl out without proper authority and she'd got away from him, but that's all I heard and I may have got it wrong.

Jonas had made it clear from the very beginning what he intended to do with me when the chance and time came, even though the older one, Higgy, kept going on about seniority. The crazy thing is, I ought to have been really upset that they were discussing who was going to have me first and yet the only thing on my mind was that I wanted it to be Jonas, if possible. The other crazy thing is that, when it looked like Higgy was going to exercise his privileges first after all, I accepted it quite placidly, like it wasn't any right of mine to choose.

In the end, Higgy was called away somewhere. There was a tall woman – she had weird eyes, a bit like a reptile I thought – who seemed to be in charge and all the grooms were scared stiff of her, I could tell. She wasn't there much, but when she was about she had a sort of presence, an aura. It wasn't evil, I don't think, more a sort of neutrality. Coldness, that was it. She was really cold, as if she had absolutely no feelings at all, like a machine on legs.

My nipples were still in their clamps, I was still belled and everything else about my rig was exactly as it had been throughout the races. The girth corset no longer seemed tight – though my legs were beginning to ache from standing on tiptoe in those hoof boots for so long – but I knew Jonas wasn't going to worry about my immediate comforts.

He led me into an empty stall – I think it was the one where I had been bridled earlier, though I'd gone past recall or caring anyway – and just hitched my rein to a hook on the wall, then unclipped one end of my bit and took it out. The tongue plate remained – he didn't want me speaking, after all.

'You know what's going to happen now, don't you, Sassie?' he said. He was so nonchalant about the whole thing, standing there, hands on hips, but he was also so good looking and strong that the nonchalant attitude just added to the feelings I was getting of being so completely in his power. Not that I knew it at the time, but without one of those special personal master tags, it meant I was available for anyone who took a fancy to me, visitors or staff alike.

I looked at Jonas and nodded. My mouth felt dry, but I was making up for that between my legs and I knew he could see that. The rubber body suit was keeping my exposed nipples aroused above and my pussy lips thrust well forward down below. It was crude and yet not crude, a simple emphasising of availability and, I suppose, surrender.

Jonas must have understood, but then he was probably very experienced, even though he didn't look very old. He took a plastic bottle and held the nozzle up to my lips, squeezing to produce a thin jet of water.

I drank, gratefully, greedily almost, but he was wary of letting me drink too much all in a rush. Instead, he grabbed my bridle and kissed me and I couldn't believe the length of his tongue. It probed everywhere inside my mouth and into the top of my throat, and I thought I was going to choke.

I kissed him back, though I couldn't respond with my own tongue, but he held my bridle so that I couldn't exert any real pressure with my lips, either. It was the most bizarre kiss I had ever experienced and yet probably the most erotic. He was kissing me and yet I wasn't allowed to kiss him, at least not in the normal way, though the lack of anything normal shouldn't have surprised me any more.

The kiss lasted a long time, and then he started on my nipples and I saw just how long his tongue actually was. I was really suffering now, grunting and groaning, scraping the ground with my hooves, like a mare in heat, I guess. I wanted him to take me straight away, but he wasn't going to be hurried. Instead, he kept flicking his tongue from one nipple to the other, making those little bells jangle as he did it and my nipples just carried on getting bigger and harder and throbbing like they were going to burst at any moment.

And then, without a word, he broke off, stood back, unhitched my rein and turned me around to face away from him. Instinctively, I knew what was expected of me and I bent forward, until my back was parallel with the ground, my buttocks thrust back and I knew my sex was just so visible and available. I could hear him doing something with his clothing, but the blinkers meant I couldn't see backwards and I tensed myself, waiting to be entered, except that at first it was his tongue that pushed inside me, and it found its target first time.

I came immediately and I would have fallen forward if he hadn't grabbed me by the hips. Now I started to push back, thrusting myself into his face, but he didn't seem to mind. Instead, he just kept going with his tongue and I squealed and whinnied as one orgasm blended with another until it all just became one. I was vaguely aware when he finally stopped, for he cried out something, but before I could react, or even start to come back from the peak, he fucked me.

It sounds crude, saying it that bluntly, but that was exactly what he did, without ceremony and without further ado. One minute he was using his tongue, the next he simply pressed himself against me and slid straight in, filling me with the longest cock I had ever known, and then pumping in and out until he came, a torrent that filled me and at the same time, pushed me completely over the edge.

I must have blacked out then, though only for a few seconds, and I did not fall, presumably because he kept hold of me. When I came to again, I was standing upright once more and he was holding my bridle. I peered down as best as the collar would let me and saw that he was still rigidly erect. The sight of that shaft was as awesome as it had felt.

He was built like a stallion – truly magnificently endowed beyond anything I had ever believed humanly possible. His cock had to be at least a foot long and he was only too well aware the effect the sight of it was having on me.

'Now you've been properly broken, Sassie,' he grinned. He patted my cheek and then kissed it. I simply stood there, shaking all over, my knees weak. 'Ready for some more?' he asked. I think I nodded, though I don't suppose it would really have made much difference whether I had or not. He turned me around again and I bent forward, powerless to resist even had I not been so rigidly and helplessly bound . . .

'Eat the way any pony does,' he said, understanding the question I was unable to voice. 'Get your snout in there and suck it up. Don't worry about the mess – I'll clean you up again afterwards.'

The stiff rubbery plastic stuff from which my face mask was made did not help me, for where the fabric curled in over my lips, it desensitised them considerably and I made more than just a mess of trying to feed. However, the porridge-like stuff tasted surprisingly good and, even though my stomach was still compressed within the tight girth corset, it felt empty and hollow and I knew I needed to get something sustaining into it.

Jonas laughed uproariously at my pathetic efforts, but he was patience personified, standing there with the tray and occasionally using his fingers to scoop stray dollops of the mixture back between my lips, so that eventually I managed to consume a good three quarters of the meal, with less than a quarter of it smeared around my rubberised face or splashed about my feet.

'Good girl,' he murmured, when I swallowed the last mouthful, and even before it had started downwards he was fitting the snout back across my mouth, the bit following in short order. Holding me tightly by my bridle, he reached out and caressed the tips of each of my nipples in turn and immediately those awful, fantastically beautiful bolts of fire began shooting through me again.

'Whoa, what a randy little filly you are!' he exclaimed, gleefully. 'Up for another good tup, by the looks of it.' He turned me slightly and patted me on the left buttock. 'Not now though, girl, much as I'd like to. Been on duty all night, I have, and I'll be needed again just after lunchtime, so I'm off for a few hours' shut-eye.

'Don't you worry, though,' he said, in what was supposed to be a consoling tone, 'Higgy'll be back down here soon. He wanted first go with you anyway and he was a bit pissed off when he was needed for other duties. Still, that's the crack, as the Irish say.'

He led me to the very back of the stall area and pointed a finger downwards towards the straw, which had been piled thicker here than it was by the doorway.

'Settle yourself down now,' he advised. 'I'll not hook you to anything, so you can stretch yourself out. Just lay back against the wall and let yourself slide down, mind. Takes a while to get used to not having your arms to help, but it's better than sleeping standing up, which is what the four-legged pony varieties do, of course.' He chuckled to himself and turned away for the door, without waiting to see whether I might need any help in carrying out his instructions.

'See you later, Sassie gal,' he said, banging the bottom section of the door closed once more. He grinned and tipped a mock salute at me. 'Good tight fuck you are, I'll give you that. Hope I'm around when you're next free, eh?'

And with that he was gone, leaving me standing there, back against the wall, totally bemused and feeling inexplicably frustrated by this latest turn of events. A good tight fuck, he'd said, and yet he was now more interested in sleeping than in repeating the experience. Despite the fact I knew deep down I should feel completely humiliated by this, my overriding thought was how long it would be before Higgy did make an appearance again.

My treacherous damned body, resplendent in its pony-girl finery, was already beginning to yearn yet again and, whilst Sara would have been horrified at the prospect, Sassie was already at the point where one cock was pretty much as satisfactory as another – the satisfaction was now the key concern, not who gave it to me!

Higgy was plainly unimpressed with having had his regular routine disrupted and, I suspected, with having been usurped by one of the younger grooms in the pecking order when it came to me. He also looked as if he hadn't had much sleep, if any, and he banged around, in and out of the other stalls, shouting out instructions to another couple of younger men who appeared shortly afterwards. Finally, after what must have been about twenty minutes, but which seemed to me like hours, he appeared at the door of my stall, leaning over it and peering in at me.

I lay motionless in my straw initially, feigning sleep, waiting to see if he would disturb me, knowing as he must surely have done that I had been on my feet for several hours, even without the additional exertions associated with the usual pony-girl activities here. He disturbed me all right.

'On your feet, you idle fucking filly!' he roared, kicking against the door with his heavy boots. 'C'mon, let's have you up and make sure that little bastard has sorted you out properly!'

Tired as I was – I yawned as I struggled to get myself into a position from which I could rise unaided – I felt the little electric surges starting up anew. Vaguely I did hear that same little voice asking me just what I thought I was acting like, but I quickly thrust it back down where it had come from and, once I had regained a standing position, sashayed over to Higgy with what can only be described as complete arrogance. He seemed surprisingly pleased at this.

'Ah, I do love to see a properly proud pony,' he chuckled. 'Makes it all the more satisfying when I whip her hind quarters for her, you see?' I could see that, all right, for I was learning fast, but I continued to regard him impassively, chewing ever so slightly against my bit, blinking as seldom as I could possibly manage.

'Let's have you out here then,' he said, swinging the lower door aside. 'You need a damned good brush, get rid of all those bits of straw and then I reckon a good hosing down will do you no harm. Got a lovely new skin suit over there, jet black with just a white flash and blaze – reckon you'll make a fine sight in that, especially with a pretty silver harness set against it.' He reached in and caught hold of my short lead rein, tugging my head firmly, just in case I had forgotten who was in charge, it seemed to me, though there was little chance of that.

'Fucked you good and proper, did he?' he whispered, as I came out alongside him. 'Well, you ain't seen nothing yet, Sassie my girl, I can promise you that. And this time, old Higgy's going to make sure he gets his oats before he feeds you any more of yours and turns you out for the hoi polloi to have their fun with you!'

My master for that morning appeared to be reasonably young, though the mask-hood that covered his head and face made it impossible to be sure. However, the tight white breeches and sleeveless top he wore displayed a well-muscled body and a healthy bulge between his legs. He stood watching, as Higgy harnessed me between the shafts of one of the lightweight gigs and although my blinkers prevented me from getting a good look at him – his eyes in any case were the only part of his features visible – I sensed his approval at what he saw.

'Sassie's not one of our regulars, Master Harvey,' Higgy explained. Harvey – was that his first or last name? Not that it mattered, for unless he decided otherwise, I wasn't going to be addressing him at all and even then it would be only as 'master', I knew.

'Apparently she's quite something, however,' the groom continued. He pulled harshly on the strap between my shoulder harness and the left side shaft – perhaps a trifle too harshly, I thought, wincing as I was tugged sideways. Higgy was annoyed, I knew, as the sudden arrival of Master Harvey put paid to any notion he was entertaining of having his own turn with me immediately.

'I watched her running last evening,' Harvey said, nodding. 'I was surprised her own master and mistress haven't placed her on the reserved list. If I owned such a fine creature, I doubt I'd be so keen to share her.' He spoke with a soft Midlands accent, his tone and pitch suggesting maturity without great age, much as his body did.

'Still,' he continued, and I saw him wave a hand airily. 'I've never been one to look a gift horse in the mouth, so why should I start with a gift pony, eh?' He chuckled at his own joke and I felt a shiver run up and down my spine, as the import of his words struck home. A 'gift pony' – yes, that was exactly what I had become, whether by the deliberate design of my own master, or by an oversight on his part, it mattered not.

I had been left here in these stables, dumb, defenceless, available and with no way of expressing my own wishes. Neither did I have any idea how long this state of affairs might continue. What if anything happened to Colin, my real master, the one who knew I was here? What if the true purpose of our mission was discovered? I could become Sassie permanently, I now realised, but although the reality of that brought another shudder, I was not entirely sure whether it was of horror, fear, or simply just . . . anticipation?

No, surely not? A game was a game, but that . . .? And yet I truly felt no trepidation, only excitement and, as Master Harvey moved around to get a better view of my front, desire to please and satisfy. Two grey eyes regarded me through narrow slits in the leather.

'Nice tits,' I heard him murmur. Beside me, Higgy nodded – I couldn't see him, but I felt the slight movement transferring through his arms and marvelled at how sensitive I was becoming to these things. 'I think maybe a tit harness,' Harvey continued, stroking his masked chin thoughtfully. Higgy released his grip on my tack and walked around to stand beside him, adopting a suitably subservient pose.

'Yes, good choice, Master Harvey,' he agreed, after a few seconds in which he was apparently considering the suggestion. 'A harness makes a pony more aware of her tits, for sure.'

I soon realised the truth of this.

The tit harness was a thin tube – it looked like stainless steel – at each end of which was a small round spring clip, designed to snap to the nipple rings. There were different lengths of bar and Higgy brought a selection, holding each one up to my chest in turn, until Master Harvey selected his choice. It was then only a matter of seconds before it was attached and I was astonished by the effect.

The bar chosen was just long enough that it pushed each of my nipples about four inches wide of its natural position, at the same time distending my breasts slightly in an outward direction. This constant pressure immediately began to take its toll on me and my whole body began to respond in the only way it now seemed to know. Something in my demeanour must have betrayed this fact, especially to Higgy.

'Ah yes, sir,' he muttered, nodding eagerly. 'Yes, that's made all the difference. Want me to check and see how wet she is?' He moved forward, apparently not anticipating a negative response to this offer and probed between my legs with his fingers, immediately finding the evidence of my arousal.

'How about a crotch strap with a vibrating plug? Guaranteed she'll come and keep coming all the time you've got her out. I know some drivers really like that effect and I can fit her with a tail plug, too – very nice effect, the two together.'

Master Harvey nodded, slowly.

'Ye-es,' he said, eventually. 'Yes, do that, Higgy, if you're sure it won't tire her to the extent of making her useless?'

'Not if you handle her right, sir,' Higgy said. 'I'll fit a vibrator with a control – there's a thin wire and a handheld button for you to switch her on and off. Oh yes,' he added, as he started to move away, '– it don't hurt none to rest her up at least every twenty minutes or so.

'That might not seem very long, I know,' he grinned, 'but believe me, it'll seem like a week to her!'

I had almost forgotten about Colin, as I had forgotten largely the original reason for our coming here; to investigate these curious islands. I gave it little enough thought at the time, it's true, but now I think I understand what happened to me, though I know I should not take any pride in the way I let things just take me over.

The dildo Higgy had inserted inside me felt snug and fat, filling me completely, yet not stretching me. The same was true of the butt plug that held my tail: it had been carefully sculpted so that there was a thinner part just before the flanged base that prevented it going completely inside me and my sphincter muscles settled around this quite happily. However, as soon as I began to trot and Master Harvey activated the vibrator for the first time, the combination of the two intruders all but sent me into a delirium.

I climaxed within only a few steps and I wanted to stop, to squeeze with my muscles and savour the feeling, but this was clearly not part of Harvey's plan.

'Trot on!' he commanded, flicking the whip over my head as I made to halt, and I remember biting hard into the rubber of my bit in order to force myself to obey him. Then, as I gathered speed again, everything became a complete blur as the multiple orgasms blended together in one long and shattering surrender to the inevitable.

When I next regained my senses I realised, to my astonishment, that I was still running – loping slowly now, rather than trotting as I had been before. The vibrator had stopped, but I could feel its presence down there, along with that of the rear plug: the swish of my tail against the backs of my thighs above the tops of my boots added another layer of stimulation.

'Good girl,' I heard from behind me, followed by a low chuckle. Clearly my unconscious performance had met with Master's approval. I tossed my head and this brought another laugh.

'Atta gal!' he cried. 'Show everyone what a proud pony you are!' At this, I suddenly realised just how many other people there were out there. Other ponies trotted by every few minutes, singly and in pairs, pulling a variety of vehicles and driven by an even greater variety of handlers. Some, ponies and drivers alike, had their identities hidden behind masks and I found myself wondering if any of them were my friends.

The vibrator started up again, but this time only for a matter of seconds, and then it became still again. However, even that short burst had proved sufficient to stir my juices again, and all thoughts of anything or anybody beyond my current position and current master were banished as I lurched towards orgasm once again.

'Steady, Sassie.' I felt the slow drag on my reins which signalled me to slow down and I did so with reluctance. Only a few days earlier the mere presence of a dildo inside me – the mere fact that I was helpless in my pony regalia, the feel of the bit pressing back into my mouth and the breeze blowing gently against my naked flesh – all those things combined would have kept me in a state of permanent orgasm, but now I knew I needed more still. Permanent arousal I had, yes, but now I was an experienced pony-girl and an experienced pony-girl needed driving to her climax.

Trying to smile around my bit, I slowed as required and snorted as a sudden gust of wind blew directly into my face. No hurry, I told myself, peering sideways to where the sun was less than halfway up the eastern sky. The day had really barely begun yet and I had the feeling I was in the hands of a master who knew only too well what a pony-girl needed.

I dropped to a walk as we entered one of the clearer spaces that appeared to be everywhere among the tracks here and wondered how long it would be before the mechanical beast in my vagina would be replaced by a real, throbbing, flesh and blood one. Not too long, I hoped . . .

SLAVE-MINES OF TORMUNIL

Aran Ashe

Aran Ashe has been a stalwart of the Nexus list from its inception, creating a lyrical world of fantasy erotica which contains a myriad of possibilities for bondage, submission and domination, all written with a touching sense of the characters' internal feelings. After a hiatus of a few years, we published *Slave-Mines* in 2002, and we're very pleased to have Aran Ashe back on the list.

CHOOSING LOVERS FOR JUSTINE
THE SLAVE OF LIDIR
THE DUNGEONS OF LIDIR
THE FOREST OF BONDAGE
PLEASURE ISLAND
THE HANDMAIDENS
CITADEL OF SERVITUDE

F ew of the inhabitants took heed of the stranger riding through the dirt-dry streets: the eve of the market saw many travellers. But there were glances of appreciation for his young concubine, who clung behind him, riding bare-back and astride.

When they reached the little square the horse went straight to the wooden trough beside the well and the stranger dismounted. The horse drank. The girl stayed on his back and stared about. Her pale and delicate flesh drew more onlookers into the bright sunshine – even some of the masters taking bare-breasted girls to the stables paused to stare. There were no obvious marks of sexual punishment on this new girl's skin. Her master appeared young, perhaps inexperienced in knowing how to deal with a slave. Thoughts of barter seeded the minds of these watchers. Her breasts were small. All she wore was a shirt. A little ruby-studded touchable gold chain glinted between her bare girlish thighs. Some of the watchers stood on tiptoes to achieve a sweeter view.

The shirt, a man's shirt, skimpily buttoned, parted just above her deep umbilicus, a black, smooth well in the whiteness of a naked, hairless belly whose lips were full, as if from coaxing. Perhaps her young master was not after all so lax in attending to her flesh. Her naked sex lips pouted provocatively and were linked by the little chain.

By now an interested group had gathered by the well. The stranger singled out the grizzled wise-man, stood before him and said:

'Sir, my name is Josef Stenner. I pass in peace across your lands.'

The old man signalled to one of the others, who drew water from the well. 'Drink, friend.'

The stranger took the overflowing ladle but gave it first to the girl. Then he drank. He wiped the dripping liquid from his lips. Someone in the crowd gasped and pointed.

'He wears the Talisur!'

The old man showed no emotion until he took the stranger's hand and with trembling fingers touched the mystic ring. Then he sighed deeply and shook his head. 'Our village is well-graced, my lord.' He bowed slowly.

'I crave no special favour, and beg that you treat me only as an honest traveller. But you can help me.'

'Only say the means.'

'I seek a man – a Tormunite lord named Malory.' The onlookers stared blankly. 'His party must have passed this way two or three days ago. He had soldiers with him, and a girl.' Still there was no reaction: such sights were commonplace. 'Someone must have seen them passing through?'

Amid the vacant glances the old man shook his head. 'I know of no Malory, my lord. No soldiers have been here – save the drivers.' He stared up.

'Then there is a market here?'

'In the next town, it is but a few minutes' ride.' He nodded down the road then stared up at the semi-naked girl on the horse. 'Think not ill of me for saying this, but she is comely. And there is a spark of generous hunger in her gaze. At the market – Talisur or no – there will be those who scheme to spirit her from your arms by any means. Therefore keep her on a near-tether and sojourn in that town no longer than you must.'

* * *

218

Josef watched Leah murmuring and moving in her slumber. He had stripped the warm shirt from her back, up over her head, and had bound it securely round her wrists to leave her body naked and her hands imprisoned so she could not touch herself. He had fastened a soft leather thong around her narrow waist and pressed his middle finger gently, deeply into her umbilicus. Her little nipples had come erect in expectation. Then he had threaded a length of rough sisal rope from behind, up between her legs, under her sexual chain, intimately between her virgin sex lips and close against the mouth of her bottom. Slowly drawing the rope upwards, deep between the small, round, buttock cheeks and tight between the pink lips, he had finally secured it back and front to the waist-thong. These last few nights he had done this to her before putting her to bed. Tonight her anticipation had been stronger. When he had turned her face-down and pressed his palm into the small of her back, steadily pushing her belly firmly into the bed while drawing her rope tight, he had felt a shudder ripple through her body from front to back and travel up his arm. Leah had twisted round, her small face thrust between her fastened arms, and hungrily she had kissed him, sucked his lip and tried to reach down to kiss his naked penis.

Her body was beautiful and sexual. The evening light now caressed it as it moved against the sheet. What was she dreaming about?

Josef thought of what had happened that afternoon after she had bathed in the warm, slow river – how she had stepped lightly, nakedly, over the dry, flat stones, her fine, gold sexual-chain glistening and tinkling between her smooth, denuded thighs. Clothed only in this chain she had stood before him and stared expectantly up into his eyes, the eyes of her new master, a master she had chosen. It seemed to make no difference to her that he sought another, and that this

219

was the purpose of his mission. As far as Leah was concerned, she was his charge, and he was obligated to observe the Tormunite rule – to punish her, to cherish her, and to train her to his preferences. Josef had not yet grown fully accustomed to sexual ownership but with Leah he was learning quickly.

Day by day on their travels she had grown hungrier for pleasure, wanting him to draw it forth from her by elaborate and demanding means. She would recount to him the sexual things that had been done to her in the Abbey. And he would see the fervour in her lovely blue eyes as he held her naked white body close, cupping her sweet, chained, pink sex in his fingers till it yielded honey. These last few days she had repeatedly driven him to intense pleasure. But still she wanted to be shared with other men. 'It will teach me how better to please my lord,' Leah had said.

Such sharing was the norm amongst the Tormunites, but Josef had found it too difficult to permit. Here in the roadhouse public sharing was commonplace. When they arrived there had been two men on the stairs with a girl wearing only a thin wet top. While Josef carried Leah past the two men, Leah was staring at their wet erections. When they reached the room she had wanted to know why the girl's breasts and the men's sexes were so wet, and whether it was with the girl's honey, or the men's fluid. 'She made them give good measure,' she had murmured wistfully. Then, with her brow furrowed deeply, she had caressed Josef's penis and closed her eyes, and he knew she was imagining and desiring those other men. But he would never want to let her come to harm.

She had slept fitfully, wanting Josef to hold her, making him cup her roped sex in his fingers from behind. Eventually she had fallen into a deeper sleep. She had made a little moisture which remained on his fingers until it dried in the warm air. He could hear noises in the street and eventually he went to the balcony.

His room was high on a corner and overlooked much of the town. In the distance he could see the marketplace. Closer by were several small inns and a larger building which was the house of pleasure. A platform had been constructed in the yard behind it and wooden spars and supporting frames were being added to it. People were beginning to congregate. There seemed to be a clear division in this town between the quiet natives and the brash Tormunite masters who used it as their base for trade. Diagonally opposite the roadhouse a girl with bared breasts was being held with her back to the wall. Her breasts stood very full and proud. Her masters had begun to loop a leather cord around them to bind them.

Josef turned and looked again at Leah, whose breasts were very small, and yet, he thought, she was beautiful indeed. Her dried sexual honey was smooth upon his fingers. She had turned on to her back, her fastened arms still stretched out above her head, her thighs slightly open, arousing delicious pangs of wanting in him as he looked at the thin love-chain stretched across the rope lodged between her spread sex lips. The chain, symbolically sealing her lips, was the sign of her virginity.

Her eyes, softly blue, half opened. She tried to reach for him. He unwound the shirt from her wrists. 'What is my lord thinking?' Leah whispered, stretching up, reaching her fingers around the back of his neck.

'That, were I the air, how I would cling to your soft, sweet skin.' He clasped her gently round her slender ribcage, lifted her completely from the bed and kissed under her arms, tasting sun-salt there despite her ablutions. Her little nipples brushed against him as he lowered her feet to the floor. Her head was level with his chest and her mischievous fingers were against his leg, seeking, wanting to know he was erect for her. She smiled in satisfaction, then gasped as his fingers intruded under her chain, around the rope, under it a little way, opening her very slightly, finger-tasting the salt-sexy glaze there, warmer than mulled wine. He eased her gently back to the bed. There he unfastened the rope, carefully lifted it away from the adhering hot flesh, and removed the rope completely. Then he opened her sex to the waning sunlight, stretching its beautiful bare lips, making of it a split pink chained fig with a polished bulb of erection at the tip. As Leah lay across the bed, head back and down, her perfect belly trembling open, Josef slowly masturbated this open fig. Each time a soft murmur started in her throat he pinched her nipples, which had become fuller over the last week though her breasts were still small. When she felt the Talisur ring touching just inside her body, gently probing her virginity, she began to shudder and tried to press the ring against her clitoris, seeking swift satiation with it. But Josef took charge of her aroused flesh. She was moaning as he replaced the rope with a thin strip of cloth between her legs, arranging it so it pouched her tightly, sealing the longing into her puffed-up sex. He secured the cloth pouch to the thin leather thong around her waist. Then he lifted her limp body from the bed, clothed her with her wrinkled shirt and took her downstairs.

As they came out into the busy street, Josef could feel the sexual tension in her body. He could feel it in the way she reacted to his hand against the small of her back, propelling her to a fate just beyond her control. And he almost felt that he was playing out the role of a true Tormunite lord, who might at any moment choose to stop her, draw her to the middle of the street and publicly whip her perfect buttocks while a stranger's searching fingers, clutching her cloth pouch, slowly milked the delicious goodness from her.

At the marketplace many pairs of eyes were distracted by Leah. The low sunlight gave way to torchlight and the glow from the cooking hearths. Droves of people moved slowly past the stalls while the scent of herbs, yeasty bread and roasting meat laced the air.

'Apothecary!'

'Honey-roast pheasant!'

'Harness! Tackle!'

'Trinkets for the damsel's hair!' The beaming girl swathed in necklaces pushed up to Josef, proffering an armful of brooches. Josef chose for Leah a pink pearl grip. He slipped it into her hair then ushered her down a side street towards the sound of drums. When the scene opened before them, Josef stood behind Leah, holding her gently by the shoulders. She was trembling. 'Who are they?' she whispered. 'Why are they chained so?'

They were nude girls fastened to a single long copper chain. They had evidently been chosen for the beauty of their figures and their breasts. The guards were preventing idle onlookers from entering the enclosure.

Josef simply held up the hand bearing the Talisur ring and the sentinel buckled into subservience. 'What mission are you charged with?' Josef asked him.

'A consignment for Menirg, my lord.'

The name meant nothing to Josef, but he was unwilling to reveal his ignorance by enquiry. 'May we inspect them?'

'Of course.' The sentinel's gaze fell on Leah, whose shirt was open and whose cloth pouch had ridden up, clasping high between her legs.

From inside the building came the distinctive sounds of spanking. As the chained girls outside froze, the sentinel explained that a second team was in the building and was being punished for a clique of elders of the town, who preferred to keep their sexual predilections private from the masses. Leah clung to Josef as he took her inside.

Their entry stirred little notice from the elders, though it coincided with a lull in the punishment. There were about a dozen chained slave girls. All had been depilated according to the Tormunite custom, so as to leave the sex bare to the viewer. Some faced forward and others faced the wall, their buttocks reddened, their legs outspread. The elders were comparing them in vulgar tones which heightened Leah's trepidation. A blonde girl wearing only a footman's open brass-buttoned bright-blue jacket and boots had been administering the punishment with a leather belt, and had presumably dictated which way each girl should face to receive it. One girl at the end of the line was crouched on a stool.

The blonde girl did not seem to belong with either the soldiers or the elders. She now refastened the leather belt around her bright-blue jacket at the waist, but left her breasts still visible. Each girl had a large, gold, circular, hinged clasp inserted through a fresh piercing in one of her labia, usually the right one. The clasp fastened her sex to the copper chain. A tiny lock across the jaws of the clasp could be opened by a simple key carried by the guards. The blonde girl took the key and moved slowly down the line, passing breasts of breathtaking fullness and tight, trembling buttocks striped with weals.

Josef moved Leah gradually closer as the sexual inspection proceeded. The elders, seemingly keen for her to watch, made way. Josef grasped the thong at the back of her waist and gently drew it tighter, making Leah's chained sex bulge against its cloth as he walked her through the cluster of men.

The blonde girl had stopped in front of one girl. She now inhaled the warmth rising from the naked slave-body which looked little younger than herself. There were red marks inside the frightened white thighs which straddled the copper chain. It passed high up

224

between the girl's legs, behind one buttock and across the front of the other thigh. Her gold labial clasp was pushed upwards by the locked links of the chain, forcing her sex slightly open on one side, creating a sweet distortion in the lip, as if an invisible fingertip were lodged there and the lip were gently sucking it. Josef wondered how much sexual arousal she had undergone. Was her gold clasp hot when the blonde girl touched it? As it was being unlocked it seemed the movement transmitted to the partly open sex induced a tiny tremble in the slave girl's belly. The chain fell away and the blonde girl now ordered her to stand in the middle of the floor with her gold clasp dangling open, a glittering bait. Then one of the soldiers lifted the slave into a sitting position on the table while the blonde girl stared at her, silently demanding access, her expression an eerie blend of desire and chill.

Josef glanced at Leah, who gazed transfixed as the girl on the table obediently and tearfully opened herself with her fingers. There was neither murmur nor movement from the elders. The chained slaves watched with half averted eyes.

The gold clasp through the girl's labium was of a thick gauge. At the point of insertion the flesh of the lip had been forced out all around it to leave a stretched, raised rim. The blonde girl had clearly identified this as a focus of sexual pain because her fingers went straight there and squeezed the stretching. With the first definite gasp she took hold of the clasp itself and drew the lip widely aside and upwards, to expose the clitoris but not to touch it. Then she again squeezed the focus of sexual pain in the piercing. She moved to one side so all could see precisely where her victim was being squeezed. It was as if she wanted to instruct her audience in how to make the slave girl gasp. The girl cast pleading looks about her. Amid the gasps the blonde girl's eyes slowly challenged the room. The slave girl did not know what to do with herself. Her breathing became uneven as the blonde twisted the now-yielding sex lip by its clasp and rubbed the exposed clitoris directly but very gently.

Josef could feel Leah's trembling. He slipped his fingers between her legs, holding her pouch, which was moistly hot and tight because her lips were so swollen. He could feel the fine chain links through the cloth. And he could feel the proud flesh around her clitoris.

The blonde again took off her leather belt and clipped its buckle to the girl's gold clasp. The weight of the belt hung down between the girl's legs and over the edge of the table, drawing the tortured labium down and making the clitoris stand a little askew for the blonde to play with. The touching was keener now, not gentle, and the tip of the belt was swaying just above the floor. Its steadily strengthening movements were fed by the heightening arousal of the girl. On instruction from her mistress her knees were now bent and her heels were on the edge of the table. Her naked sex was thrusting out over the edge to meet the rough pleasure of the rasping fingers. Then the blonde grasped the leather hanging between the girl's legs and stroked it, as if it were a heavy dangling phallus. The girl reacted as if the phallus were hers; fluid began seeping down it.

The blonde called for assistance. With the leather drawn tight, the groaning girl sank slowly back. One of the elders moved round the table and the girl suckled him. Another reached across and held the spare nipple pinched tightly between his fingers.

The girl was inexperienced, it seemed to Josef. Her responses were strong because they were probably coming for the first time. Her mouth was open; her head was rolling from side to side. Her slim legs were shivering, her feet standing up on their toes on the table, to permit this sweet violation as the tongue of the belt was now being inserted. Josef's fingers could feel

226

Leah's mounting sexual excitement oozing through her cloth, which now clung to her like a second skin.

The blonde had furled the end of the belt to make a tube which she was very slowly inserting not into the sex but into the anus, pushing firmly as the anus progressively opened in small, chaste, shy gulps and one by one the eyelets in the tube of leather disappeared.

Leah kept pushing back against Josef. She must have known even before touching him that he was in erection. She stood on tiptoes and opened her buttocks: she wanted him to push his fingers or his penis under her cloth and touch her anal skin.

Just as he stretched the cloth aside, the girl on the table gasped loudly: the leather belt had gone into her as far it could and her throbbing clitoris protruded like a bulb. The blonde in blue now began to draw the instrument of stimulation out just as slowly and steadily as she had pushed it in. The eyelets popped out one by one. Each emergence seemed to cause a little echoing pulse of retraction in Leah's anal skin, which Josef had been very gently caressing with two fingers. The girl's clitoris bulbed throughout the withdrawal.

The elders, their penises poking, began to crowd closer to her, blocking the view completely. Leah whispered: 'Shall she have to drink their yield?' Again Josef thought about Leah's envy of the girl with two suitors on the stairs.

Josef drew Leah by the thong and led her to a quiet corner.

'Feed me, master,' Leah whispered, touching the hardness of his penis through his clothes. And she surely knew that he was already leaking. Her sweet mouth was open suggestively, wide enough to take the thickest penis. She started to kneel in front of him but he stopped her. He rolled up his sleeves, that his bare arms might embrace her nakedness.

He found something deeply satisfying about playing with her when she was already aroused almost to the point of no return. Her lips were warm and searching; her underarms were moist and hot against his bare forearms; her little breasts were trembling. She was at the stage of receptiveness where he might easily have put her to one of the prurient elders for pleasure, and her flesh and mouth might gladly have received it. Josef gently teased her, scratching her bulging pouch until her honeyed lubricant welled through the cloth and ran under his fingernails.

The blonde girl had stood back, her blue jacket open, her leather belt now dangling from her hand. The first groans of pleasure were coming from the elders and Leah's eyes peeped keenly round Josef's elbow. He moved to one side so she could see the semen begin streaming. These men, though old, gave copiously. He knew that Leah loved to watch such scenes. Each splash upon the girl's breast and neck made Leah's bright eyes glitter. Leah's lips spread again as if in suck upon a penis. Josef pulled her shirt over her head, up her arms and bound her wrists with it. With one hand he pinned them above her head and against the wall. Her little breasts now looked fatter; her belly bulged as her legs bowed open. He lifted her pouch to one side and she murmured as her sex protruded through the gap. Her eyes were fixed upon the scene but her sex responded to his fingers, now skin to skin with her. 'Would you like me to put you to the elders like this?' he whispered teasingly in her ear, 'with this little bud out for them, so tight and near to bursting?' And a fleeting stab of pleasure seemed to tremble through her thighs.

The girl, with a spurting penis in each hand, was drinking the leaping silver broth of passion. Other girls were now being penetrated while still chained together – a leg would be lifted and a rampant penis would push aside the gold clasp and slide in above the copper chain.

The wet, chained lips of Leah's sex slipped hotly through Josef's fingers. Her clitoris reacted to his teasings like the hypersensitive tip of an exposed bone which kept retreating back into its swollen fleshy hood. He pressed it in and twisted his fingertip gently back and forth against the tip, while on the table the girl's face, neck and breasts were being drenched in semen. A clear, watery fluid was trickling down the girl's arm from the wrist that was doing the masturbating. Leah was moaning; her legs were shaking. Josef's fingertip allowed the sensitive tip of her clitoris to come out once more, only for him to press it into her again, tormenting it. Her oil ran down his finger and coated the Talisur ring. He whispered to her: 'When we return to the roadhouse I shall hire two young men for you and you shall feed upon their semen.' She groaned and tried to kiss him. He nudged the ring up against the hot place where his fingertip had been pressing, making intimate contact, mystic ring to sensitive clitoral tip, and suddenly her eyes rolled upwards and a jerk that felt electric went through her body. The climax seemed intensified because she was standing. She was trying to keep on tiptoes for it, trying to keep her clitoris barely touching, trembling, dancing against the ring. Her mouth was wide open, gulping the air that was impregnated so thickly with the scent of semen.

When the pleasure waves were finished Leah slumped forward against Josef. 'Don't stop,' said a voice behind him. He turned sharply on the intruder only to find it was the uniformed blonde girl. 'You must not stop,' the girl persisted. 'I sense that she is barely started.' She was looking at him with an expression of mild playfulness. 'My name is Roanen.' She brushed casually against him but stared at Leah. 'One could not help but notice her plight.' Without seeking leave she now unwound the shirt from Leah's wrists and, pressing it to her face, breathed in its scent. She ran her fingers down Leah's cheek. 'She likes men?'

'She is a virgin,' Josef warned.

'I noticed her chain. But you like attentive men, my sweet?' Leah's eyes closed softly in assent and her cheek pressed against Roanen's palm. The first pangs of possessiveness stabbed at Josef's heart. He tried to fight these feelings. The girl was beautiful and sexual and Leah was aroused. She wanted these attentions.

'Lift her for me,' Roanen whispered. 'Let me touch her love-chain.' Josef cautiously lifted the trembling Leah and held her cloth to one side. He could feel her heart beating through her back. The slim hands went straight between her thighs, seeking out the points of puncture, squeezing each one tightly against its gold insert, rubbing it and drawing Leah fully open against the constriction of the chain, making her gasp. Her heart was bursting with excitement. 'See,' said Roanen, 'how wide her lips are now parted, despite their chain, how open-mouthed and willing her cunt is, how pliant to the touch.' Leah's thighs were shivering. Roanen's slim thumb went in a little way, a little way into Leah's body, but it could not go too far. It came out again with a heavy drop of liquid at the tip. Roanen held it up as if it were precious essence. She glanced sidelong at Josef but spoke to Leah. 'If your master will consent to leave you with me then your night is scarce begun.' Leah was looking up at him pleadingly.

'I must have her back in my room at the roadhouse by –'

'Dawn,' Roanen interrupted.

She raised her thumb to Leah's open mouth. 'Quick my sweet, for it is dripping.' Leah's small tongue peeped and stroked off the shiny sexual droplet as tenderly as if it were the pre-emission at the tip of a penis.

DOLLS

Aishling Morgan

Aishling Morgan is a fantasy and period erotica writer with a difference – just as you get used to one set of sexual extremities, she pulls out all the stops and gets even weirder. From her period novels which feature the rakes, scapegraces and hangalluses of eighteenth-century Devon, through her present-day pagan erotic fiction, to the fantastical, timeless stories which feature lyrical, gothic fantasy worlds peopled by curious anthropomorphic beasts and which draw firmly on her own zoological training, Aishling Morgan is an erotic writer like no other. What follows is a short story which is exclusive to *New Erotica 6* and which appears here for the first time.

By Aishling Morgan and published by Nexus:

THE RAKE
MAIDEN
PURITY
TIGER, TIGER
DEVON CREAM
CAPTIVE
DEEP BLUE
PLEASURE TOY
VELVET SKIN
INNOCENT

A zai paused as they reached the shop, catching sight of her face in the reflective black-copper glass of the window – snub nose, freckles and a slight blush of embarrassment. Her sister caught her hand, pulling her towards the door.

'Come on in, Azai. You're not a little girl any more, so there's no need to act like one.'

'Sorry, Jana,' Azai replied automatically.

Jana pushed open the shop door, Azai following. Within, the room was furnished in the same dark glass, mixed with black leather and bronze. Comfortable couches stood against two walls, a desk against the third, with a door beyond. A young woman sat at the desk, her hair and face immaculate, her blouse cut open in the latest style to reveal firm, bare breasts. At the sight, Azai felt an immediate self-consciousness for her own chest, with her breasts displayed through her first open-front top. The young woman stood, smiling as she spoke.

'Ladies, good afternoon. I am Amaranth. How may I help you?'

Jana spoke before Azai could decide what to say.

'We would like cock, please, for my sister. Her first was last week.'

'Jana!' Azai exclaimed, the blood rising to her face. 'You don't have to tell everybody!'

'You should be proud,' Amaranth stated, 'and you are beautiful, your breasts especially.'

'I keep telling her that,' Jana said. 'I took ages to get her into her top this morning.'

Amaranth responded with a light laugh.

'I'll show you around myself,' she offered. 'It's not every day we have a first. Do come in.'

She had opened the door behind the desk, and held it wide as Jana stepped through, Azai following less confidently, into a small, square cubicle. A scent struck her immediately, somewhat animal – musky, leathery – bringing her nipples to embarrassing erection. Jana giggled and reached out to tweak one stiff bud. Amaranth gave a knowing smile.

'Did you have anything particular in mind?'

'We don't have a great deal to spend,' Jana responded, 'but we would like to see a full range, if we may?'

'Certainly,' Amaranth replied. 'Our policy is to value all our customers. After all, a girl who buys a Teasing Feather one time may come back to order a full staff of dolls.'

'We'd like to see some dolls, please,' Azai managed.

'Naturally you would.'

The two older women shared a wink. Azai felt her blush rise again as Amaranth pressed a finger to a pad beside the inner door, which swung back. Immediately the animal scent grew stronger. Azai swallowed, painfully aware of her arousal. Jana's tongue flicked out to moisten wet lips, her hand rising to touch a breast. Amaranth seemed unaffected, leading them down the corridor to yet another door, this time a steel grid, with cages visible beyond.

'This is the Stopes range,' she said, casually indicating the row of cages. 'Functional and affordable, although naturally you don't get the style of the top names. This is the Brad, for instance.'

Azai looked into the cage Amaranth was standing by. She felt her stomach flutter as she saw the creature within. It was standing, its chin at the level of the top of her head, placid blue eyes staring out from an expressionless face. There were no breasts, only a hard, muscular torso, with tiny nipples, above a flat belly, a tangle of dark blonde hair, and male genitals, the penis thick and pale, resting on the bulging scrotum.

'It's so ugly!' she said, trying to fight down the revulsion welling up inside her, to war with her arousal.

'Ugly, yes,' Amaranth agreed, 'but if that cock was inside your little pussy, my sweet, you wouldn't worry about how he looks.'

'It's polite to say "he",' Jana remarked, 'not it. Look, watch, Azai. He can smell our cunts. He's getting excited!'

She finished with a giggle, and put her arm around her sister's shoulder. Sure enough, the Brad had begun to take an interest, grasping his cock and tugging at it, with his big, pale eyes flicking over the women's breasts and down to the tight Vs of their crotches. Azai found herself giggling nervously, her eyes locked to the rapidly growing pole of male meat as she wondered how it would feel inside her body. Suddenly the Brad stepped forward, brandishing his now erect cock. Azai stepped quickly away from the bars.

'Down, boy, not now,' Amaranth said, firmly, yet calmly. Immediately the Brad slunk back to the corner of his cage.

'All the Stopes models have unquestioning obedience built in,' Amaranth went on. 'It makes them easy to handle, of course, but it does mean one rather has to control the fuck.'

'How much is the Brad?' Azai asked.

'Twelve thousand,' Amaranth answered, 'or at twelve-five there is the Brad Ballman, with a larger genital package.'

'What are the specs?' Jana asked.

'Seven long, six around for the basic Brad. Eight long, seven around for the Ballman. Both are designed

235

to amply fill a typical vagina. Insemination is available as an optional extra, at five-hundred on all models.'

'Insemination?' Azai queried.

'Yes. Some women prefer to feel they have been impregnated during an act of sex, although naturally the sperm is drawn from the banks in the usual way.'

'Naturally.'

'Delivery takes a little longer, as a minor operation to the testes is needed,' Amaranth went on, ' but you'll both be far too young to be thinking of pregnancy?'

'Yes,' Jana agreed quickly, Azai nodding. Amaranth went on.

'The top of the Stopes range is the Clinton, here, and then there's the basic Dave, or the Kirk for those who prefer an older look. The six inch Dave starts at eight thousand, a Clinton Ballman with insemination and high-capacity testes would be twenty thousand five-hundred. Stopes don't offer programs.'

'Programs?' Azai asked.

'Special features,' her sister said, 'like cuddling after sex, or cunt licking.'

'Cunnilingus is now standard in most models,' Amaranth added, 'but for programs we really need to see a more up-market range.'

'Do you have Rebus and Sacs?' Jana asked.

'Certainly,' Amaranth answered, her eyes showing no more than a trace of doubt as she glanced to Azai's sister. 'A specialist company, of course, but their dedication to quality is not to be faulted. This way.'

She led them back into the corridor and through another grill, on which Azai recognised the Rebus and Sacs motif from Jan's bedroom wall. Again there were cages, again containing males, only this time each stood behind a double layer of steel bars. Lustful growls greeted their entry, and Azai noted that Amaranth kept carefully to the middle of the space between the cages.

'Oh, my, a Bull!' Jana exclaimed, turning to a cage in which a huge male sat hulked on a low bench, his great red genitals hanging low between his spread thighs, the cock already stirring.

'You know your dolls,' Amaranth said, with another doubtful glance to Jana. 'He's a Bull, yes, ten by eight, half . . .'

' . . . litre capacity, arousal receptors, forced cock sucking as standard,' Jana took over, 'with six programs to choose from, including Viking Marauder. Oh, what a beast!'

'Also with ten metres of heavy chain, voice controlled winch and electric prod,' Amaranth added, 'all for thirty-three thousand seven hundred and fifty.'

'I wish,' Jana sighed. 'Oh well, one day.'

The Bull had come forward, his face set in an expression of feral lust, eyes blazing from beneath heavy brows, great muscles working in his torso and along his arms. His cock was hard, a huge red pole that had Azai thinking instinctively of her virgin sex and backing away from the cage. Amaranth moved on hastily, only to find that the other males had also come forward, erect cocks sticking up, hands reaching ineffectually through the bars. Jana's neck and upper chest were flushed red, her nipples straining to erection.

'Would you like to see the Millefiori range?' Amaranth asked. 'We have their Adonis in, at one hundred thousand, complete with . . .'

'What is this?' Jana asked, ignoring Amaranth as she came close to another cage.

Inside was another male, his skin dark bronze, taller than the Bull and almost as massive, his body hard, sculpted muscle, a good ten inches of rigid penis projecting from his groin above massive balls.

'A custom model,' Amaranth explained, moving cautiously closer, 'special order for a certain wealthy actress. His body is an upgraded Intruder, eleven by seven, with one litre capacity . . .'

'One litre! Oh my, oh my . . . Would he force me to suck his cock?'

'Yes, with a random chance of coming in your mouth or over your face and breasts. He'll position you himself too, at random . . . very rudely.'

'I have to go in with him, Amaranth.'

'Jana!' Azai exclaimed.

'He's reserved, a virgin, I'm afraid,' Amaranth said.

'Oh, please!' Jana begged. 'I can pay.'

'He's going out at eighty-seven thousand,' Amaranth answered. 'If he's not virgin, we lose the sale.'

'Oh . . . but how will she know? It's not as if he can tell her!'

Amaranth laughed at the joke, but shook her head.

'Please!' Jana begged. 'Look how he needs me.'

Sure enough, the Intruder's cock was straining out towards them, and his eyes were fixed on Jana's bare breasts. Clearly he sensed their physical excitement, and possibly even understood something of the conversation.

'Shit!' Jana swore. 'I need a fuck so badly, Amaranth, a really good filling too. Do you have anything else one litre?'

'Well, yes,' Amaranth said doubtfully, 'there's an upgraded Slutmaster Boss, but . . . .'

'Slutmaster?' Azai broke in. 'That doesn't sound very nice.'

'An Australian company. They've only just started exporting . . . .'

'He sounds rough.'

'He is.'

'I don't care. Put me in with him, Amaranth!'

'Jana, really! I'll tell Mummy.'

'Oh sh, Azai! I just want a good rough fucking while we're here. I'll put two hundred towards your choice too, okay?'

238

Azai hesitated, feeling the tingling in her own sex and wondering how it would feel to watch her sister being put to one of the big male's cocks. There was really no choice. She nodded.

'You will be purchasing?' Amaranth queried.

'Yes, absolutely,' Jana assured her.

'Okay,' Amaranth replied, 'in the interests of gaining new customers. Come with me.'

They left the Rebus and Sacs males, seven pairs of glaring eyes and seven stiff cocks following them from the room. A little further down the corridor Amaranth opened another grill, letting them into a room with a single occupied cage. The male within was tall as always, but relatively slender, with pale gold skin and a shock of tawny hair. A long cock hung down between his thighs.

'The Slutmaster Boss,' Amaranth said proudly, 'exclusive to us. Ten by six, one litre capacity, rape as standard, with three programs to choose from : . .'

'Let me in!' Jana exclaimed.

Amaranth laughed, with just a touch of nervousness, and turned to the cage. The Boss was standing, and stroking his cock.

'A treat for you, Boss,' Amaranth stated, pressing her finger to the panel by the cage door. 'All yours, Miss, but you'd be wise to undress first.'

'No,' Jana replied, stepping eagerly into the cage, 'being stripped is half the fun. He is programmed not to tear my clothes, isn't he?'

'Well, no . . .' Amaranth answered.

It was too late. The Boss has already closed on Jana. She reacted with a giggle as his powerful hands took her breasts, kneading the plump globes of flesh, his cock stiffening and drool starting to run from the side of his mouth as he pawed her. Her hands went to her trousers, getting the button open just in time before his thumbs were pushed hard into her waistband. Her

239

trousers came down, intact, baring her petite bottom even as the twin, fleshy globes were pushed hard to the bars of the cage. He was grunting, eager, his cock fully erect as his hands grappled for her panties.

'No!' she squeaked, but too late as the tiny piece of silk was torn off her hips.

Azai watched in fascination as her sister was lifted, her thighs spread wide, the Boss's cock searching for her hole, only for him to be frustrated by her trousers. His response was immediate, and simple. She was twisted over, bottom up, so that she had to grab for the bars. Her mouth went wide as the big cock was thrust unceremoniously up into her body from behind. She gasped, pleasure mixed with pain and shock, and she was being fucked, her breasts swinging to the motion as he pumped into her, grinning in glee, his hands locked in the flesh of her hips.

Jana's eyes had gone glassy with pleasure as she was fucked. Her mouth hung slack, spittle running from one corner. Azai stared, entranced at her sister's reaction to the harsh, animal fucking, and wondering how she herself would take the same treatment. She was shaking, and her sex felt in urgent need of her touch, but she held back, embarrassed to do what needed to be done in front of Amaranth, despite Jana's open display.

Boss was getting frantic, faster and faster, until Azai was sure he would come, and she would see her first male orgasm, delivered up her sister's hole. The thought was too much, and she let one hand sneak up to her chest, to play with a nipple. Amaranth gave a knowing smile in reaction, and Azai found herself blushing. Not that it stopped her, and she was wondering if she dared undo her trousers and slip a hand down the front of her panties when the Boss suddenly moved.

In three quick motions Jana had the big cock pulled from her sex, was spun around, and dragged to her knees. Even as she gaped wide her mouth was filled with erection, the Boss taking her by the hair to force himself deep in. Jana's cheeks blew out, her eyes going wide in reaction, as the long, thick penis was jammed down into her throat. She was trying to suck, but the Boss was too eager, too rough, and too strong, just fucking her head without the slightest consideration for her needs. Azai gave Amaranth a nervous glance, but the only response was an arm laid gently across the young girl's shoulder.

Jana's face was going dark, and she was clearly choking, but the instant she began to panic, and to slap her hands on the Boss's legs in apparent futility, he stopped. The long glistening shaft was pulled from her mouth, leaving her gasping, with a ring of saliva and her own juice smeared around her lips.

The Boss gave Jana no time to recover, but turned her about once more, onto her knees, bottom high, his erection resting between her upturned buttocks. Jana blew out her breath and managed a weak smile for Azai even as the Boss took hold of his cock, to slide it down between her buttocks. Jana gave a little mew of satisfaction as the big cock head was slid up her once more, gently this time, slapping in the juicy opening to her body as he moved it, rubbing from clit to anus. Jana began to sigh, her mouth going slowly slack once more, her eyes closing, only to jerk open in shock.

'No! Ah, no, not . . .'

She ended in a gasp, a sound mirrored by Azai as she realised that the Boss was trying to bugger her sister.

'Stop him!' Jana gasped, but it was too late. The cock head was in her rectum, and the Boss was not going to forgo his pleasure. 'Oh shit . . . he's in my bumhole . . . the dirty animal!'

Amaranth's hand had gone to her mouth in wordless shock, and she cuddled Azai close. They watched in horrified fascination as Jana was sodomised, the thick penis jammed inch by inch past her straining anus and up into her bottom. She took it gasping, breathless, as more and more was fed into her rectum, until she began to mumble obscenities, under her breath, then aloud.

' . . . oh shit, not my bumhole, not my bumhole . . . . . . oh that feels so dirty, so fucking dirty . . . oh, no, not that . . . oh so dirty, so dirty, up my bum . . . up my dirty bum yes, fill me up . . . I can feel it . . . so hard . . . bugger me . . . yes, bugger me so hard . . . ah!'

She gasped as the last couple of inches of penis were forced hard into her protesting anus. The boss began to rock, grinning down as he held Jana's buttocks apart with his thumbs, to watch her distended anus as it pulled in and out on the fat plug of his cock. She was gasping, her mouth wide again, a streamer of spittle hanging from her chin, her eyes closed in shame filled ecstasy.

Azai could only stare, watching her sister's spread buttocks and the obscene way her anus moved on the Boss' cock. Worse still, Jana was clearly enjoying being buggered, whimpering with pleasure at the use of her anus, her torso down, to let her nipples rub on the hard floor of the cell to the motion of her swinging breasts. The Boss was getting faster too.

'He's going to come,' Amaranth whispered, squeezing Azai to her. 'One litre . . .'

Even as she spoke, the Boss grunted. Jana's eyes went round with shock, and she screamed. Again the Boss grunted, jamming himself up Jana's bottom to the very hilt, and again she screamed, and started to babble.

' . . . no, it's too much . . . I can't . . . I can't not up my bottom, not . . . oh, shit!'

She broke off, gritting her teeth as the Boss began to withdraw from her anus, the thick cock shaft sliding out, moist and slimy with her juices, until the head popped free. Jana's anus closed behind the cock end as she once more began to babble.

' . . . oh no, oh no, not that . . . no, don't look, Azai . . . don't oh fuck . . . that is lovely, so, so lovely . . .'

As she had spoken, her anus had opened again. Most of the litre of sperm which had been put up her exploded from her bottom in a thick white arc, to splash over the Boss's cock and balls as she sank, moaning to the floor. She gave in, abandoning herself completely, her hand going back to her sex, with the sperm still bubbling out of her anus, to run, thick and sticky down into her gaping vagina as she started to masturbate.

Azai gaped, shocked, as she watched her sister in ecstasy. Jana was rubbing hard, come spattering her thighs and falling into her lowered panties and trousers in thick white gouts. Nor was the Boss finished. Grabbing Jana by the hair, he twisted her around, to force his filthy, sperm soaked penis into her mouth. She sucked, not just eager, but frantic, masturbating with desperate urgency as she mouthed and slobbered over the huge penis that had just been withdrawn from her rectum. Her eyes were shut in rapture, her breasts jumping and jiggling to her motion. Dirty sperm burst from around her lips and the Boss gave her a final mouthful, and she was coming, her muscles twitching in orgasm, her body locked in ecstasy.

Neither of the watching girls said a word, until Jana at last slumped down in the pool of sperm and juice beneath her. She was filthy, her face soiled, her breasts smeared, her panties full of dirty sperm. The Boss took her by the hair, holding her as his cock went slowly limp, then casually proceeded to urinate over her prone body. Jana took it gasping and wide eyed, but made no effort to stop it happening as her bottom, then her breasts and belly were pissed on. At the end she was smiling, red faced with embarrassment, yet still smiling.

243

'Back now,' Amaranth ordered, and the Boss retreated, immediately to curl up on his sleeping bench.

Jana crawled from the cage, only pulling herself up on the bars when she was out, to stand giggling and red faced, her body dripping urine, sperm running down her thighs. Azai found herself speechless.

'You had better wash,' Amaranth commented. 'The bathroom is at the end of the corridor to the left. You'll find everything you need, including a dispenser for paper panties. I do apologise for that. I thought he was on standard, but one of my colleagues must have been showing a customer programs.'

Jana just fled, clutching at her still lowered trousers, bare, dirty bottom wiggling behind her as she went. Amaranth finally removed her arm from around Azai's shoulders, speaking carefully.

'Your sister, she will accept what happened to her, I trust?'

'Yes, Azai answered, sulkily, but with certainty. 'I just wish she wouldn't be so dirty in front of other people.'

'She had little choice.'

'Believe me, she loved it. She reads that magazine Rebus and Sacs do. That little scene could have come right out of it. Still, I think she got a bit of a shock when it was put up her bum.'

Amaranth gave an understanding nod and began to steer Azai along the passage. They passed several more grills, before coming to an ordinary door, which Amaranth held open.

'Feathers, puddendolls, appenda,' she explained. 'Things I imagine will be more within your price range.'

Azai nodded as she looked around the room. Nearest was a tank of Feathers, creatures she recognised from her mother and sister's bedroom. Engineered from phasmid stock, each was a long quill like structure

244

supported on six legs, with the insectoid head at one end, and the trailing, Feathery tail at the other.

'We have an offer at present,' Amaranth remarked. 'Three for the price of two, two nipple-ticklers and a cunt-tail. Or there's something your sister might like. The Tri-Tease, those bronze coloured ones. They're engineered to stand over the anus, with the Feather tickling both holes and your clitty.'

Azai giggled, partly at Amaranth's joke, but also thinking of her own shy and illicit experiments with Jana's Feathers, and how good it felt to come under the exquisite tickling sensations they produced. Each creature was engineered to seek out a particular part of a woman's body, drawn by distinctive scents and tastes, then to stay put, tickling with the long Feathery tail, until removed.

'They start at twenty,' Amaranth remarked, 'and you may test them if you wish.'

Thinking to detect a note of expectation in the young woman's voice, Azai found herself blushing. There had been something familiar about the comfort given as they watched Jana buggered, and for all Amaranth's apparent insouciance, it was hard to believe she had been unaffected. Certainly Azai herself had not.

'Thank you, no,' she answered. 'May I see the puddendolls?'

'Certainly.'

Amaranth moved a little further into the room, to indicate a yet larger tank. In it, several dozen of the bizarre creatures stood to attention. Azai had seen them before, sneaking peeks at both her sister and mother as they masturbated, but never so close. Both Jana and her mother kept their puddendolls carefully locked in their cages, denying Azai the chance to experiment, and making the creatures all the more fascinating. Each was a large, permanently bloated phallus, a cock sprouting up from a thick scrotum that housed the enormous balls and the remainder of the creatures organs, with one or more secondary spurs rising in parallel with the cock. Most were pink, some a fleshy bronze, or even a rich brown shaded with purple. Each stood on four squat legs.

Some of the puddendolls had clustered around the feed dishes at the back, their absorbent fans spread to take in the nutrients from the solution. More simply squatted on the floor of the tank, straining up to catch the tang of the girls' pheromones. Occasionally a wave of peristalsis would pass along one or another. One in particular caught her attention, a great brown monster with testicles twice the size of most others.

'That's the Rude Boy, a new release from Jersey Genetics in the States,' Amaranth said, noting Azai's interest. 'He's powerful, dual clitty-spur, as you see, with a four-hundred CC capacity and a great refresh rate. Hungry, naturally, but if you want the best . . .'

'He's so big!' Azai mouthed. 'I'm . . . I'm not sure if I could.'

'He might be a bit of a shock, first time!' Amaranth laughed. 'How about this little fellow, GWC's Pussyeater, basic, but effective, one-hundred CC, single spur . . .'

'No,' Azai interrupted her. 'It just wouldn't be the same. Have you got the Rude Boy in white?'

'No, I'm sorry, but there's the Cuntjammer from Brovary Laboratories near Kiev. They haven't quiet got the knack of product names yet, but he's sturdy, single spur, but a full half litre capacity, which is as high as they go. Where is he now?'

Azai followed Amaranth's fingers, to a fat pale puddendoll, whose rounded knob rose a good two inches above his companions in the feeding bowl. Amaranth reached it, to gently grasp the big puddendoll and lift it from the feeding dish. The absorbent net lifted from the fluid and sucked up into an opening like a tiny anus, which quickly closed to a point.

'He's heavy, fully laden,' she remarked. 'Be careful.'

Azai nodded, and gingerly took the puddendoll in her hands. It squirmed in her grip, and, remembering how Jana soothed her own puddendoll during masturbation, she began to stroke the thick shaft. It felt smooth, warm and fleshy, with a delicious firmness. Just touching it sent a shiver the length of her spine, with the thought of how it would feel inside her. There was also anticipation, with a touch of fear, at the realisation that if she chose it, the fat pink head would soon be puncturing her hymen. Turning it to her face, she wondered how it would feel to suck on, with her mouth wide around the bulbous tip, or gaping with it pushed right in, the way the Boss had forced her sister's mouth.

It would feel good, she was sure, and the rich, musky smell of the Cuntjammer was making her want to take him in her mouth. She stroked more firmly, but held back, unsure if it would be thought polite. Amaranth was going to speak, when the fat puddendoll jerked in Azai's hands, expelling a good quarter-litre of spunk full in her face with a single powerful ejaculation. She gasped in shock, only to receive the second spurt full in her open mouth, the third catching her across her breasts and top as she jerked the puddendoll away, the fourth merely oozing out over her hand.

She stood back, arms spread, mouth wide in surprise and disgust, sperm running slowly from her open mouth, to hang in a curtain from her chin and fall in thick gouts to her breasts. One eye was closed, there were blobs in her hair and down the side of her face, more hanging from her nose and one ear. Without a word, Amaranth passed her a box of tissues and took the now somewhat deflated puddendoll from her hand. Azai began to clear up, only to realise that there was far more in her mouth than the tissues could possibly absorb. Grimacing, she forced herself to swallow the mouthful of thick, slimy, sugar-sweet come, gagging slightly at the texture as it went down her throat.

'There is a spittoon,' Amaranth remarked, 'but if you prefer . . .'

'Too late,' Azai answered her. 'Yuck! Do they always do that?'

'The Cuntjammer is perhaps a little over sensitive,' Amaranth admitted, 'and he had just been feeding. Some girls rather like it.'

'Good for them.'

Amaranth waited patiently, holding a waste paper basket up for Azai as she cleaned her face and breasts before speaking again.

'Now with the Rude Boy, that would never have happened. You need to really jerk at them to get them to come unless they're inside you. All the sensitivity is in the head. Can I tempt you?'

'Well . . . How much is he?'

'Five hundred, but they are the top of the range. The Cuntjammer is three hundred and fifty.'

'No, thanks. Five hundred? That's a lot of money . . .'

'I'll throw in a Feather to make up for your unexpected face-full.'

'Well, it's tempting, with the two hundred Jana promised . . .'

'Try him.'

'Here? What, properly?'

'As you please. I'd be honoured to see your first time, or you can take a private room, with Jana perhaps. It is better with someone to hold you.'

Azai bit her lip, uncertain, but Amaranth was already holding out the big black puddendoll. The head twisted, straining to find the source of female smell, the twin spurs writhed, making Azai's clitoris twitch in anticipation. With a wry smile she reached for the creature. Amaranth responded with a nod of understanding and went to take a towel from a rack, which she spread on a comfortable looking leather couch opposite the tanks. Azai felt herself start to colour up again, but the feel of the big puddendoll in her hands was getting to her.

'Would you like to undress?' Amaranth asked.

Azai nodded, telling herself that her embarrassment was inappropriate, and that she should try and behave more like her big sister. Her top was already slightly soiled, but it was something Jana had warned her might happen, and she had a spare, also fresh disposable panties. Nevertheless, it was obviously sensible to be naked.

She was still unsure, yet Amaranth seemed to expect her to do it, and she knew Jana did. So did she, having promised herself before setting out that she would go through with it. Actually surrendering her virginity was not so easy. Handing the now squirming puddendoll back to Amaranth, she began to undress. Quickly, she slipped off shoes and socks, trousers, her top, and finally her panties, to expose the neat puff of pubic hair on her mound, shaved that very morning into a stylish shape.

Amaranth gave an appreciative nod, watching without embarrassment. Azai returned a shy smile, and sat, coyly, her thighs together. Amaranth passed her the puddendoll. She took him, trembling as she forced herself to spread her knees, exposing her sex as Amaranth sat down beside her. Determined not to make a show of her innocence, she feigned a casual attitude, pressing the Rude Boy between her thighs. Just the feel of it against her sex made her gasp, the fat body squirming on her flesh, with increased vigour as it sensed her.

'May I?' Amaranth asked. 'He has several rather fine features, for instance . . .'

She took the puddendoll, holding him gently to Azai's sex. Fighting down her embarrassment, Azai forced herself to keep her legs wide, making her sex fully available to the other woman. Amaranth gave her a reassuring smile, and squeezed the Rude Boy's balls. Immediately he began to shiver, sending a powerful vibration straight to Azai's clitoris. She gasped, and her thighs went wider still, this time by instinct.

'That is nice! How do you do that?'

'Just squeeze his balls. Not hard, or you'll hurt him. Always remember, he's a living creature. You try.'

Azai reached down, to curl her hand gently around the Rude Boy's huge, turgid scrotum. She squeezed, tenderly, and again a delicious trill ran up the fat shaft, straight to her clitoris.

'I want him in me, Amaranth. Where's Jana?'

'Still in the bathroom, I imagine. She can't go anywhere else on her own. Did she want to be with you?'

'Yes, if I was going to take anything into me. I think I'm going to.'

'A moment.'

Amaranth rose, and walked quickly from the room, leaving Azai to tease herself with the puddendoll, squeezing the balls over and over again, to send shock after shock through her clitoris, and bring her ever nearer her climax. By the time the door opened once more she was wondering if she could hold back at all. Amaranth came in, immediately followed by Jana, in nothing but a pair of disposable paper panties.

'Oh my, little sis, do you look beautiful! And what is that!'

'He's called a Rude Boy,' Azai answered happily, 'and I rather think I like him.'

'I'll bet you do! If you get him, I want to share.'

Azai just purred and squeezed the puddendoll's balls one more time. As the vibration ran through her she gasped.

'I think you've got a sale here,' Jana remarked. 'So, do you want to let him in, or do we wait until we get home?'

'I want to, I'm a little scared,' Azai answered.

'I'll hold you,' Jana promised.

'Both of you,' Azai said, stretching to push out her sex against the Rude Boy.

She was going to do it, she was sure. It would just take a little comfort. As her sister cuddled in beside her, she found exactly the comfort she needed.

'A moment,' Amaranth said. 'I want this to be special for you.'

Azai smiled, watching as Amaranth went to the cage of Feathers, to select two elegant green creatures, nipple ticklers. One was placed on each of Azai's breasts, which she pushed up as their feet settled on her tender flesh, the Feathery tails immediately setting to work on the straining nipples. Jana giggled, and reached out, to tease the curve of one of her sister's breasts. Azai sighed, once more squeezing the Rude Boy's scrotum to send a shock of pleasure through her body.

'Two last touches,' Amaranth said, speaking from beside the third of the tanks on the far wall. 'A Clittytease from GWC, and a Brovary Labs Poo-Pusher. Like I said, they haven't really got the hang of the names yet.'

'What does it do?' Jana gilled.

'It's a modified puddendoll,' Amaranth explained. 'It goes in the anus, and swells as it feeds . . .'

'I'm not sure . . .' Azai began, but Jana had already taken hold of one leg, lifting it to roll her sister up and exposed the tight hole Amaranth needed.

Azai moaned and surrendered, thinking of how her sister had been so rudely buggered by the Boss, and realising, to her shame, that she shared some of the same dirty needs. Her other leg came up, her eyes shut and she was showing, deliberately flaunting her bottom hole. She felt Amaranth's finger between her cheeks, actually on her anus, and she squeezed the Rude Boy to try and knock the agonising shame it brought from

251

her head. Even as she sighed in pleasure her bottom hole was being worked open with a well lubricated finger. She squeezed again, her orgasm rising as the taut bulb of the Poo-Pusher pressed to her anus.

'Push out, my sweet,' Amaranth ordered.

Azai obeyed, and felt her anus open to the little creature, and close on his neck, leaving her bottom neatly plugged. Immediately it began to squirm in her anus, a sensation at once exquisite and filthy.

'Show yourself, Azai,' Jana whispered.

As her sister cuddled her tight, Azai moved the big puddendoll, exposing her sex to Amaranth. Immediately something else touched, sucking on to her clitoris to make her cry out in shocked pleasure. Her thighs went up as Amaranth settled beside her, and it was happening, her muscles tightening, even as she put the head of the Rude Boy to her vagina, to feel her hymen pull taut against the turgid flesh.

Now was the moment, she had to. As the Clittytease sucked once more she gave a sob, and pushed, hard, to feel the pain, stop, only for her sister to take the puddendoll in hand, guiding it in, gentle but firm. Azai cried out, sharp pain blending with her still rising orgasm, begging her sister to stop, only to scream as Jana pushed again and her hymen tore wide.

She was coming anyway, clutched tight in the girl's arms, her nipples straining, her anus stretched on the fat bulb within, the Rude Boy crawling up into her body past her burst hymen, her clitoris burning, her head swimming with ecstasy and emotion. Nor did it stop, her body twitching and shaking in reaction even as the peak of ecstasy faded. The Feathers still tickled at her nipples and breasts. The Rude Boy was still going in, pulling up her, with wave after wave running down his fat body. The Poo-Pusher was still swelling, stretching her anus and bloating out her rectum. The Clittytease still sucked on her clitoris, keeping her speechless and gasping in the girls arms.

As the full, fat bulk of the Rude Boy came into her she felt his balls press to her flesh. The double spur wrapped to her sex lips and she knew it was going to happen again. Her pleasure was soaring, and at any second he would spunk in her, for her first time, her hole, her cunt, filled with sperm. It happened, her insides twisting as she was filled with sperm. She screamed again, a second orgasm tearing through her, peak after peak, in time to the pulsing of the pudden-doll's body, over and over, until at last it began to subside and she went limp in her sister's arms.

Amaranth had already begun to remove the creatures, gently, returning each to his proper place. Azai simply lay slack on the couch, spread and naked in bliss. The Clittytease followed the Feathers, then the Rude Boy, drawn carefully from Azai's not open vagina, and last the Poo-Pusher, slipped out to leave her anus agape, with sperm running down into the hole from her vagina.

'Better clean up,' Jana said softly, 'tuck the towel up between your legs so you don't make a mess.'

Azai nodded, and let her sister lead her from the room. Half-an-hour later, and after a giggling lick at Jana's sex, they returned to reception.

'I trust you're satisfied?' Amaranth asked, smiling sweetly.

'Absolutely,' Azai answered. 'I'll take the Rude Boy, please, and a Feather if the offer is still open.'

'Certainly.'

'How much is the Clittytease, and ... and that Poo-Pusher?'

'Fifty for the Clittytease. The Poo-Pusher's not cheap, I'm afraid. He's a special addition, at two-hundred.'

'I'll save. It'll be something to look forward to.'

'I'm going to save too,' Jana added, 'for a Boss, if it takes me ten years!'

Amaranth laughed, then spoke briefly to one side. Minutes later another young woman appeared, holding two large boxes and two instruction manuals. Azai paid, her hand still shaking as she completed the transaction. Both kissed Amaranth and they left the shop.

They were still giggling as they walked down the street, with Azai holding her precious packages close to her chest. They passed another person, small, weakly built, lacking all aggression, and with none of the girls' vibrancy, a typical man. Neither so much as glanced to the side, nor saw the look of pathetic entreaty which followed their carelessly wiggling bottoms as they walked away from him.